Lacey didn't see him at first and when she did, her chest heaved a rasping sigh. She scanned the length of his body, beginning with the toes of his worn but obviously expensive boots. Molded denim and weathered cowhide gloved a body that ignited fear and sparks of passion. The wide brim of his hat covered most of his face, but not the smirk on his upturned lips. The shadow of a beard was evenly spread over a granite chin. Drops of moisture clung to his face. He was leaning against the treated cross-timbers that held the Camp Noepe sign. The toe of one boot pointed down into the gravel.

No one spoke.

He shifted his stance and pushed the black brim back from his face. Trapped in his stare, her muscles tightened and her heart pumped. He was in Lacey's world, but she felt like she was the stranger on exhibit. His cutting eyes danced with cerebral pleasure, as though he had already read her mind and owned her heart. She crossed her arms over her chest and searched for words to describe him.

Simply beautiful.

Too spectacular to be safe.

OAK BLUFFS

JOAN EARLY

Genesis Press, Inc.

Indigo Love Stories

An imprint of Genesis Press, Inc.
Publishing Company

Genesis Press, Inc.
P.O. Box 101
Columbus, MS 39703

ISBN: 978-1-58571-379-0
Manufactured in the United States of America

First Edition

Visit us at www.genesis-press.com or call at 1-888-Indigo-1

DEDICATION

To my African, Irish, and Native American ancestors and all others who embraced their differences in the face of grave hostility and left a rainbow of love that outshines all prejudices.

ACKNOWLEDGEMENTS

I am grateful to the readers whose support and encouragement are my inspiration, and to my family and friends for showing pride in my accomplishments.

I want to especially thank my children, Jeff and Ashley, my beautiful granddaughter, Devon, and my dear husband, Dale, for their unending love and faith. Thanks to my family in Houston, Memphis, New Orleans, Chicago, and Woodville, Mississippi.

Thanks to my special "sisters" who have been in my life for as long as I can remember. Dorothy, my shadow and partner in crime, and Deloris, whose strength and love are immeasurable. I love you guys! Thanks to those wonderful teachers back in Wilkinson County, Mississippi, who gave me a strong foundation.

Above all, my humble thanks to God, who makes all things possible.

CHAPTER 1

Lacey Daigle had driven the mile-long road along Aquinnah Cliffs many times, but still marveled at the colorful diagrams of history in the rows of clay, sand, and fossil-filled gravel. Streams that had formed from melting glaciers cut through the low hills and valleys along South Road. The red brick lighthouse that overlooked Vineyard Sound had guided many sailors around the treacherously rocky shore.

She found the beauty and the history of Martha's Vineyard equally fascinating. She loved Aquinnah, the rolling hills of Chilmark, and the up-island area of Oak Bluffs, where her family had owned land since the 1800s. Her ancestral home, Powan House, was built around 1907, when Cottage City was renamed Oak Bluffs. It was that piece of family history that had brought Lacey back to the island.

Looking in the rearview mirror, she caught a glimpse of her image and smiled at the pairing of bloodlines that defined her heritage. Her skin was black. Her features were delicate. High cheekbones were half-hidden behind sheets of raven hair. Dark eyes were heavily hooded with lashes that fanned out like butterfly wings. Her mouth was wide and full, her lips artfully defined. Her father's

African American and Native American roots were visible, as were the Caribbean influences from her mother's family. She was tall and willowy. The strength of her heredity was hidden, but easily called upon.

She drove quietly past farms and grazing lands on Middle Road, admiring the backdrop of sparkling water until they reached the vibrant cottages at Oak Bluffs.

"Maybe I'm being unreasonable," she said to the woman sitting next to her. "I just have to try, Mother Pearl."

"You're not unreasonable." The older woman's eyes clouded with memories. "Powan House is very special to this family. It's certainly special to me," she confided. "That's where your grandfather first kissed me and held me in his arms."

"Your love for Papa rivals all of the love stories ever written. He must have been blind not to notice your feelings sooner. I want that kind of love."

"And you shall have it very soon. Your future is clear in my head."

Pearl, like Lacey's grandfather, was born on the island. Her cooking skills were well recognized, but Lacey was the only one in the family who believed in her predictions. Because of that, Lacey's heartbeat quickened when Pearl declared she would soon find love. "You mean I haven't found love with Mason?"

"I can't say for sure. The faces are not visible. I just see white lace and a big halo of happiness."

Lacey parked at the county square, but sat behind the wheel, unmoving. Her heart quivered in her chest. So much was riding on the decision of strangers. She removed her wet palms from the steering wheel and placed her forehead where they had been.

"Come on, honey," Pearl said. "Let's go in and face the music."

Forty-two minutes after the meeting was called to order at the Dukes County Courthouse, Pearl and Lacey were making their way back to the center of Oak Bluffs. Lacey held her coat collar tightly against her throat and looked up to the rooftop of an old church in the town square. Sunlight sparkled off a clump of snow that was buried in a crevice near the steeple, creating an almost heavenly glow.

"Well, I guess that's it, Mother Pearl," she spoke with deflated resignation. "There's nothing more we can do. We could fight it in court, but unless I miss my guess, Treadwell has the time and the money to wait us out."

"I blame myself for this. I just—"

"Don't." Lacey placed her hand on Pearl's arm. "We all saw the change in Papa. Even Dad said the radiation treatments might have affected his memory. There was no way you could have known he had not paid the taxes on Powan House, or that notices had been sent advising of foreclosure."

They walked down Circuit Avenue toward the car Lacey had rented in Boston two days earlier. She stopped after hearing her name called, and turned to see a flurry of denim hurrying toward them.

"Miss Daigle, I'm so sorry. I can imagine how you must feel."

"Thank you, Miss Gosling." She nodded in Pearl's direction. "This is Pearl Choate Daigle, my grandmother. Mother Pearl, Miss Gosling is a realtor. I found her sign on the property when I first came here." Lacey's mind was whirling. "Are there any more properties for sale around here, Miss Gosling?"

"Well, there is one I can show you, and please call me Fran. It's tied up in probate now, but I have the listing. The land has a partial oceanfront view, but the buildings are in need of repairs, and no one knows when the probate will release it. The owner died some time ago. Young man. Only fifty-two. The court can't locate any relatives and there were no wills."

"The property is abandoned?"

"Not really. He left livestock out there. The feed and grain store in Chilmark advances supplies. A man who had worked for the owner still drives in from Aquinnah to look after the animals. He's been doing it without pay since the owner died."

"Where is the property located?" Lacey asked.

"The area is called Ocean Cove." Fran took a map from her briefcase and pointed to a spot on the right of the V-shaped coast between Oak Bluffs and Vineyard Haven. "I'm sure it would have sold long before now if the probate matter had been resolved."

Lacey thought of her grandfather's pride the last time they visited Powan House. He had marked off a section to build a stable, bleachers, and a riding arena. "Would you take us there, Miss Gosling?"

Lacey immediately fell in love with the scarred buildings in a breathtaking glen. Walking cautiously across the old floorboards, she added the estimated cost of renovations to the purchase price, and knew it was a great deal. She met Yank Whitefeathers, the caretaker, and felt a strong kinship. He was a full-blooded Wampanoag and a crusader for ancestral rights.

"Do you need to get back to New York or can we stay long enough to gather information on this place?" Lacey asked Pearl.

"Stay as long as it takes," Pearl assured her. "I don't come out here nearly as often as I should. I'm enjoying this visit with my family."

Lacey arranged to return to the property with a real estate appraiser, and without Fran Gosling.

"So, what do you think?" she asked Pearl during the drive back to the home of Pearl's sister, Minneola.

"I've got mixed emotions. We wanted to build that camp on family land for Asa. Are we still doing this for him, or because we're too stubborn to let it go?"

"Mom thinks I'm being totally irrational and Mason says I'm grief-stricken. It doesn't take a genius to see that I'm still hurting, but we can do this. I have insurance money from Daddy's plane crash that I will only spend on something with real value."

"And I have the insurance money from Asa's death. I have nothing more to lose, but your life is just getting good, honey. You'll lose a great career."

She watched the cliffs rise in the distance. "No, I'll interrupt my career. I'm just approaching thirty. I can always go back. Daddy was wise enough to insist that I minor in education just in case I needed something to fall back on. I can get that place up and running, get licensed, and open a riding academy. It was Papa's dream, and now it's mine. You're the one who said the bold dreams of our youth predict our capabilities. I know I'm capable of turning Papa's dream, my dream, into reality."

Lacey used the services of her New York attorney, who was also licensed in Massachusetts, to help settle the probate issues. There were no known living relatives, making the wait much shorter than anticipated. The property was a steal, just as Powan House had been for Ramsey Treadwell.

She did not know the man who had purchased Powan House. Feeling mutual trust and respect with Yank encouraged her to seek his help. She left Pearl to browse through the Breckenridge art exhibit at Cousen Rose Gallery and made one last trip to her newly acquired property before heading back to New York.

"Yank, what can you tell me about Ramsey Treadwell?"

"I don't like the man." Standing tall and proud, he brushed a lustrous lock of hair from his face. "I've done work for him a few times. He's a tightfisted tyrant. I think he has a Napoleon complex. He's a little pip-squeak, so he tries to act like a tough SOB."

"Do you know where I can find him?"

"Sure do."

She followed Yank's truck for the short drive down Old County Road. They parked inside a natural cleft bluestone wall and walked up aged steps to the Victorian house with gables, turrets, and scores of fancy wooden lacework.

"I'll stay with you," Yank said. "I don't trust Treadwell."

"Thank you. I don't expect anything good to come of this, but I have to try." Lacey rang the doorbell and waited in the entryway until the housekeeper directed them out to a large deck that rested high on a cliff over-looking the ocean.

"This is a lovely view," Lacey said after Treadwell offered them a seat.

He turned to face her. "I'm sure you didn't come here to discuss the scenery, so what can I do for you, Miss Daigle?"

"I just want to make one last offer for our family homestead. The offer I made was more than fair, but I'm willing to pay whatever you're asking."

"The property is not for sale at any price, Miss Daigle, and I don't think you'll be getting Ren Foster's place in Ocean Cove. Certainly not any time soon."

She was not going to tell him the probate issues had been resolved. "Well, those are my plans. I would like to have the camp ready for next spring. I also hope to have a contestant for the Junior Equestrian Roundup at the end of the season."

His eyebrows lifted in annoyance. The bald spot on the top of his head turned beet red. "Now how in the world do you plan to do that? You don't even have a camp but you're already planning to enter the contest? My champions are islanders, not vacationers. My people work with them year-round."

A slow, infuriated smile spread across her face. "Thanks for your time, Mr. Treadwell."

She stood and so did he. Thinking Yank was right about his complex, she turned to leave.

"I'll make a deal with you, Miss Daigle. If you can get a camp up and running by spring, and by chance win the contest at the end of the season, I'll give you title to that property." He pursed his lips and extended his hand. "Deal?"

She gripped his hand in a firm shake, and returned his steely gaze. "It's a deal, Mr. Treadwell."

From the corner of her eye, she saw a wide smile spread across Yank's face. He was her people. He knew what was at stake. His life had been devoted to fighting for the rights of Native Americans on the island. He would help win back her family legacy.

Six months later, Lacey walked down the driveway of Camp Noepe, wondering if she had made a big mistake. The riding instructor she had hired, sight unseen, from Denham Wells, Texas, was three weeks late. He had promised to arrive on the Tuesday morning ferry. Thinking she had mistaken the dates, she had driven in to the ferry landing each Tuesday morning.

Smothering her anxiety beneath a smile, she waved to Pearl and prepared to make a final drive to the landing. The beauty of a New England morning went unnoticed as she drove down Barnes Road. She had staked her future, her money and a sizable chunk of her pride on an idea that almost no one believed would work. She shooed flies of failure from her mind. She would succeed.

She had the property—a small strip of breathtaking land—and she certainly had the equipment, the horses, and a ton of determination. She drove into town, realized she was much too early, and parked her Jeep in front of Grand Harbor Gourmet. Heading north to the junction, she paused in front of Grove's General Store, smilingly admiring the picture-perfect scenery. Oak Bluffs was the tourist center for Martha's Vineyards, but even the digital temperature gauge and other modern eye-catchers failed to distract from the scenic beauty of history preserved. It was a moment frozen in time.

Lacey pushed back a brown corduroy sleeve and checked her watch before going into Evan's Bakery. Without looking at the menu, she ordered black coffee and a pecan-crusted sticky bun, removed the woolen glove from her right hand and fished three $1 bills from the back pocket of her jeans. Balancing the hot coffee and waxed-paper-covered roll, she walked over to look at the cork bulletin board on the wall.

"I see your ad for a riding instructor is still there." Fran Gosling pointed to the green flier Lacey had tacked to the board two weeks earlier. "Mary Clair is excited about the camp. I've also recommended it to several friends," she said, touching Lacey's sleeve. "Are you sure you'll be able to open without that riding instructor?"

"We'll open." Lacey smiled and turned to leave. "Tell Mary Clair to practice her mounts, and don't forget to send me that mailing list you promised when I bought the property."

Feeling her heart could no longer support the smile on her face, she hurried away. Monroe Faulkner had answered her ad and accepted her offer without hesitation. He had sent an impressive résumé and she had sent him a check.

Placing the Styrofoam cup in the holder below the gearshift, Lacey leaned her head on the steering wheel. "Small towns," she mumbled. "Everyone knows your business."

She had arrived in September, and, even with the disappointment of losing her property, her soul was now anchored in Dukes County, Massachusetts.

She fastened her seat belt and continued her drive, drinking in the rustic splendor of early morning. Sprinklings of sheep feasting on the rolling hills, the smell of the ocean, and a reverent nod to American history. Her heartbeat quickened during the last mile of her drive. She parked and waited at the ferry landing, holding her breath until she felt her chest would split in half. She watched the cars and foot travelers disembark, but Monroe Faulkner was not among them.

Lacey's drive back to the camp was filled with disappointment. She squinted against the sun, swallowed the tremors of panic and reminded herself that fear was an emotion she could not afford.

"I have to win," she said in quiet assurance. "I knowingly stepped out on a cardboard deck against the advice of 99 percent of my family and friends. This is no time to think of drowning."

After parking under the carport, she walked around the stable and tried to press the wrinkles of doubt from her brow before entering the kitchen.

"Well, he didn't show, Mother Pearl." She removed her jacket, stuffed her scarf and gloves in the pocket, and hung it on one of the wooden pegs that ran along the back hallway. Rubbing at her temple, she took a glass from the drainboard next to the sink. "I don't know what I'm going to do," she sighed, suddenly full of doubt.

She turned to look at the frown on Pearl's russet face, and watched her brush wisps of silver from her noble cheekbones. In Pearl, Lacey saw a picture of assiduous fortitude. From her suede loafers to the bun resting on a yoke of denim, Pearl epitomized strength, directness, and stamina. Her love for Pearl was immeasurable.

"I just don't know why this man would accept the position and not show up. If something happened, he should have called. They do have phones down in Texas." Pearl turned back to the stove and asked, "Just how much money did you send him?"

"Two thousand dollars. It's not the money, Mother Pearl. He gave his word. Besides, he never cashed the check." Suddenly the burden became too heavy. "I checked out his references and read the newspaper clipping of his rodeo exploits over the past five years. I verified his certification. There were no photographs with the clippings, and I couldn't ask his age, race, or anything outside of his qualifications. I don't know what he looks like, but I do know he's eminently qualified to teach horseback riding. He has no criminal background, and the one reference that I spoke with made him sound almost saintly."

"Well, there are saints and then there are saints." Pearl shook her head. "Quit beating yourself up over this, honey."

"I'm just disappointed. This is not the first time I've had to make shepherd's pie from sheep droppings, but this is a new world for me. What the hell made me think I could do this? I shouldn't be here."

Clouds of age circled the murky brown discs in Pearl's squinting eyes. "You know, honey, I believe in destiny. A place for each of us. Some people get to choose their vocation, but often times the vocation chooses us, because that's the plan. If you shouldn't be here, then where should you be?"

She set the baking dish on the counter and wiped her hands on the thick cotton apron that shrouded her sturdy frame. "I was the first to hold you when you were born. The first to change your diaper. I can't find words to describe my feelings about that tiny life in my arms. You fought so confidently and yelled your disapproval in octaves seemingly impossible for such small lungs. Your father cried when I placed you in his arms. I cried. We knew you were someone very special."

She smiled, touched Lacey's face, and paused thoughtfully as if she was remembering every detail from the past. "It wasn't just your looks, though God knows you were the prettiest baby I've ever seen. It was strength and courage beyond all expectation. You were tiny, so small it was difficult to find you in the folds of bedding, but you were not to be denied. You've always known what you wanted, Lacey, and you were never afraid to go after it."

Lacey turned on the faucet, allowed the water to run cold, and held her glass under the stream. Taking a stool next to the counter, she supported her chin in her palms and enjoyed the reflective journey from a woman who had long been the balm to her pain.

"This place, the island in the streams, is the beginning of a strong branch of the Daigle family tree. Your life's blood is here. I don't know of anyone who belongs more than you do."

"And I don't know what I would do without you. You're right, Mother Pearl. We can make this work. I can use Yank as a riding instructor, but I have a ton of brochures claiming to have a champion rider and roper to teach the kids."

"Yank can handle it," Pearl assured her.

"I'm sure Yank can handle it. He could probably do a better job than this bozo from Texas, but you know as well as I do that people want to see credentials. This man had all of the right accreditations, along with a laundry list of accomplishments. Substituting Yank would mean a delay in getting the license. Having a Native American instructor would be a good drawing card. It would also be further exploitation of a wonderful man and already exploited race—the thing that sparked this whole idea."

She slammed her fist down on the counter. "This man answered my ad all the way from Texas. Sent a long list of references and promised to be here the first Tuesday of February. It's damn near March, his phone is disconnected, and my last letter was returned with no forwarding address. It's too late to wait for a response to another ad. I've asked around the island, but no one is interested in seasonal work at a girl's camp. There was that one man, but his credentials weren't as impressive as Yank's, and he smelled like a distillery. I wouldn't trust him with the horses, let alone the children."

"Don't worry, it will work out somehow. It has to," Pearl said, pouring water from the hissing teakettle and stirring the contents of a large bowl with a wooden spoon. "Go ahead and mail the flyers. If this man doesn't show, Yank can handle it."

"I've sunk more money than I intended to spend into renovating this place. I've purchased furnishings and equipment. Those damn horses that keep eating me out of house and home. Nobody is going to buy me out. No wonder Fran smiles like a Cheshire cat every time we meet. I'm probably the only fool in the continental United States who would try something like this without experience."

"You have experience," Pearl answered, her voice vibrating as she grated yams over a large granite bowl. "You ran a luxury hotel in Atlanta when you were only twenty-six and moved on to an even larger one in New York. You're educated and determined. You'll make it work, with or without this cowboy from Texas."

"I think I may have acted strictly on impulse. That's what Mason said, and though I would rather eat dirt than admit defeat to that pompous son of—"

"Lacey." Pearl's eyebrows descended in a deep frown. "Let's not get worked up over this."

"You're right. I can't allow myself to give in to the frustration. All I have to do is think of that smug smile on Ramsey Treadwell's face. " She raised her head in a defiant toss. "Where the hell is Denham Wells, Texas, anyway?"

∞

By sunset, Lacey had walked a dozen miles. She roamed around the property, killing time and swallowing the bitter taste of panic. The older, established camps were already laboriously competing for business.

In order to open and become profitable, she had to impress the parents of potential students. She needed a name with notable credentials. The man who answered her ad was a true cowboy. According to his résumé, most of which she had verified, he had ridden in twelve rodeos and won top prizes in bronco busting, bull riding and calf roping. He worked on a large ranch and taught horseback riding on the side.

She stopped at the stable and helped exercise the horses, allowing the bay she named Champion to nuzzle her face. "A little drippy, old boy, but still the nicest kiss I've had in a long time."

After combing the tangles from his tail, she led him back to the stable and returned to direct a delivery of feed and grain to the covered shed where Yank was working the horses. Leaving them to unload the truck, Lacey took a bottle of water from the cooler, stood at the side of the building and viewed her property. With or without a camp, the real estate had been a spectacular purchase. She headed back to the kitchen. A cold wind slapped her face when she rounded the side of the building. She snuggled her chin down in her collar and hastened her gait.

She didn't see him at first, and when she did, her chest heaved a rasping sigh. She scanned the length of his body, beginning with the toe of his worn, but obviously expensive, boots. Molded denim and weathered cowhide gloved a body that ignited fear and sparks of passion. The brim of his hat covered most of his face but not the smirk on his upturned lips. The shadow of a

beard splayed evenly over a granite chin. Drops of moisture clung to his face.

His skin was the color of perfectly browned toast.
Heavy eyebrows were arched in a quizzical frown and
the hair around his neck was long and curly. Lacey stood
back and stared. Seeing a young black man on foot in
that area was quite unusual. He casually leaned against
the treated cross-timbers that held the Camp Noepe
sign. The toe of one boot pointed down into the gravel.

No one spoke.

He pushed the black brim back from his face. She
couldn't help noticing that he was handsome to a fault.
He smelled of leather and sweat and, she guessed, was
well over six feet tall. His shoulders were strong and
erect. Plaid sleeves were rolled over bulging biceps.

Trapped in his stare, her muscles tightened and her
heart pumped erratically. He was in Lacey's world, but
she felt like the stranger. Cutting eyes danced with cerebral pleasure, as if he read her mind. She crossed her
arms over her chest and searched for words to describe
him.

There were no vehicles in sight and she wondered
how he got there. She had been outside for over two
hours. The delivery truck was the only vehicle in the
area, and it had no passengers.

She waited for him to speak, but he stood back and
stared with unmistakable brashness.

"Can I help you?" She tried to sound brazen but
flinched at the shades of danger in heavy-lidded eyes.
There were no threatening moves, yet she felt assaulted

by his intrusion and his scowl. She looked around, hoping Pearl or Yank would come around the side of the building.

He cocked his head to one side. "Maybe."

His cactus drawl pricked her skin. Beads of sweat cascaded down the center of her chest. She moved cautiously, staring at the metal trunk, brown saddle, and worn duffle bag next to his feet, fighting the urge to scream for Yank. Even if he wasn't dangerous, he was harmfully handsome. He seemed to be studying her as if he had seen her before, and was trying to remember where. She stood still, trapped in his stare.

"I'm looking for Lacey Daigle," he said matter-of-factly.

"I'm Lacey Daigle, and you are?"

His smug expression quickly changed to one of desperation. He looked up and down the road and finally turned back to Lacey, stammering bewilderedly. "Monroe Faulkner. I was hired by Miss Daigle...by you, I guess, to teach horseback riding."

Hot breath gushed from her throat. "Mr. Faulkner. Thank goodness you're here." Relief surpassed the anger that had grown during weeks of waiting. "I went in to meet the ferry. I thought you were coming by ferry." Her voice caught in her throat and she swallowed hard. "How did you get here?"

"Hitched, mostly. I'm sorry I didn't call to say I would be delayed." He removed his hat and mopped his brow with his shirtsleeve. "I had a few unavoidable obstacles to overcome. Hope it didn't cause you any trouble."

"No harm done, Mr. Faulkner. Or should I call you Monroe?"

"Seems you're the boss." He slipped his hands into his back pockets. "Call me whatever makes you comfortable."

She studied his somewhat bemused reaction and tried to compare his face and his voice with the one on the telephone. Nothing matched. "Very well, Monroe, and please call me Lacey. We're very informal around here."

He delivered one firm shake to her outstretched hand, released, and drew back abruptly as if her skin was hot to the touch. His eyes had not left her face and his stare was much more disarming than she felt it should have been. Her insides contracted sharply.

"Bring your gear and I'll show you to your quarters." She waited for him to hoist the trunk to his shoulders and marveled at the strain of muscles that extended down his neck. The brief contact had been very revealing. Just enough time to feed her growing skepticism.

"What does it mean?" he asked.

"Excuse me?"

He stood tall and strong, like the trees behind him, and flicked his head to the right.

"The name Noepe. What does it mean?"

"Oh. It's an old Algonquin name for the island of Martha's Vineyard. It means 'island of streams.' The area was given several names over time. One was 'island that spoke by hand' for the large number of deaf people born here. Bartholomew Gosnord bestowed the name that stuck in 1602. He named it for his daughter, Martha, and for the wild grapevines that cover a good portion of the terrain."

Without smiling, he followed her to the back of the main house. She slowed and moved to his side.

"Since you're from out west, I'll be happy to share my knowledge of the island. In the six months I've been here, I've read every bit of local history I could find. As you no doubt are aware, this is a very historic region. There are three main areas to the island: Martha's Vineyard, the Elizabeth Islands, and Noman's Land. The seven towns here in Dukes County are Aquinnah, from the Algonquin meaning 'the land under the hill,' Chilmark, Edgartown, the county seat, Oak Bluffs, Tisbury…"

She kept talking because she was too nervous to stop, but he did not appear to be listening. She guessed he had expected someone older and probably white. So had she.

"This is the main house," she continued. "The office, kitchen, private dining area and main dining hall for the kids. My quarters are here for now, but I'm moving to the bunkhouse when the campers arrive." She stopped and pointed to her left. "Let me introduce you to the lady who holds me and the camp together. Mother Pearl, this is Monroe Faulkner."

He put down his gear and tipped his hat. "How do, ma'am?" He turned an annoyed frown back to Lacey. "Is my room somewhere close by?"

"It's a cabin and it's right down that path," she answered.

"Don't you think it would be a good idea to show me where I can store my gear before giving me the grand tour? I'm not a pack mule." His words were mocking and spiteful.

Lacey looked at Pearl, her face blanching with anger. "Yes, of course. Right this way."

She led him back though the kitchen and breezeway to the garage. "The first one is yours." She pointed to a row of bungalows. "It's not fancy, but very comfortable. There's a—"

"Thank you," he interrupted. "I'm sure I'll be able to locate everything I need."

Her eyes followed his long strides, broad shoulders, and the tilt of his head. She struggled with indescribable emotions, and the sting his rebuff had left on her cheeks.

"Hey, Monroe," she called after him, but he did not turn around.

"The cowboy has arrived! I told you everything would work out." Pearl rested her hand on Lacey's shoulder. "He's here and he's got a burr under his saddle," she said, laughingly. "Was there anything in his references to explain that?"

"He's certainly not the friendliest cowboy to come out of the West, but I don't care. I can breathe a little easier now and start getting this place ready to open. It's hard enough already. I don't need employee problems. I'll coddle and cajole Mr. Monroe Faulkner if that's what it takes to get the job done."

"I'll say one thing for the cowboy, in spite of his surly attitude, he sure is a looker. I knew they grew them big in Texas, but that's one fine man." Pearl gave her a cursory glance.

"I hadn't noticed," she spoke softly and blushed, wondering why she felt the need to lie.

"Oh, come on, child. You'd have to be dead not to. I'm an old woman and he makes my juices boil. The man is gorgeous from head to toe, and in my eyes, that gruff exterior just makes him more desirable. A fine stallion, yours for the taming." She hugged Lacey's shoulder. "Of course, I'm positive he noticed you. You're even more beautiful when you're embarrassed."

"I'm only concerned with his qualifications and his contribution to Camp Noepe." She spoke with confident detachment, but felt completely ill at ease. He was, without a doubt, the most appealing man she had ever seen. His scent lingered around her, pure male, a magnificent aphrodisiac. She wondered if frosty mannerisms were part of his hard drive or the result of some recent bout of unpleasantness.

"I want him to work. I have no desire to tame him. I came here with a dream, and it wasn't finding a man. That's a good thing, because this man is not my type."

"Let's just wait and find out. Is he joining us for dinner?"

"I have no idea. He brushed past before I could ask him. I tried to call after him, but I figured going hungry might diminish his conceit. I'm still trying to determine how he got here. Surely he didn't walk, but I didn't see a vehicle, unless he was dropped off further down the road. He said he hitched."

"That seems far-fetched." Pearl frowned. "I don't know many people in this area who would pick up a stranger. The main thing is that he's here and you can quit worrying.'"

"You think so? I'm not so sure." Lacey took four glasses from a row on the bottom shelf of the cabinet. "Several things just don't add up. He's three weeks late, he doesn't sound anything like he did on the phone, and his résumé is longer than my arm. I don't think he's lived long enough to have done the things he claimed."

"I'm sure there's an explanation."

"There's no explanation for his hands," Lacey mused. "They're softer than mine. I don't think Mr. Faulkner has done any hard work lately, certainly not anything involving getting his hands chapped. How tall would you say he is?"

"About six-five. All fine, dark meat. I love good-looking black men in cowboy hats." Pearl's hearty laugh filled the room. "I predict the two of you will get to know each other a lot better, but for the time being we'll all keep our eyes open. He could be a—"

"Curb your fertile thoughts, Mother Pearl." Lacey shook her finger. "We'll know of each other only what's needed to get the job done, so downshift your imagination. I'd love to photograph and fingerprint him, but we both know I need him here, so I'll just have to trust him. I'll alert Yank to keep his eyes open."

"Did you at least tell him dinner is being served?"

She looked down the path. "I was about to, but he didn't give me a chance."

Pearl spoke with aimless intensity. "A man would never travel from Texas to Massachusetts for this kind of job unless something was chasing him, so let's hope it didn't follow him. I didn't sense any danger."

"So you think he's running? Hiding from something? I submitted his résumé and certification along with the package I sent to get this place licensed. According to the state of Massachusetts, he had no criminal history anywhere in the United States."

"I didn't say he's a criminal, but I do see a clouded past. I also see decency and a lot of strength in his face. I'm not making predictions, mind you, but I think he's a good man. I think Monroe Faulkner is just the kind of man you need in your life."

Before Lacey could answer, Pearl grabbed a large metal bell from the counter. "I'm going out and ring the dinner bell. If Mr. Too-Good-Looking doesn't come to dinner now, he'll just have to eat with the horses."

CHAPTER 2

A battered oak table stretched in an unbroken line down the center of the rectangular room. Cane-back chairs stood, like fence posts, along the sides. Large pillows of oak, wrapped in comfortably worn leather, framed each end. They were man-sized chairs, rugged and roomy. Lacey made several trips from the table to the cabinet. Each time she passed the window, her eyes darted to the space between the cheerful yellow curtains and down to the row of bungalows. The front of the one she assigned to Monroe was in her direct line of vision. He had opened the blinds on the front window. She stretched her neck.

Her business soul wanted him to stay and finish out the season. Her thick layer of protective instincts was unsure. The only certainty she felt was an overwhelming desire to wallow in the big man's arms, but that would only happen in her thoughts. She hoped he was productive, finished the season, and caused no further disturbance than the one he already caused her heart.

Once the table was set, she stood back and smiled. A wagon-wheel chandelier sprayed yellow beams on place settings of denim mats and Blue Willow dishes, all purchases from a store-closing sale at Chantilly's. Lacey and Pearl learned the small bridal and gift shop on Tea Lane in West Tisbury had advertised going out of business prices for four years. Lacey did not complain. She had sixty place settings, matching mugs, and blue tumblers for the price of a couple of Waterford flutes.

Pearl had thought it was an excellent deal and Lacey deferred to Pearl on all matters of kitchen supplies. Pearl was also the undisputed authority on dining etiquette, having worked in New York's finest restaurants. She staunchly declared dinner a time for relaxation. No television, and only soft music to aid digestion. She complemented her meals with fine wines, though not necessarily expensive ones, including her own vintage made with grapes from the island. Serious or disturbing conversation was forbidden at Pearl's table.

Lacey felt that she and Pearl were a matched pair. Pearl bragged on Lacey's business savvy and Lacey knew of no one who prepared a better meal or had more knowledge of foods, wines, or the character of a person's soul. Pearl had already achieved what skeptics said was impossible, recognition by "Continental Chefs" and a successful bakery in bustling New York.

A wild thought crossed Lacey's mind. She smiled and increased the pieces of flatware. Pearl leaned against the sink, chin in hand, and watched. The furrows in her brow increased and she finally spoke.

"Now, I'll admit, I'm pretty finicky about my dining conditions, but I never asked for this. Have you added a few more courses to our evening meal?"

"It's just a little test." She smiled at Pearl, her eyes filled with mischief. "I have a feeling about our new riding instructor, and I want to see if I'm right."

Before Pearl could question her further, Yank pushed through the door.

"I'm hungry as a bear when the snow melts." He quickly sat at the table, his shiny raven hair pulled back into a band of cowhide. "Seems like three days have passed since we had lunch."

Lacey joined him at the table. Visibly dwarfed by the massive chair, she cautioned Yank about their newest addition. "Did you meet our riding instructor?"

"Saw him walking to the cabin, but we didn't meet. I might be mistaken, but he seems to have his ass on his back. What's his story?"

"I wish I knew," Lacey said. "I'm skeptical about this whole deal. Too many things don't add up. I want you to keep your eyes and ears open until I feel comfortable with him being here. Hopefully, he'll stay long enough for that to happen."

"Lacey thinks he lied about his qualifications," Pearl said.

"I don't know what I think, but I'm not gullible enough to buy something I can't explain. I hope I'm wrong, but I smell a great big Texas rat."

"Don't worry. I'll keep him in my sights as much as possible," Yank assured her. "As long as he does his work and doesn't give you ladies any trouble, I can handle him on my end. He's a big dude, but I can kick his butt any day of the week."

"Well, I think you should go tell Mr. Faulkner that dinner is being served. That's only polite." Pearl looked at Lacey.

"I'll go tell him," Yank offered.

The living room door opened just as Yank stood to leave. Floorboards creaked under the slow, deliberate steps of a large man's weight. Lacey, Pearl, and Yank's eyes moved in unison, coming to rest on Monroe's passive face. A natural skeptic, Lacey tried to convince herself that the handsome stranger was indeed the man to help get Camp Noepe up and running. His smooth good looks would, in no way, entice her to do what she had sworn against.

He hesitantly approached the table and spoke to no one in particular. "Excuse me. I heard a bell."

"That was the dinner bell," Pearl said. "Yank was about to come and get you. He and the other workers are usually out of earshot, so I use the bell for breakfast and dinner." She motioned to the chair next to Yank. "Come on in, Mr. Faulkner. Have a seat."

"Thank you, and please call me Monroe." He removed his jacket.

Lacey fidgeted as Pearl made the introductions.

"Monroe, this is Yank Whitefeather. He tends the horses and does everything that needs doing around here, including most of the hiring and firing. Yank, Monroe Faulkner, Camp Noepe's riding instructor."

The two men regarded each other with slight interest before shaking hands.

Pearl bowed her head and the others followed. "Dear Lord, we're about to embark on a problematical journey. We will need your guidance and strength every step of the way. Bless us collectively, and fortify us individually in all of our endeavors."

After a communal amen, Pearl passed the basket of homemade rolls. Monroe filled his plate with baked chicken, yams, smoked corn, and peas. Lacey observed his deftness and lack of hesitation in choosing his utensils.

Taking the basket of rolls from Yank, she allowed her eyes to cascade over the engaging profile of her new employee.

"Delicious." He swallowed and spoke. "I must say I'm a little surprised to see such an elaborate table for a regular meal—or is this a special occasion?"

Thinking nothing had gone unnoticed by the handsome stranger, Lacey offered a quick explanation. "Oh, just something we like to do from time to time. We work hard during the day and occasionally treat ourselves to a helping of elegance in the evening. Yank, would you please pass the wine?"

She smiled slightly and blinked against the shivers of excitement that cruised her spine. Hatless, he looked more like a male model than a riding instructor for a youth camp. Pearl had immediately noticed the cleft in his chin that deepened when he spoke, but Lacey was fascinated with the dimples his smile drilled into his smooth cheeks. She felt an awakening that she had been too preoccupied to worry about.

"I'm glad you came here, Lacey," Yank said between bites. "Life is supposed to be easier everywhere, but that isn't always the case. It's hard for those of us who live here year round."

"And the number of black-owned businesses has decreased, not increased," Pearl said. "Back in the 1950s and 1960s, there were more black-owned guest houses and dining halls because blacks weren't welcome in most of the white-owned establishments, except to serve. It was funny how many blacks came here from down south during the summer. Young men from Morehouse came to work as waiters, and herds of professors from Tuskegee Institute came to vacation. That's all changed now that we can go wherever we want."

Attentive during the discussion, Monroe joined in with a question. "I thought this area was more racially integrated."

"Whites were more accepting of non-whites, but it was still segregated," Pearl answered. "African Americans were present on the island long before the American Revolution. Slavery was banned in the colony in 1783, but indentured servants were still bought, sold, and even willed as personal property. There was even a state statute that totally disregarded the 1780 Declaration of Rights in Massachusetts, and assessed taxes on 'Negroes and mulattoes under the government of a master and mistress' until 1793."

"Massachusetts was a stop on the freedom trail," Yank said. "I remember the story of a white woman in Nantucket who hid an escaped slave by dressing him in women's clothes. The story said every family in Nantucket helped get that man safely out of the state."

"My West African family came here in the 1780s." Lacey did not look at Monroe but felt his eyes on her. "We have records of Obias Diaglnar, a West African whaler, coming to the island." This time she looked at Monroe before continuing.

"He settled up-island. That's where we are now. It was called Eastville back then. Obias Diaglnar was listed as a 'colored for'ner' on county records. He worked at a lobster hatchery, and married a member of the Wampanoag Tribe with the last name Powan. Their children were listed as 'mixed for'ners' in the Dukes County records. They built a home on family land during the Methodist Campground development back in 1835."

"My folks, the Wampanoags, clung to their ancestral lands down-island in Aquinnah," Yank said. "And so did members of the Mashpee Tribe."

"That's right," Pearl affirmed. "The Daiglnars changed their name to Daigle and settled along Seaview Avenue, close to the beach. They called the area Cottage City after those colorful gingerbread-style houses were built. A handful of African Americans became homeowners by purchase or by marriage to a Wampagnoag or a Mashpee who had held onto their property. The Campground Association limited the number of lots that were leased to 'colored people,' but some of them hung in there."

Monroe looked at Lacey. "Interesting history. I'd like to know more about the camp if you don't mind talking shop over dinner." Monroe's voice was weighted with charm.

"Not in the least," Lacey began. "Camp Noepe is designed for young girls to learn horseback riding, as well as an appreciation for the land. I hope to draw children from all over the country. I've developed a summer program that encompasses swimming, fishing, camping, crafts, and many other activities designed to teach kids about nature and the...what?"

She felt, rather than saw, his shock. His frown-filled face lifted. His eyes met hers.

"Why are you staring at me that way?"

"I'm sorry. I know the camp is seasonal, but I had no idea you were just starting out."

"Yes, I am, but there's no need to be concerned. This is a carefully thought-out plan and it's going to work. I have at least a dozen tentative reservations. I just needed to fill the instructor's position before I—"

"Surely you're not doing this alone?"

His raised eyebrow was more insulting than the cynicism in his voice. She stiffened with anger and gestured around the table. "As you can see, I'm not exactly alone, but what would be so amazing if I were?" Her anger built with each word.

"Nothing, but you have to admit, it is a bit out of the ordinary," he said.

"And so am I," she said. "Are you doubting me because I'm a woman? Are you insinuating that I lack the know-how to make this work? You don't know a damn thing about me, Mr. Faulkner."

Pearl rested her fork on the plate and placed crossed fingers in her lap. Yank simply stared in silence, a twinkle of amusement in his eyes.

"I came here to work in what I thought was an established summer camp, not some experiment for bored socialites." His voice quivered with anger. "Why are you doing this?"

"Excuse me, Mr. Faulkner, but you have no right making that kind of assumption. You know nothing about my reasons for opening this camp and even less about me. I'm sorry if you feel you've been misled, but come to think of it, I don't know that I got such a great deal with you. You're certainly not what I expected. You sound nothing like you did on the phone, and your hands are smooth as silk. For all I know, you could be an imposter, unable to distinguish a piebald from a pinto. I'm taking—"

Pearl placed her index and middle fingers together in her mouth and blew. Yank gulped loudly.

"Hold on now. Both of you just hold on. The way I see it, you need each other. You're here for your reasons, Mr. Faulkner, and Lacey needs a good riding instructor to make this camp work. Believe me, Mr. Faulkner, it will work."

Lacey fumed, sorry Pearl had intervened. His skepticism reopened old wounds. She had heard the same doubt from her mother and Mason.

"I have a masters degree in business management, Mr. Faulkner, with an undergrad degree in education. Prior to coming here, I managed a five-star hotel in

Atlanta and one in New York. Just little ole me. I had a part-time job as a hotel clerk when I was sixteen. I'm not some spoiled socialite out for an adventure, and this is no damn experiment. My grandfather worked every summer of his life on this island, teaching wealthy white kids to ride horses. My grandfather was half Native American, Mr. Faulkner, and one of the finest men I've ever known." A well of tears halted her words.

"Honey, just let it go." Pearl coaxed. "The things you say are only important to those of us who remember when the world had four corners. Mr. Faulkner could never understand." She reached across and placed a hand on Lacey's arm before turning sideways, her jaw firmly set and her eyes afire. "Mr. Faulkner, I can assure you this is no frivolous undertaking. Lacey and I have personal reasons for coming here, for purchasing this place and for what we plan to do with it."

"I'm sorry. I didn't mean to upset everyone. It just seems like such a giant mission, or maybe I should have postponed my assessment until I knew all the facts. How many people do you have on payroll, and what makes you so sure you're going to get an enrollment that will support this operation? What will you do with the facility in winter? The animals still have to eat."

Lacey's nostrils flared in annoyance. Mason had said practically the same thing, but with more arrogance. Even her brother, whom she could count on to take her side, had been in their mother's corner when she announced her plans. Pearl had been the only one to fully believe that she could make the camp work. Faced with the same cynicism from a man she didn't know, she fixed her gaze on his challenging brown eyes.

"We'll have a full staff when the campers arrive. During the preparation, Yank will have his father, Tedera, his wife, Shale, and their son, Micah, to help us prepare. They're back in Aquinnah—that's the Wampanoag aboriginal land—but they'll be here shortly. Shale will teach beadwork, basket weaving, and pottery to the kids and help Mother Pearl with the domestic duties. Yank's brother is a carpenter. He'll be here to help construct the arena."

"Do you mean corral?" he asked.

"A corral, but with bleachers. We'll need an observation area for the students to watch the trainers and each other work with the horses. I'll hire additional help as needed. For now, you and Yank will care for the horses and the—"

"Just a minute. I never agreed to be a stable boy. I only agreed to teach horseback riding."

"Mr. Faulkner, I don't know how they do things back in Texas, but here we all wear many hats. There's no separation of duties."

He shrugged impatiently and drummed his fingers on the table.

"Your notion that Camp Noepe was an old, established camp did not come from anything I said or any of the printed material I sent to you."

They stared at each other with matched irritation. She fought her anger as she watched his expression change to an impudent scowl that pinned her to the chair. She also noticed the delightful little curl in his upper lip, the way he held his pinkie, and the assuming twinkle in his eyes.

"If you're such a stranger to hard work, maybe you should just leave right now." She shot back with contempt. "Go back to whatever rock you—"

"Now, now. We're jumping off track again." Pearl's quietly commanding voice took center stage. "Mr. Faulkner, we're talking about three months of preparation and three months of operation. Six lousy months, total. If things don't go well, just leave at the end of the season and go on back to whatever life you had before. Lacey and I are committed to this. Yank's loyalty is unquestionable."

"We live here," Yank contributed. "Year-round work is hard to find. My wife teaches and my father drives a school bus, but bills don't stop during the summer. I was laid off after almost ten years with a company in Boston. I take what I can get, but this is more than a job to me. I understand why Lacey is doing it and I want her to succeed."

Lacey's anger cooled. Pearl and Yank shared her feeling about Camp Noepe. The determination in Pearl's voice fueled her desire to make the camp successful. She also saw total dedication in the ruddy face of a man she had come to admire more than most. A man whose people had known untold hardships. Lacey had spent many nights listing and trying to understand Yank's convictions. So far, she knew he was one of the most determined people she had ever met. The fact that he was one of only two million surviving Native Americans had made her weep. The story of how his family fought to regain title to their tribal land of Aquinnah filled her heart with anguish and pride. Yank, and the rest of the Wampanoags, were her people, her blood.

"I wish you could have seen the camp when Lacey bought it." Pearl heaped her plate with sliced tomatoes before passing the platter to Yank. "We've renovated and furnished this place, purchased horses and riding gear, canoes, a tractor, and everything you see before you. My granddaughter gave up a high-paying job in New York, everything she had worked to achieve, to come here. No one in their right mind does something like that on a whim."

Lacey stole glances at Monroe's bowed head as the intermittent sound of eating utensils cut through the silence. Tension eased when Pearl and Yank began discussing the berry patch in back of the stables and its bounty that went into the making of dessert. Monroe squirmed uncomfortably. When Pearl left the table to dish up the cobbler, he tried to make peace.

"Answer one question, if you don't mind. I walked around the stable before coming to dinner. I know the price of good horseflesh, and you'll have to admit, this is quite an elaborate setup. It takes time to put something like this together. You certainly can't blame me for thinking the camp had been around for a while."

"Actually, Mr. Faulkner, that was the deciding factor in purchasing the camp. Most of the horses came with the property. The owner died without a will and with no known heirs. My vision is clear to me, but you're not the first—and undoubtedly not the last—to question my ability to make it work. I will make it work, Mr. Faulkner. Rest assured of that. "

She stared up through thick black lashes, awaiting his next comment. When he continued his meal without speaking, she asked, "Is there anything else I can clarify for you, Mr. Faulkner?"

He shook his head. "No, but I would appreciate a tour of the place after dinner, if you don't mind."

"Why not?" As much as he irritated her, she knew she needed his help. She no longer thought of Monroe as a threat, but as someone whose arrogance had probably alienated everyone around him. Knowing there was little to be gained by increasing the tension, she forced a smile.

"Everything you see here was achieved during the past six months. The first three were sheer hell. The house in back, the bunkhouse, was in total disrepair when I purchased the property. I moved here, and the three of us, along with Yank's father and son, worked twelve-hour days, seven days a week. I had carpenters and electricians here for the major renovations, but we pieced this place back together, board by board. Pearl, Shale, and I painted, made curtains, and rummaged around the county for affordable supplies."

He half smiled and she continued.

"The kitchen appliances were all outdated and had to be replaced. That was another fortune. Everything had to be up to standards and pass inspection before I could get the necessary license to open and operate a camp. That's a lot to go through if you're not serious about your undertaking. I'm not wealthy, but I managed to do this without a loan. I have to make this work, Mr. Faulkner, come hell or high tides."

He kept his head bowed over his plate.

Lacey knew she had to motivate him to stay, but she had no intention of losing her dignity in the process. "I don't expect you or anyone else to have the same commitment I have. I have four students already signed up for the entire summer, and it's my dream to have at least one winning entry in the Junior Equestrian Roundup at the end of summer. This gives us a little over two months to turn a greenhorn into an able horseback rider. Yank, or anyone in his family, can train the campers. I needed your experience as a drawing card."

"Is this some big deal, this Roundup? I mean, with only a few months to prepare, why bother?" He waved his hand in yet another dismissive gesture.

Lacey thought of the frosty doubt on Ramsey Treadwell's face. She wanted to tell Monroe why she needed to win, but did not dare. She also wanted him to know that the event came on the heels of summer vacation and was a major island highlight. Had been for many years. It was the first thing she noticed on the Treadwell Riding Academy brochure. A win for Camp Noepe would be a groundbreaker for the recognition Lacey wanted in honor of her grandfather. Feeling she had already provided too much information, she settled for a snappy reply.

"It's a big deal because I want to win. Camp Noepe isn't the only boarding camp on the island. I want it to stand for something. I want to put Camp Noepe on the front pages of the local paper and beyond. I want to come back here next summer and the summer after that." She paused. "Let's just say I have something to prove, on behalf of someone who's not here to prove it himself."

A smile toyed with his lips. "In that case, we'll do our best, but how do you know that one of these girls will be interested, or even capable? In my experience, young people usually want to listen to rap music, play video games, and invent excuses for failing."

"So cynical, Mr—"

"Call me Monroe, and I'm not cynical, just realistic. I love success stories, Ms. Daigle. I really do. I would certainly like to see one happen here. From everything you've said and what I've seen, you've made a great investment of time and money."

He made a dollar sign with his index finger. "Big investment. I saw the cost of admission on your brochure. Now call me cynical, but I wouldn't bet the farm on turning a child whose parents can afford a fancy summer camp into a proficient competitor for your little race. I didn't lie on my résumé. I'm very knowledgeable about horses and everything else on a ranch. I can't say I'm good at teaching young girls because I've never tried, but if you'll just show me the ropes, so to speak, I'll do my best to train a champion rider for this contest."

They finished dinner and cleared the table. Yank laid a reassuring hand on Lacey's shoulder, and she smiled her thanks.

"Ready for your tour, Mr. Faulkner?" Lacey pulled up to her full five feet, eight inches, and tried to smile.

"After you."

Monroe went back to his cabin and sat wearily on the edge of the bed and removed his boots. He rubbed at the ridge of anxiety along his forehead. He could not believe what had happened.

He took the cell phone from his belt and called home. "I'm here, Pop, and you'll never believe what I found. A beautiful black woman who looks enough like Debra to be her twin owns this camp. Same mocha skin, same saucer eyes, only they're jet black, and so is her hair. She's part Native American."

He listened to his father's updates and concerns, his mind still fixated on Lacey's beautiful, angry face. "I want to leave, but she needs help. I can't just walk away. I don't know the whole story, but she's committed to this, she says to honor her grandfather's memory. She's a strong woman, Pop. Strong and so beautiful she takes my breath away. I can't get close to her or let her get close to me. There's no room in my heart to love another woman."

CHAPTER 3

When Lacey questioned Yank later in the week, he reported that all was well. "He's a nice dude. Never said one word about his personal life, but that can be a good thing, too. He's not a braggart, and he does seem to have a knack for hard work. His hands may have been soft when he arrived, but that won't last long."

Feeling slightly relieved, Lacey's thoughts turned to her brother's law school graduation. She dreaded going back to New York and facing her mother's nagging.

"I don't care how much you protest, Lacey, you know you have to attend your brother's graduation." Pearl pushed a plaid sleeve above her elbow and worked on the mass of white dough in the floured circle. "Don't go, and Amanda will never forgive you. Knowing her as I do, she'll surely find a way to blame me."

"I know. I want to be there for Nicholas, but I don't know if I can face my mother right now. I sure as hell don't want to see Mason. It's hard enough to ignore them while we're miles apart. Mom calls with her continued attempts to make me feel like a first-class fool, and Mason e-mails every day."

Pearl stopped and stared. "I didn't realize you two were communicating."

"I said he e-mails me. I didn't say I answer. I did when I first arrived, but only to ask him to leave me alone." She turned a quizzical eye to Pearl. "You never did like Mason, did you, Mother Pearl?"

"I wouldn't say that. I like Mason just fine. He's a nice young man with a great job and a promising future." Pearl preened. "He's also very pretty."

"You were the only one who didn't jump for joy when he asked me to marry him, and the only one who didn't call me crazy when I returned his ring," Lacey remembered. "Tell me why."

"I just never saw it," Pearl replied, with a gentle toss of her head. "I saw the two of you together, but you were never white-laced and beaded." She grunted softly. "And, I might add, you were never happy."

Lacey chuckled. "Amazing. Why didn't you say this before?"

"I'm just like any parent, honey. I want for you the things you want for yourself. If Mason makes you happy, I want to see you with Mason. If he makes you sad, I'll spit in the ocean and burn a lock of his hair."

"Mother Pearl."

She gave Lacey a knowing smile. "Now go and pack your bag so Yank can drive you to the airport. Miss your flight to New York and I'll have to plug my ears to drown out the sound of your mother's screeching. I almost have to do that anyway. She told everyone in New York that I'm the reason you gave up your job and came out here. I know you don't want to face them, but you're the only buffer between Nicholas and your mother, and you're stronger than he is."

"You don't know how bad it was before I left. Mother had that sticky-sweet sarcasm that drives me batty. And Mason. His ego will never allow him to believe that I gave up the life he offered for anything other than another man. He had become intolerable even before I announced my plans to come to the island."

"It will be okay. You're tougher than they are."

"It's more than not wanting to face them. I hate leaving Camp Noepe at this stage." She saw Monroe walking near the stables. She still did not trust him, or particularly like him, but he did something to her heart.

"There's nothing here for you to do right now. You've spent the last week in your office, faxing, phoning, and stamping brochures. You've hauled enough supplies to that craft room to decorate New England, got the fliers out, and sent packages to the schools on your list. The camp is ready except for that arena Yank and Mr. Wonderful are building."

"I don't know if he's Mr. Wonderful or a demonic fiend, but I've told him what has to be done to get Camp Noepe ready for the season. I just hate leaving you to handle this place while I'm back in New York attending the extravaganza that I'm sure Amanda Victoria Norris-Daigle will throw."

"Honey, you have the hard job. Don't spend a smidgen of your time worrying about me. I'd much rather be here with Yank and Mr. Wonderful than smiling through one of your mother's fancy-shmancy dinners, and being stared at by that crowd of shallow, pretentious assholes. 'Oh, look,' " she mimicked. " 'An Indian.' I told that snobbish bitch that Indians are people who live in or migrate from India. My people were here when her folks crawled off the Mayflower, or more precisely, were scraped from the bottom of it."

"Don't hold back, now. Say what you feel, Mother Pearl." Lacey laughed. "Frankly, I'd rather be here, too, even with the tension I feel every time Monroe and I cross paths."

"Never mind that." Pearl waved her hand. "The tension is purely sexual. When the time is right, you and that Texas stud will have one fine time together."

Lacey's face blanched. "On that note, I'm going in and pack."

Dressed in a new, blue pantsuit, Lacey felt strangely inappropriate without her jeans and work shirts. Between the Cape Air flight to Boston and the Continental flight on to New York, she had plenty of time to think. She tried to review the remaining tasks that needed completion before Camp Noepe opened, but thoughts of Monroe sneaked past her defenses. His soft but commanding voice, freshly calloused hands that he tried to hide, and the rush of excitement she felt when he entered the room were all mind-boggling. She didn't want to want him, to need him, or to have his face peering out of her every waking thought. Losing her will to such an abrasive stranger made her feel weak and vulnerable.

She took a cab from LaGuardia Airport and mentally prepared for what she knew would be an unpleasant confrontation. Pausing on the steps, she took a deep breath before using the key she still kept and unlocking the large mahogany door to the house in Strivers Row.

Her parents moved to the spacious home, which was centered on West 138th between Seventh and Eighth Avenues, when Lacey's father, Nathaniel Carlton Daigle, began his private practice. Her mother had added modernity to old opulence. Once she achieved the desired indulgences, she begged to move, but after Nathaniel's death, it seemed the home was what held her together.

Lacey had watched Amanda suffer the loss of her love. Her former social circle had all but abandoned her when she became a young and beautiful widow. Amanda's answer was to use the home that she had lavishly furnished to throw grand parties that rivaled the ones she had given when her husband was alive. Within months she not only moved back into the circle, she dominated it.

Lacey smiled at the thought of huddling with Pearl and snickering at the outfits, the perky silicone, and the number of husbands and wives who drank too much, spilled their secrets, and often left the party with someone else's mate. Now she would have to face the hoard of insincere revelers without her confidant.

She slipped in, unnoticed in the hustle and bustle of party preparations. The furniture was polished, crystal chandeliers sparkled, and the aroma of lemon was everywhere. Hiram, the piano tuner, was busy at work, because everyone knew Mandy Daigle would never have a party without live music. Lacey smiled at Maurice, the caterer, dodged two men in gray uniforms, and slipped into her old bedroom. Before she had time to fully settle in, her mother swooped in and interrupted her thoughtful pilgrimage around a roomful of memories.

"Darling! Why didn't you let me know you were here?"

Enfolded in the familiar fragrance of Chanel, Lacey hugged her mother carefully so as not to wrinkle the creamy blue suit. "I just got here, Mom. From the fuss out there, I assumed you were busy. How's everything coming along?"

"Your brother is going to be so surprised, and the two of us have a big surprise for you as well." She stood back. "Let me look at you. Oh, baby, I've been so concerned. I'll just never understand how that woman was able to talk you into going into the backwoods and starting a horse camp, of all things. You don't belong there, Lacey. You should—"

"Don't start, Mother." Just as Amanda used Lacey's full name to get her attention, "Mother" was substituted for "Mom" whenever Lacey wanted emphasis. "As happy as I am for my brother, I dreaded coming home because I knew you'd start criticizing my decision and attacking Mother Pearl. How many times do I have to tell you, this was my idea, not hers. I talked her into going to Martha's Vineyard, not the other way around."

"You just think it was your idea, darling. Pearl always had a way of planting her notions in your head and making you believe they were yours. She does that to people who allow themselves to fall under her witchcraft."

"I will not stand here and listen to you speak of her that way. Mother Pearl never professed to be a witch. Far from it. She's also never attempted to profit from her visionary powers, and if you think they're fake, why call her a witch?"

"Anyone can lead those who are willing to follow, but let's not talk about Pearl. You left that wonderful Mason here alone to run off on this mission that none of us understand. How long do you think this man will wait? Surely some other woman will steal him away."

"When I returned Mason's ring, I certainly didn't expect him to wait. Let him marry someone else. Our relationship is over. I'm doing what I want to do, and I'm happy. Doesn't that count for something?"

"I know you're still distraught over your father's death, and that woman has taken advantage of it. She's persuaded you to do something you would never consider doing. I'm appalled—"

"Cut it out, Mother! That couldn't be further from the truth." She wrung her hands in frustration. "I've tried to explain how much this camp means to me, and the only one who understands is Mother Pearl. Let's change the subject. Tell me about this girl my brother is so taken with. Do you think we'll hear wedding bells soon?"

"Not if I have anything to say about it. This girl is completely wrong for Nicholas. She comes from a family of nobodies."

"Okay, let's change the subject again. Tell me how you've been. I swear if you get any thinner, you won't be able to cast a shadow."

Amanda smiled and then smirked. "Is that another of Pearl's witticisms? When you see the rest of the family, you'll compliment me for staying thin. Wait until you see your aunts. Both of them have hips that span the globe, and your poor cousin Shelby is the size of a small horse."

Lacey had already tuned her mother out, though she felt a great measure of sadness for her brother. She could handle Amanda, whereas Nicholas always caved under her persistence, even as an adult. He attended the college of his mother's choice, accepted the career path she had lain and unless he took a stand, would marry a woman chosen simply because of her family connections. She made a mental note to encourage him to make up his own mind about the woman he was dating. Thinking of the woman Amanda would probably select for Nicholas, Lacey saw a female version of Mason and scowled.

As Lacey expected, the graduation ceremony was well attended by family and friends. Nicholas surprised his sister by announcing he would begin his career with the law firm of Phipps, Schaeffer, Mott, and Phipps, the last Phipps being Mason. Lacey mused at her mother's never-ending plan to control the lives of everyone around her, and pitied her brother's inability to sidestep the interference. The people in Amanda's circle of friends, even most of her family, were more impressed with titles than looks or character.

Lacey thought of the change in Mason's attitude once he met Amanda. She had fawned over him while assuring Lacey he was the one. Lacey knew her feelings had been real, but Amanda's matchmaking had taken over. Mason became arrogant and condescending.

The graduation celebration was another of Amanda's displays of grandeur. It was Nicholas's party, but as usual, Amanda was the center of attention. Lacey watched her work the crowd, dispensing smiles and compliments to those she wished to impress. A former dancer with enough vanity and money to maintain her youthful appearance, she strutted in four-inch heels amid the rustle of designer threads, and thumbed her nose at everyone who did not measure up to her meticulous scrutiny.

Amanda had called upon a bevy of friends—celebrities, politicians, and entertainers—to add intrigue to the gathering. Having a dance studio in the heart of Manhattan, she amassed an impressive list of connections and she used it to her full advantage. Everyone wanted an invitation to Mandy's shindigs. Lacey knew it was not because they liked Amanda or desired her company, but because of her imposing register of acquaintances whose elbows they hoped to rub.

Amanda found Lacey in the kitchen. "Honey, Mr. Rydell is going to grace us with a few selections. Would you lend your beautiful voice to the festivities?"

Lacey smiled at her mother's formal title for the man who had been her companion for the past eight months. Larry Rydell was a nightclub owner and restaurateur, also with social prominence. He sent flowers and gifts on a regular basis and, though she wondered if Amanda felt any real attraction, Lacey was pleased to see her mother smile again. She stood behind Larry and sang two of her mother's favorite songs before slipping away from the crowd with her brother in tow.

"I'm so proud of you." She hugged his shoulders and winced at his strong resemblance to their father. "I know Daddy wanted both of us to go into medicine, but I'm sure he's proud of you today. So, what's next?"

"I'll be working with Mason's firm and studying for the bar. I'm also going to add maritime law to my degree, so I've still got a ways to go, even though I'm truly sick of classrooms and digging through dusty law books."

Lacey felt more protective than she thought the three-year age difference warranted, but her realm of worry for Nicholas's happiness had tripled after their father's death. "Nicholas, I want you to be happy. I want you to have the world." She took his arm. "Please don't allow Mom to plan your life. Make your own choices, or you'll regret it and you'll resent her for forcing you into her mold."

"She's only trying to make our lives easier. I understand her attempts to help, but I am making my own decision. I wanted to consider medicine, but let's face it—I'm too squeamish. I'd never make it as a physician. Law is the only field I've ever considered."

"But with Mason's firm? Was that really your decision or Mom's? And what about this woman you've been dating? Is it serious?"

He dropped his head and Lacey hugged his shoulders. He had their father's butter smooth skin, dark curls and manly chin.

"Just between us, I think I'm in love," he said, smiling. "I know Mom doesn't want to hear this, but Greta makes me happy."

"Is she here?" She stopped and looked back at the crowd. "Why haven't I met her?"

"She's with her parents. They were at the graduation but had another stop before coming here. You'll like her. Just promise to help me keep Mom from clawing her eyes out, please."

"I've got your back, little brother." She hugged him and remembered the days she spent consoling him after their father's death. "If you love Greta, stand up to Mom. It's the only way you'll ever be happy. Mom loves us, and she does mean well. She's also focused on background and breeding more than anything else. That's fine if you're a racehorse. If you want to be with Greta, please don't let Mom interfere."

The party was in full swing, but Lacey slipped back to her room. She never enjoyed her mother's formal gatherings or her friends. Most were superficial phonies.

Taking the photo album that chronicled her childhood, she sat on the bed with her legs folded beneath her, giving no thought to the Carolina Herrera original dress her mother had waiting when she arrived home. She stepped back to a time filled with laughter, with her father's arms there to guide her, along with her grandfather's wisdom and wit that always made her smile. Carried away by the memories, she failed to lock the bedroom door or to hear it open.

"Hi, baby."

She jumped upright and quickly wiped the memories from her face. "Mason. What are you doing here?"

"Surely you didn't think I'd miss your brother's graduation party. I would have been here sooner, but I had to rid myself of two pesky clients." He sat on the bed and pulled her into his arms. "The only reason I haven't already swam out to the island is that I knew you'd be here today. I've missed you so much. Everything in my life is different without you."

Regardless of her feelings for Mason, Lacey admitted missing their sex life. His touch enlivened a heart filled with months of loneliness. She almost surrendered. "It's good to see you. How've you been?"

"Going crazy for you." He smothered her face with kisses. "Lacey, I keep thinking I'll wake up and realize this is all one horrible nightmare. Please, baby. Forget this nonsense and come back home. I'm sure you'll be able to get your old job back, and if not, you'll have no problems finding another one. You belong here, with me. Every time I think of the plans we made, I feel like I'm going insane."

"What I'm doing is not nonsense." She pulled free. "It's my life. The one I've chosen."

"Bad choice of words." He stood and paced. "You and I had a wonderful thing going. You can't deny that. We had plans to build a future together, have a family and a life together. You can't just throw all of that away without good reason. I'm here for you. I love you, but I won't wait forever." He cupped her chin and tilted her face up to his. "Your appetite for sex was just as great as mine. How do I know you're not up there with another man?"

"You don't." She pushed his hand away. "Your life is no longer my concern, and what I do is my business. I expected you to find someone else to sleep with, and to marry if that's what you want." She watched his expression and knew he had too much pride to readily accept rejection. She took his hand and held it tightly. "The only thing I want is for you to find the happiness you deserve."

"You know, I absolutely refuse to believe the woman I fell in love with has thrown away a damn fine job, abandoned everything she had going, and moved off to start a damn horse ranch! I didn't want to believe your mother, but she's right. It is that woman, your grandmother, putting these ideas in your head? You're acting like you've lost your—"

"Okay, that's it. Get the hell out of my room." She reached behind her for one of the whirling figurines in a row of dance trophies and threw her weighted hand over her head. "Get out!"

"What on earth is going on in here?" Amanda dashed in and quickly closed out the merriment. "Honey, this is your brother's celebration and you're creating an embarrassing scene." She smiled and held out her arms. "Hello, Mason, darling. I didn't see you come in, but I'm very glad you're here. Are you as happy as I am to see this beautiful lady?" She busily smoothed the skirt of Lacey's dress. "Make her understand how much we've missed her."

"That's what I was trying to do." The anger had drained from his face. "Lacey, you've got to get over this obsession of—"

"What I've got to do is get the hell away from here as soon as possible. I am not obsessed. I'm doing what I want to do. Just because it doesn't meet with your approval doesn't make it inappropriate. And that goes double for you, Mother. 'Show passion for the things you love.' How many times have you said that to me? I love where I am and what I'm doing."

"That's what everyone says when they're being duped by some kind of controlling force." Mason reached for her hand and turned to Amanda when she pulled away. "She didn't listen to me before and she's not listening now. It's almost as if she's a different person. It does seem that someone is controlling every move she makes."

Lacey's eyes glistened with anger. "I could also say you're different. I'd like to think I fell in love with a considerate man, not a cynical snob. You want to know about obsession? I'll give you my definition. Obsession was your attempt to impress your associates by spending weeks, uh, make that months, on the golf course trying to measure up to what you felt was critical to your career. Did I make fun of you?"

"That was not an obsession." He pouted. "My father wanted me to learn to play so I could entertain clients. It was another way of helping my career and helping the firm."

"But you couldn't even hit the ball, Mason. I watched you, blistering in the sun, day after day, trying to fit into something that was clearly not your scene. I'm not like that. I know who I am. I've never tried to be anything else. I'll return to New York when the season is over, but only after I've proven that I can make this camp a success."

"But you don't need—"

"You know what?" she interrupted Mason. "Neither of you have expressed even the mildest concerns about the camp. You didn't ask if things were going well because you're too busy telling me what a mistake I'm making. How foolish and obsessive I am. Camp Noepe is a dream, my grandfather's and mine. I'm going to make it happen. So please, just leave me alone."

Amanda placed her arm around Lacey's shoulder while drawing Mason into their midst. "I have a wonderful suggestion that I'm sure both of you will accept. Since you've already spent money on this camp, why don't you stay there until it gets off the ground and then come home? Leave Pearl to manage it and you can go back as often as you like. I'm sure Mason will even go with you sometimes. The island can be a lovely retreat for the two of you. You can plan your wedding—oh, I've got it. Have your wedding on the island. Wouldn't that be perfect?"

"I love Lacey. I'm willing to cooperate. If this thing is so important to her, I'm willing to wait until she finds the success she's seeking. It's hard, but I'll do it."

"Now there. Isn't this the perfect solution?" Amanda smiled and pulled the two of them together.

"Mother, I can't believe you just engineered a line of condescending bullcrap that I'm supposed to appreciate," Lacey fumed. "I don't want Mason to wait for me. I assumed he would have someone by now. In fact, I'm also sure he's had someone by now." She held out her hands. "I've tried, though unsuccessfully, to make both of you understand why I've made the choices I've made, but now I don't care whether you understand or not. I'm not giving up on this camp. I will give my grandfather something to feel proud of and I don't give a damn what either of you think. If you loved me, loved me unselfishly, the way you should, you'd understand."

"Your grandfather is dead, Lacey. He has no knowledge of what's going on here. If he did and was still in his right mind, he'd suggest that you come home. Besides, your grandfather was not a failure. He was a professional who lived a good life and provided a good life for his family. I think it was very selfish of him to let his pride keep him from admitting his inability to take care of his business affairs, but there's no use worrying about that. You're worrying about the dead while this wonderful man here loves and wants to marry you. Surely you can—"

"I don't want to argue. As you just said, this is Nicholas's night. Just pretend I'm not here." She turned. "Mason, I loved you. I was confident in the future we had planned. I was happy and you were supportive, but that was when everything was done your way. As soon as I expressed my desires, my dreams, you became almost abusive in your refusal to try and understand. Get married. Get any damn thing you want, but don't tell me how to live my life."

She tilted her head and screwed her face into a beseeching smile. "Can't we end our relationship on the same positive note it began?"

CHAPTER 4

"You should have heard her, Mother Pearl," Lacey spouted. "My own mother conspiring with that insipid, anal bore. I don't know what I ever saw in him. It was all I could do to keep from screaming at her, and closing his drooling little mouth with my fist. "

Pearl looked on amusingly as Lacey vented her anger. "What about Nicholas? Did he enjoy the party?"

"He did until Mom damn near attacked the poor girl he's in love with. Just devoured her."

"Is she a pushover or did she retaliate?" Pearl questioned.

"She tried to fight back, but you know Amanda. Her questions are always innocent. 'That outfit is just so right for you.' Not pretty, just right, and then she asked if Greta 'found it in a specialty shop.' She's a big girl."

"Oh, Lord. Nicholas should've known his mother would attack the girl if she's overweight."

"She's not exactly overweight. She's probably a size 10. When I say big girl, I mean big." She held her hand in the air. "She towers over Nicholas, and he's almost six feet tall. Mother kept quizzing her about everything, and then publicly enumerating her short-comings, or at least her views of them. 'You've never been abroad? I thought everyone had been to London. It's just right across the water.' Nicholas told me later that he thinks Greta has a fear of airplanes. She's graduating law school next year and she's very intelligent. I think she's perfectly delightful, and I hope Nicholas will tell Mom to mind her own business, but I know he won't. I don't think he can."

"If he loves this girl, he'll stand up to Amanda. God knows he's seen you do it enough times. I know that wasn't easy for you." Pearl's voice was laced with compassion. "Your mother's opinion of me is no secret, but I still say you have to be patient with Amanda. Things aren't always what they seem."

"Meaning?"

"Meaning there's more to your mother than she'll allow anyone to see. We all have ways to protect our heart from pain, and I know she wants what's best for you."

"She doesn't care what's best for me. She just wants me to marry Mason, and that's not going to happen. I was angry as hell for the way she embarrassed Nicholas and Greta, and I told her so. I left the house four hours before my flight time, and took a cab to the airport."

Lacey noticed the changes that had occurred in her absence. "Micah is becoming a very handsome young man," she remarked. "The older he gets, the more he resembles Yank." She noticed the large bouquet of roses and remembered Micah telling her that his grandfather, Tedera, had a crush on Pearl.

"And just where did those roses come from?" She smiled up at Pearl. "Don't tell me Dean Greenup mistakenly sent the wrong bouquet?" Since opening Camp Noepe, Lacey had purchased a bouquet of blooms each week, along with her produce, from Greenup's Nursery and Produce Mart just outside of Bettlebung Corners. "I didn't order roses. Did you?"

Pearl blinked and sighed. "I don't want to hear this from you right now."

"Hear what? You mean the roses didn't come from Greenup's? Who then?" She smiled at Pearl's discomfort.

"I know what you're doing, so knock it off."

"Come on. Surely you're not keeping something from me. Are those from a secret admirer? Mother Pearl's got a boyfriend," she chanted.

"Stop this nonsense right now." Pearl rolled a dish towel in her hands and swatted Lacey's backside. "You know better. Tedera is sixty-five years old."

"So?" Lacey had argued with Micah that being seven years Tedera's senior would bother Pearl enough to prevent a romance. "Who cares about the age difference?"

"I do. Haven't you learned that women's bodies keep functioning while men get old and limp? That man is too old for me. If I go out on a limb for a man, he'll have to be able to put a smile on my face. The only thing Tedera can do for me is point the way to a

younger man. I'm not spending my time with that
relic, but since you want to start a fuss, I'll just give it
right back to you. Guess who was asking about you
while you were gone, and moping around like he'd lost
his best friend?"

"If you mean Monroe, I'm sure he just wanted to
know if I planned to return and sign his paycheck."
She had seen him watching as she and Micah drove up.
She had thought of him, especially when she was with
Mason. She even compared the two men, knowing
Amanda would not give a second's consideration to a
wandering cowboy. If anything, that fact made him
even more attractive.

"Don't try to snow an old lady. I know you're
attracted to Monroe Faulkner, and he to you. He asked
where you were, when you were expected back, and he
did so with a gaga look on his handsome face. The
man has it bad."

"Come on, Mother Pearl." She blushed. "Monroe
isn't interested in me. He doesn't even like me."

"He's not only interested, his tongue is wagging
like old Crow when he sees a soupbone." She looked
down at the sleeping black lab lying across the
doorstep. "And you know what? I see the two of you
together, and this time there is lace and…" She
blinked against the tears in her eyes. "There's lace and
gaiety, and happiness. I want those things for you. I
want them very much."

"Mother Pearl, I'm shocked. You don't tear up very
often." She snaked her arm around Pearl's waist. "I

want them one day, and they'll happen, just lay off the predictions. If you saw us together and I was wearing lace and beads, it was anything but a wedding."

Pearl shook her head. "I can't identify the occasion, but you looked very pleased."

Lacey smiled. The two women were equally protective of each other and shared a closeness that few, including Lacey's mother, understood. Lacey believed Pearl could see the future, but a future with Monroe Faulkner was not a possibility in her mind.

Micah and Tedera provided the extra hands needed to accelerate the readiness of Camp Noepe. They made rapid changes, both inside and out. The days began early with a clank of the breakfast bell and a hearty spread with plenty of hot coffee.

Pearl and Shale quickly cleared all evidence of breakfast, and everyone went about their daily routines. Lacey spent a lot of time in the large room of the main house, making daily schedules and training manuals for the campers. She also made regular trips into town for necessities. She and Shale rummaged through sale bins for reasonably priced items to keep the campers and themselves occupied.

Monroe went out each morning with Yank, Tedera, and Micah to tend the livestock and help construct the arena. Knowing their varied schedules would place them all in different locations, Pearl did not summon them for lunch, but placed trays of sandwiches and sweetened iced tea or lemonade on the table. Lacey noticed that Monroe finished his meal at the table instead of grabbing a sandwich on the run like the others.

She smiled at the back of his head and watched him languidly amble out to the stables. According to Yank's reliable report, Monroe did his share of the work and more.

"It's almost as if he pushes himself beyond the limit just to see how far he can go," Yank had whispered to Lacey. "I keep telling him he'll wear out before the camp opens, but he just smiles and keeps on working. Still hasn't said anything about his personal life. I saw him walking around out back and talking on his cell phone the other night. I guess he was looking for clear reception."

Yank rubbed his hands together and smiled. "I laugh every time he asks me or Micah to find out something from you. It always starts with 'Would you ask Lacey.' You were standing right there the other day when he did it. Even Micah started telling him to ask you himself."

Lacey had overheard and had wondered. The words spoken between them, other than hasty saluta-tions, did not exceed the number of sunsets Monroe had worked at Camp Noepe. "As long as he does his work, we'll be okay," she told Yank.

She tried to sound dismissive, but her curiosity heightened. Why was the man from Texas so secretive and so far from home? She searched on the Internet for information about him, but found nothing. She even tried searching using his name and social security number. The result was the same—zilch.

When the dinner bell called them together in the main house for the evening, she watched him enjoying Pearl's flavorful meals. He was accustomed to finery. She could see it on his face. Pearl still declared him "harmless and handsome," but Lacey secretly thought he was far too handsome to be harmless.

April had brought enough warm weather to encourage a blossoming mélange of wildflowers. The landscape came alive with yellow and purple blooms, bits of reds and orange foliage draped over a mass of green. Lacey spent as much time outside as she could spare. Far away from the day spa she had enjoyed in New York, she jogged along the beach in the early morning, and when dinner preparations were in the final stages, she enjoyed her other love—horseback riding.

She had chosen her favorite from among the horses, or more precisely, he had chosen her. She and Champion galloped along the beach, followed the sun's orange highlights into beds of buttercups, or trekked along the damp sand, always taking a different route. The open spaces brought her in touch with her spirit. Tension drifted off in the freshly scented breeze. She returned calmed, and usually with a giant appetite.

The one thing she tried to avoid at all costs was being alone with Monroe. It wasn't that she didn't trust him. She didn't trust her own love-starved heart. Their encounters had been relatively pleasant. She met his smiles with her own, but directed her comments regarding work to Yank or Micah. Even during dinner the two of them seldom spoke directly to each other but Lacey often caught sight of his intense, icy stares. She felt the attraction, and a large measure of unexplained resentment.

During dinner the women usually talked among themselves, and so did the men. Ever mindful of his nearness, she fought to conceal all traces of emotion. The combination of her need and his overpowering manliness wheedled away her willpower each time he was near. No man had made her feel so alive, yet so afraid.

When her hard work began to pay off and she felt confident of her endeavors, Lacey wanted to celebrate with a special dinner. Pearl was more than happy to prepare a feast. Lacey's eyes sparkled with excitement as she surveyed the scrumptious roast duck with plum sauce, wild rice, and butter beans. After dinner, there was Pearl's special Swiss chocolate cake, along with aromatic coffee.

Everyone gathered around the table, talking about their day, the weather, and work still to be done before the opening of Camp Noepe. Lacey was touched by the exchange of sly glances between Pearl and Tedera. Knowing Pearl had found a companion made her heart feel light, but seeing their nods of affection only served to identify what was missing from her own life.

She saw Monroe watching her. Her mood was always set by the feelings in her heart, and for the first time in quite awhile, her heart felt light. She could hardly contain her enthusiasm during dinner. Everything seemed to be working well. Monroe looked more at ease than on previous occasions, which made her confident he would stay. Yank happily reported that the arena was near completion. After a round of praise for the cook, they gathered around the fireplace, and Pearl sat at the old upright piano that came with the building, plucking aimlessly at the keys.

Lacey disappeared into her office and returned with an accounting ledger. "I have an announcement that I think will ease some of the uneasiness regarding the success of Camp Noepe." She squinted in Monroe's direction before filling seven glasses from Pearl's reserve stock.

"Go light on this, Micah. It's another of Mother Pearl's specials that could knock you flat on your rear." She smiled, raised her glass, and held the green-lined tablet in her other hand.

"As of today, each bed at Camp Noepe is filled for the first session, and some for the entire summer. I have also booked enough non-resident riding lessons to necessitate asking Yank to call his brother Quentin to help out during the first session. I've hired Jennifer Greenup and two part-timers to help with the campers for the rest of the summer."

Everyone yelped and raised their glasses, especially Micah. Jennifer was the seventeen-year-old daughter of Dave Greenup, and Micah's love interest. Lacey enjoyed his pleased smile and continued her update.

"We have thirty-six girls for the June session, with nine of them remaining through the second session. Our ad reached as far away as Tennessee, and we have an impressive number of locals. I have, to date, conformation of another four coming for the second session and a total of fourteen non-boarders enrolled for second session morning or evening riding lessons."

When the applause began, she raised her hand and scanned the room, carefully searching for Monroe's reaction. "There's one more bit of news, maybe the most important. I called a few contacts from my hotel days and was fortunate enough to get this." She waved a stapled stack of papers. "It's a contract with IMF Industries to rent this facility during the off season, at, what I might add, is a pretty hefty fee."

The glasses clicked and everyone cheered.

"Yank, I hope you don't mind that I waggled a tidy sum for your services, as well as an option for Shale to run the kitchen on weekends. I will go over the terms with the two of you, and if you have no objections, I'll return your signed agreement and cement the deal."

"That's my girl! I'm so proud of you, honey," Pearl yelled.

"Same here!" Yank lifted Lacey off the floor in a big hug. "Thank you, Lacey. Work is scarce around here in winter, so you're taken a load off my mind."

"Congratulations." Monroe moved forward from his position in the corner of the room. "That's wonderful. What does this company plan to do with the facility?"

"Use it for training sessions and as a corporate retreat. It's quiet here, and the large dining room will make a perfect conference area."

"What about the horses?" He moved closed and spoke softer.

"Yank is taking them to his place in Aquinnah." For reasons that she could not identify, his approval was important.

"Yank told me about Ramsey Treadwell and his runaway victories at the Roundup each year."

His eyes softened when he spoke and his lips became more irresistible.

"If even one child in your group has potential, I'll work as hard as I can to whip her into shape before the competition. Camp Noepe will have a win."

"Let's celebrate!" Pearl yelled from her position at the piano. "Come on over here." She began playing a lively version of "The Entertainer." "I don't have a great voice, but Lacey does. Sing something for us, honey. I copied a stack of sheet music for our evening song-alongs when the kids arrive, so we might as well practice."

Yank fished out an old guitar from behind the piano, and Lacey, Micah, and Shale joined him and Pearl in a medley of everything from Gladys Knight to Bobby Goldsboro. Monroe poured another drink and tapped his feet but did not join in.

"Come join us, Monroe." She waved him over.

"No thanks. I don't have much of a voice for singing."

"Neither do we, but that's not stopping us," Yank said. "Join us. Tell us your favorite songs. We do everything from dirty blues to the country ballads that Lacey sings so well."

"Country ballads?" His eyebrows lifted. "That's unusual."

"Yeah, I do country and western. Since you're a Texan, come share some of those campfire songs with us."

"No, you guys go ahead. Someone has to be the audience."

"Oh, come on." She wanted to break the barrier between stares and conversation. "I'll bet you can do a mean Luther, or maybe you're a jazz buff."

"I like jazz, but how can one not like Luther?"

"I've got it. Let's do some of the old Marvin Gaye duets. I'm sure you know those." She reached out and tugged his sleeve.

He reluctantly consented and they sang together, to each other. The words became personal and Lacey felt hot all over. Embarrassed, she felt it showed and that everyone, especially Monroe, could see that she was aroused.

"Okay, my throat is getting a little dry." She looked into his eyes. "Thanks, Monroe. You have a great voice."

"So do you. I enjoyed it. Dinner was fabulous and so was the entertainment, but I'm bushed. I think I'll turn in. Good night, everyone."

She watched from the window. He walked past the camp and into an outline of apricot moonbeams sparkling on blue water. There was something about him, maybe the mystery, that fueled her desires.

"That was a fun evening." She hugged Pearl. "Rest your feet. Shale and I will clean the kitchen. That was an incredible meal."

"It was." Shale added, "Monroe thought so. He eats better than Yank and Micah. Seemed a little troubled after the two of you finished singing. He practically ran out of here."

"You noticed that, too?" Pearl sat on her stool next to the counter. "I think something caused him a lot of pain, and he's still trying to find his way back."

"Has to be a woman." Tedera sighed, looking at the back of Pearl's neck. "Anything that hurts that much has to do with a woman. With love."

"Don't start women-bashing, okay?" Lacey cautioned Tedera. "Contrary to what you think, we're not the root of all evil."

"I never thought that," he answered, still looking at Pearl. "I think he lost someone he loved. A woman. I think he's still hurting, and he don't know what to do about it."

"I think he's in love with Lacey and don't know what to do about it." Micah said.

"Okay, let's not go there." Lacey felt a rush of blood under her skin when she heard the certainty in Micah's voice. "That man is not in love with me."

"To hell he ain't," Yank joined in. "I don't have those powers of prediction like Pearl, but I know what I see. When the two of you were singing together, I thought that man was going to grab you in his arms right there in front of everybody. You had to see it."

"See it? Feel it," Pearl said. "We were swimming in it."

"I tried talking to him a couple of times, tried to get a little background, but he clammed up. I told him I could feel his suffering and offered a shoulder if he wanted to talk about it." Tedera took a long swig of Pearl's homemade wine. "He thanked me, but said suffering was a private thing. Something to be endured, not shared. I thought it best to leave him be."

"You know what I think?" Lacey wiped her hands and took the dog's leash from a rung on the coat rack. "I think I'd better take Crow out for his walk so he won't pee in the hallway again and have Mother Pearl threaten to strangle him."

She ran from the room almost as Monroe had, her face burning under their scrutiny. Of course she had felt it, but did not want to think it was real. She certainly did not want to think of what could happen if it was real. Nowhere in her wildest imagination had she ever dreamed of wanting a man so painfully. Certainly not a stranger who could have baggage that was heavy enough to tow her dreams to the bottom of the ocean.

Crow ran toward the water, almost dragging her across the sand. "Hold on, boy." She removed the leash. "Don't go too far."

She stood in the moonlight, peppered with thoughts of her past and concerns for her future. A sprinkling of stars twinkled above, adding intrigue to the evening. She thought of Mason. He was handsome with money and potential, but it was his thoughtfulness that she had found most attractive. Her father's devotion to her mother was the yardstick by which she measured men. Mason had that devotion at first, but his thoughtfulness and consideration had ended. When that happened, her feelings for him began to wane. He had condemned her plans to come to the island, but when he declared she should be thankful for his love, Lacey knew his love was no longer wanted.

A gust of wind moved in from the water. Lacey drew her vest close to her body and looked around for Crow. She called his name, but her voice faded into the swirl of damp air. She kept walking uphill to his favorite spot, and hers. Standing atop the bank, she listened to the somber tempo of waves lapping the red clay.

A noise came from the underbrush and she called out again. Trying to keep her balance, she walked down the other side of the bank. Surrounded by scampering noises and the sound of her own weight on the dry leaves, she expected to see samples of wildlife, hopefully running in the other direction. They were mostly harmless, but the unknown activity became frightening in the darkness. She craned her neck towards the thicket ahead and called out again. Her eyes were focused on the ground, but she spied a bold flash of red through an opening in the leaves.

"Who's there?" Her heart lurched when the silhouette emerged from the shadows. "Monroe?"

"What the hell are you doing out here in the bushes?" He loomed over her.

She stopped and stared, openmouthed.

"Are you spying on me? Am I not entitled to privacy, or does exposing one's soul fall under your list of employee responsibilities?"

"Hey, I'm sorry! I'm not spying on you. I don't want you to expose anything to me."

She came closer, flames of anger dancing in her eyes. "You're here at Camp Noepe because I needed a riding instructor. I don't give a damn about your soul."

Crow ran out from the thicket. She grabbed the dog's collar and reattached the leash. A flash of awareness crossed Monroe's face.

"I'm sorry. You were just walking the dog. I thought…"

She ran away without looking back.

"Hey, Lacey! Wait, please," he called after her and began running, but she had a commanding lead.

She did not stop or look back. Her eyes were straight ahead. Anger mounted in her chest and she ran faster. She heard him shout, "Look out," but it was too late. Her right foot caught a clump of grass and she fell, face down, in the sand.

He was beside her, holding her arm and lifting her to her feet. "Are you okay?"

"Get the hell away from me!" she screamed and jerked free, more angry than hurt. "You're a real asshole. What did you do down in Texas? Ride roughshod over one of those prisons I've heard so much about?" She stood and brushed the sand from her face.

"I'm sorry. You startled me before, but I shouldn't have lashed out the way I did. I'm very sorry. Are you okay?"

"That comes under the heading of none of your damn business." She used the back of her hand to wipe the tears that cascaded down her cheek.

He passed his handkerchief. "Hey, I am sorry. Uh, don't cry, okay? I'm sorry."

"Cry? Is that what you think?" She refused the handkerchief and shoved his hand away. "I would like to see the day—or night—when you make me cry. I have sand in my eyes, not that you should concern yourself."

"I was wrong, and I'm sorry. Let me help you. You'll need to flush that sand out before it irritates your eyes, especially if you wear contacts."

She continued to brush her clothing and blink her eyes with angry rapidity. "Mr. Faulkner, I placed an ad in several trade journals for a riding instructor who was willing to commit to seasonal work. I spoke to someone identifying himself as Monroe Faulkner, and maybe I'm mistaken, but he sounded old and he sounded white."

Tasting the rough sand on her lips, she turned and spat several times. "Be that as it may, I have sunk not just my money, but some of Pearl's, into this place, and I need a riding instructor. I could do it myself or I could use Yank, but I needed someone with credentials that looked impressive on a sales brochure. The man I spoke with said he would be in on the Tuesday morning ferry, the first week of February. I drove out to meet that ferry every Tuesday for three weeks. Without any kind of warning, you show up at sunset. I don't know how you got here."

"Look, I've—"

"Let me finish." She crooked her neck and stared into his eyes. "I've watched you with the horses. I like the way you handle them and I like the work you've done on the arena, but I'm not the least bit interested in the contents of your soul, Mr. Faulkner. That brooding rural charm of yours may have been a big hit with women down in Texas, but believe me, I could care less."

She stormed away, her boot-clad feet digging deep trenches in the loose sand.

CHAPTER 5

Painfully aware of her attraction to a man who had shown only coldness and hostility, Lacey reverted to her old habit of staying clear of her new employee. He seemed to have personal issues, and she had neither the time nor the inclination to sort them out. He was good with the horses. With Yank and Micah's assistance, he had done a wonderful job with the additions to the stables. Micah said he kept to himself more than usual. He avoided the evening gatherings, and she made no attempt to seek his company.

Micah and Yank had pestered him at first, saying they needed his baritone for the Camp Noepe choir, but Lacey insisted they leave him to his solitude.

"He doesn't want to get too close to any of us, and I suggest we respect his privacy. I don't know what his problem is, and maybe it's best that way."

Without giving full details of the incident on the beach, she told them only that Monroe had ranted about what he had called attempts to look into his soul.

"He seems scared that we might learn something about him that he would rather keep secret. I don't care who he is or what he's done, as long as he can get us through the summer. Let's just leave him to his isolation."

It had not escaped her discerning eye that he was in pain, but his sadness bore a strain of superiority. He wore it like a ghost, a loner who felt that few ever attained such deep and eternal sorrow. Each time Lacey thought of trying to penetrate his wall of seclusion, she remembered the viciousness in his voice that night on the beach and continued to respect his invisible "no trespassing" sign.

The week before the campers arrived, everyone rushed in a mad frenzy to complete last-minute preparations. Lacey and Pearl had gone to town for supplies and, on their return, saw Monroe walking down the road. Lacey blew the horn and Pearl waved.

"And just where do you think he's going? He knew we were driving in for supplies. Why didn't he just ask for a ride? Has he mentioned anything about himself or his family to you?"

"Mother Pearl, the man probably has no family, not even parents. My guess is that he was hatched from one of those human incubators. He has no family and he has no heart."

Pearl smiled. "Just what am I detecting in your voice? Maybe a bruised ego?"

"What you detect is anger and frustration. I need his help, so I can't afford to do what I would like to do, which is to tell him to go to hell."

"Come on, honey. I know you. You've been out here for all of these months without male companionship, and along comes this deliciously handsome man. Sparks are bound to fly. It's only human nature."

"In that case, we're one human short. The only sparks I see are coming from the fury that man instills in me, and I'm sure the feeling is mutual. Even if I were attracted to him, which, I assure you, I am not, it wouldn't work. This man is so full of himself, it's ridiculous. You should have heard him the other day talking to Yank and Micah, giving orders as if he was Captain Hornblower. He's arrogant, self-righteous, and dictatorial."

"Mercy! He's really got you going."

Pearl was silent until they reached the driveway to the main house. "Lacey, at the risk of being told to mind my own business, I'm going to ask a personal question. Have you spoken with Mason lately?"

She swerved the Jeep into a sharp left. "And why on earth would I want to do that?"

"Now don't go running into the ditch, but the two of you were in love. You were engaged. In my opinion, all of the things you said about Monroe apply directly to Mason. He's the dictatorial fathead, but you cared enough to accept his engagement ring. I know he upset you, but isn't it possible that some of those feelings survived, that they're still inside of you, hidden under that pile of resentment you continue taking out on Monroe?"

Lacey parked without answering, took an armload of bags, and started for the back door.

"I swerved back there to avoid a squirrel, and if you really want to know how I feel about Mason, I'll gladly tell you. I feel hurt, disappointed, and mad as hell. Hurt because he didn't have enough faith in me to trust my judgment, and disappointed that I spent two years of my life in the company of a man who is tucked away in his insular, narrow-minded world without a pinch of adventure in his soul."

She slammed the bags on the kitchen counter. "I'm mad because he decided my plans were worthless, that he could wad my dreams into a ball and toss them away. I wouldn't call that close-minded mule if he were the last man on earth."

They made several trips to the kitchen, unloaded the supplies, and stored them in the pantry. Pearl removed her jacket and sat at the counter.

"Can I fix you a drink? I'm having one. I need to unwind."

"I'll have whatever you're having." She rubbed her temple with the knuckles of her right hand. "You know, Mother Pearl, I thought I had life all figured out, and then I realized my big office, fat paycheck, and all of the people around me who jumped when I whistled but wouldn't wet my tongue if I perished, were all just a great big pipe dream."

She spread her arms. "This is real. Out here, away from the rat race. One with nature. This is the life I want right now, and I'm not about to let anyone spoil it, not Mason Phipps or some bullheaded cowboy from Texas. I wish we could have done this on Daigle land, but I'm happy we're here, and I'm not going to let anyone take that from me."

Aware that children are prone to pick up on the tension between adults, Lacey looked for ways to at least alleviate the rigidity between her and Monroe. She waited until they were well into breakfast, using the time to gauge his mood. When his smile pushed deep dimples into his cheeks at one of Tedera's jokes, she decided to take a chance.

"Mother Pearl, I think we need to have a little celebration before the campers arrive next week. Everyone has worked so hard. We deserve one big blowout before we surrender our independence."

"Yank and I are one up on you, honey. We've already started planning. We've got meat marinating and plenty to drink. We're going to have a cookout and get sloppy drunk before the herd arrives."

"Great. I want everyone to take a break this next week." She found encouragement in Monroe's fetching smile, and unmanageable attraction in his wonderful upturned lips. She continued speaking to Pearl. "Do you remember my friend Christina DeLuca?"

"I do if you mean the girl with the big, pretty eyes and the boorish father," Pearl answered.

Lacey chuckled. "Yeah, she's the one. She works at the Afro-American History Museum in Boston. We had lunch last week and she gave me a couple of passes for a big museum tour. MFA is highlighting several exhibits, and one of them is the van Gogh collection that I've been wanting to see."

With everyone's attention, she turned to Monroe. "I don't know if you like art, Monroe, but if you're game, I could use the company." She crossed her fingers under the table.

"Sure." He frowned in surprise. "Sounds like fun."

"Great. We can take the ferry into Boston tomorrow, but we'll have to leave a little early. We can have lunch in Boston. There's a great restaurant on Newbury that you might enjoy."

Pearl looked on in wonder before shaking her head and touching Monroe's sleeve. "I know the restaurant. Take a bottle of Pepto."

"It's Indian cuisine, a little spicy, but great." Lacey smiled with relief.

She went into her office after breakfast. Pearl came in and closed the door.

"That was real cute." She sat in the chair in front of Lacey's desk. "You rambled sideways into that invitation, didn't you? Are you finally admitting your attraction to this man?"

"No such thing. I just want to get past where we are before the kids arrive. I'm not attracted to Monroe." She lowered her head and mumbled, "If I am, that's not the point. I have a camp to run. This is business."

That business kept her awake for most of the night. She examined her reasons for the invitation and second-guessed the idea of spending the entire day with Monroe, but knew it was too late to recant. It had been a while since she enjoyed the feel of a man's arms. There had been passion with Mason, and it was greatly missed. Monroe's arms continued to beckon her. Everything about him suggested boundless pleasures.

Her heart did a double take when he walked into the dining room for breakfast the next morning. He was dressed in houndstooth slacks, a tan turtleneck, and an expertly tailored black sports coat. His presence filled the room.

"You didn't say if the restaurant had a dress code so I wasn't sure..." he muttered.

"There's no strict dress code, but you look great." She didn't want to stare but found it impossible to remove her eyes from his perfect frame. "In fact, the relaxed atmosphere is the thing I like most about this restaurant. I think you'll enjoy it there."

They headed out right after breakfast, making small talk as she drove to the ferry landing. She kept the topics light, mostly focusing on the workings of Camp Noepe. He admired the horses she had chosen and she praised the way he handled them. She soon relaxed and began looking forward to a day away from the camp.

"Thanks for the invitation." His voice had lost all traces of annoyance. "I saw a van Gogh exhibit recently and thoroughly enjoyed it. This one focused on his portraits. I believe it was called Face to Face."

She reacted quickly. "It's the same one. You've already seen it. We can skip—"

"No, no, no. I saw it during a very short trip to New York. I like van Gogh. I love to study his brushstrokes, and there was little time for that on my other trip. I'd love to see it again. I would have gone myself had I known about it."

She smiled. "I hope you're not just saying that. I missed it in New York and was glad to have a chance to see it here in Boston, but we can skip it and go on to one of the other museums. I'm sure I'll have another chance to see it. I don't want you to be bored." She stole glances as she drove. It was hard to deny the dent he made in her heart.

"Don't worry. I'm not likely to be bored. I mean, there's so much to see. You almost have to see it twice to get the full effect."

Her heart purred in his presence and her body ached for his, but she was able to enjoy a little relaxation instead of verbal combat. Every clear thought she had told her not to get involved. They talked and laughed through three museums and dinner, which Monroe claimed to enjoy. Her attraction grew each second. They shared their mutual love for horses one more time before discussing the island and its inhabitants. She kept the conversation very general, but, on their return, they encountered a lengthy delay at the ferry landing. In trying to keep the conversation going, she stumbled into personal territory.

When he commented on the temperate climate, she spoke without thinking. "Is Texas your home?"

"Yes, it is. I was born there."

"Any family back there...I'm sorry, I don't mean to pry." She stole a glance at his face and found no adverse reaction to her question, but reminded herself that the purpose of this outing was to soothe, not ruffle, his sensitive feathers. "You don't have to answer unless you want to."

He laughed. "It's okay. I don't mind. All of my family is still there."

She wanted to ask if there was a woman in his life but didn't dare. "Tell me about Texas. My mom loves to tell the funny story of my first trip to Houston. It was during the month of February, and about ninety percent of the people we saw were dressed in Western clothing. I couldn't wait to call home and tell my brother. Little did I know that it was Go Texas Day. My friend teased me for months over that."

He laughed. "Was that your only visit to Texas?"

"Not at all. I have a friend in Dallas whom I visit often. We shop all day, have dinner, and party at night. It's the same routine we follow when she comes to New York. I'm always fascinated with the South and the West, and since Texas is labeled the heart of the Southwest, I find so many admirable traditions there. When I was a kid, I watched western movies with my grandfather. I was and still am fascinated by frontier life. And those cowboys. I don't know why they're called *cowboys*. They were real men. Were there many black ones?"

"Quite a few. Nearly a third of all American cowboys were black. They journeyed west in covered wagons, worked the land, established all-black towns and some even became wealthy. It's said the word 'cowboy' likely came from slave owners referring to the 'boys' they had placed in charge of their herds."

"I've never read anything about them." She leaned on the steering wheel. "Were any of them famous?"

"Oh, yeah. Bill Pickett was probably the most famous of all. A lot's been written about him. Hollywood had a hard time trying to create his image on the screen, but he was a legend."

"You know, I have heard of him. I don't remember how or where, probably one of those tiny blurbs in a history book."

"Yeah. There was also Nat Love, better known as Deadeye Dick. Black cowboys are still more plentiful than most folks realize. Texas. Oklahoma. Even California. Blacks still ranch and farm. Some follow the rodeo circuit. I have a good friend, Fred Whitfield, who is a three-time National Finals Rodeo Champion calf roper, and one of his chief competitors, Bud Ford, is also black."

"That's the kind of information I'd like to teach at Camp Noepe. I have a shelf of books on the cowboys, Native Americans of all tribes, but with the exception of the Buffalo Soldiers, there's no mention of black cowboys. I'll have to find a few books that illustrate just how diverse the West was and still is."

"It was a hard life for everyone back in the early years, but I'm sure many of the black men chose that over the indignities of sharecropping. The next time you're in Texas, especially Houston, plan to visit one of the museums that feature black cowboys and trail riders."

"My grandfather was familiar with the South. He even compared it, in some ways, to the island. I love Martha's Vineyard. I wasn't certain just what obstacles I'd find here, but everyone I've met has made me feel welcome. Everyone but Ramsey Treadwell."

"Did he say something to offend you?"

"He did, but I won't go into it now. I'm surprised Yank didn't fill you in."

"Yank has one pat answer for every question. Ask Lacey. I won't press, but I hope that one day you'll tell me the story of your grandfather and of Ramsey Treadwell."

"Treadwell wished me well and said another camp could help the economy, but said I didn't stand a chance of beating him in the competition." She was not ready to tell the full story.

"Yank introduced us in town the other day. I guess I saw that same look. My knowledge wasn't exaggerated. I've never taught children, but I can promise I'll do my best to wipe that smile from Treadwell's face."

His assurance eased many of her doubts. It was obvious that he was competitive.

She was sure that, with him on her side, Camp Noepe would make a fine showing. Before she could think of anything to say, he turned the questioning around to her.

"How about you? Pearl said you had gone to your brother's graduation. College?"

"Law school."

"Great. Any other siblings?"

"No, it's just the two of us. My mother lives in New York. My father was killed in a plane crash." She didn't mind talking about herself and hoped it would make him feel less like an outsider. "Just as we began to recover, my grandfather died of liver cancer."

"I'm sorry. Were you close to your father?"

"Extremely. He was a physician. A surgeon. He was on a business trip when it happened."

"And Pearl is his mother?"

"Stepmother, but she raised him after his mother died. She's a whiz in the kitchen, but don't get her started talking about it. She's also an herbalist who swears by herbs and spices as natural medicine. My dad loved her so much, and so do I. She's more like a mother than my own mother." Her voice cracked with emotion.

"I can see. If this is not a good subject, we can talk about something else."

"It's okay. Don't get me wrong. I love my mother. She's a wonderful person. She runs a dance studio in New York. She's beautiful and graceful, a former ballerina."

He turned sideways and smiled. "You grew up with a mother like that and didn't follow in her footsteps?"

"She wanted me to, but I wasn't really into it. Besides…" she looked up and sighed. "I think I grew beyond her expectations. She tried to interest my brother in ballet. He was opposed to the idea and my father concurred, thank goodness. My mother some-times thinks her way is the only way, and she's very good at convincing others that she's right."

He laughed. "There are wonderful male ballet dancers, but it's not for everyone. I'm sure she's very proud of what you're doing here on the island."

The ferry arrived and she continued the conversa-tion while driving aboard. "She was proud of my career at one time, but she thinks I'm nuts to do this." She paused for the right words.

"If you'd rather not—"

"No, I don't mind talking about it. In fact some-times it's good to share troubling things with an objec-tive person. It's just that I'm sometimes passionately expressive and I wouldn't want you to think I'm coming down on my mother."

"I won't think that. I see the way you interact with Pearl. It's obvious you adore each other."

"I also adore my mother. For lack of a better way to put it, my mother is a snob. She hates what I'm doing and she blames Pearl, which is not the case at all. This was my grandfather's dream. He loved horses and he loved children. I guess the natural innocence in both groups appealed to him. He also loved and wanted to spend his last days at our family home down on Country Road."

"So your family has property here?"

"Not anymore." She dropped her head. "It's a long story, and it makes me mad as hell to talk about it, but I enjoyed coming to the island when I was young. Got my first kiss down on Beach Road. A brat named Gerald McGillis."

"Lucky brat."

"Not after I bit him," she reported, and watched his head fall back in laughter.

"Thank you," he said with more pleasant sincerity.

"For biting Gerald McGillis?"

He smiled broadly. "For making me laugh, even if it was at Gerald's expense. I've enjoyed this outing, and I'm beginning to understand why you and Pearl want to fulfill your grandfather's dream. I think that's very admirable."

"Well, my mother thinks I'm crazy, and so did the man I was engaged to marry. He and my mother are two of a kind. Wonderful, accomplished people, but arrogant snobs. "

"Don't be too hard on them. It takes all kinds to make this world what it is. Someone once said that high society could only exist on a strong consolidated mediocrity." He amended his statement. "Oh, not that I'm calling you mediocre, quite the opposite."

When she didn't answer, he apologized. "I'm sorry. I was just babbling. I'm not saying you're mediocre at all. I don't know you very well, but from what I've seen you're very bright and wonderfully unpretentious, a quality that might not jell with the way you described your mother."

"I'm not offended by what you said."

"I certainly don't want you to be."

"I'm not. Really. I stopped talking because I was wondering about a cowboy from Texas who knows a hell of a lot about art and quotes Nietzsche."

This time he was silent.

"And now you're probably surprised that I recognized the quote," she shot back.

"No, I'm not, and I apologize again for that night on the beach. I know I'm touchy sometimes, but you are, too. I know Nietzsche because I did a thesis on philosophers, and I think most of them were mad. Nietzsche was crazy out of his mind from a syphilis virus. Some people laud his views, but as I said in my thesis, some are filled with meaning, but I still denigrate them as the ravings of a first-class nut. It's amazing how we hold onto certain theories and hypothesis and give credence to the creativity of minds that were spaced out on drugs."

"Yes, it is. I think most of the great modern lyricists, especially those from the '60s, were fruity as loons, just as Woodstock was one big open marijuana field." She turned to face him. "Damn! I wish I'd been there."

They looked at each other and laughed. The tension was broken.

Pearl and Shale began preparing for their last night of freedom just after a light lunch of sandwiches made from the previous night's roast beef. The men completed their tasks early in the day and started a fire in the big brick pit for the racks of ribs and chicken that

Pearl had marinated. Using her "secret recipe," Pearl also prepared ice cream custard to freeze for dessert, and Micah made a trip to town for more beer, ice, and Jennifer Greenup.

The men took over meal preparations while Lacey, Pearl, Shale, and Jennifer lounged on the deck with beers and sodas. A chill in the night air soon drew them together next to the fire. Lacey noticed Monroe's easy laughter and felt she had accomplished her goal of putting him more at ease.

"Mother Pearl, you and Shale have outdone yourselves. This is some good grub. Everything looks great." She stacked the plates on the end of the wooden table that Pearl had covered with a plastic cloth.

"This was an easy one for us. Thank the men. They're the ones working now."

Lacey looked at Monroe, his sleeves rolled up, muscles coiling as he turned the slabs of meat. She brushed aside feelings of longing and silently vowed to remain uninvolved.

"The food smells heavenly." She walked over and offered him another beer. "Thanks for helping out."

"No problem. Actually, this cookout is a lifesaver. I was playing poker with Yank and Tedera, and if I hadn't stopped I would have lost the shirt on my back. Literally."

"Should we tell him, Lacey?" Pearl held her head down while her shoulders rocked with laughter. "They're card sharks, honey. Both of them. Hustlers from way back. You'll never win playing them."

"Now you tell me." Monroe laughed with the others.

Micah and Jennifer loaded the disc player with, in Micah's words, "old folks music." Conversation continued until Tedera shyly asked Pearl to dance and everyone paired off, leaving Lacey and Monroe perched on the banister, sipping beers. Lacey applauded the dancers and watched Monroe's smile. When the three couples kept dancing and the two holdouts became obvious, Monroe slowly ambled over and extended his hand.

"I'm not a great dancer, but I'm game if you are."

She accepted his hand. When the bubbly lyrics slowed to a dreamy melody, he held her close and she felt his heart pounding. The moon had risen and the air was brisk and breezy, but leaning into his warmth, she felt more heat than she had while standing over the open pit.

Having consumed three beers, the man, the moon, and the moment were tempting beyond words. The music stopped and everything that was voluntary remained still, but her heart kept pounding in rhythm with his. She clung to him and prayed for another slow song.

CHAPTER 6

The opening day of Camp Noepe found Lacey in her office at five a.m., shackled with enthusiasm and second thoughts. Pearl joined her with two mugs of coffee. Hot, black, and strong, just the way Lacey liked it.

"Here, you know you can't think straight without your first cup of caffeine." Pearl's voiced her concern. "I know this is a big day for you. It is for the rest of us, too. Is everything else okay?"

"Sure. I just couldn't sleep. I suppose my anticipation was too high. Would you please glance over this sheet and see if I've forgotten anything?"

Pearl took the pad from her hand, looked it up and down and sat, a worried look on her face, in the chair facing Lacey's desk.

"Don't forget to collect money from Donnelly and Caper, and don't let anyone in here without a clean bill of health. Most of them still haven't supplied proof of current inoculations." She paused. "And tell me why I've seen those deep frowns on your face for the last few days. Is there something going on that I don't know about?"

She smiled. "Haven't I always told you everything, Mother Pearl?" The smile disappeared and her lips flattened against her teeth. "Do you think it would be terrible if—"

There was a soft knock on the office door. "Excuse me. I didn't mean to interrupt. I saw the lights on and wondered if something was wrong." Monroe stood before them, hat in hand.

"Everything is fine." Lacey breathed in fascination. He was tremendously tempting, even early in the morning. His skin was dark and creamy like a bar of fresh milk chocolate. She licked her lips, literally tasting his sweetness. "Just checking last-minute paperwork. How about you? Ready to face a stream of curious young girls?"

He chuckled. "Like they say, every day is a new adventure. I've never faced a stream of young girls before, so if nothing else, I'm excited about the new adventure. Is there anything you'd like me to do?"

"No. Thank you, Monroe. Thanks for everything."

Pearl stood to leave. "I'd better check on breakfast. I'll have it on the table in about another half an hour." She shot a hurried glance at Lacey before leaving the room.

Lacey gestured to the chair that Pearl had vacated. "Have a seat. That is, if you have a minute to talk." She waited until Pearl had left the room. "I just wanted to say that I'm glad to have you here at Camp

Noepe. This is a collective effort, and I appreciate the hard work you've done to help get ready for this day."

"Just doing my job. I know how important the camp is to you, and I'll try not to let you down."

Their eyes met and locked. A torrent of emotions swept over her. Her palms perspired, and her skin, inside the confines of her tight jeans, was hot and clammy. She finally spoke, but the words crept out slowly, hampered by her labored breathing.

"Thanks. I appreciate hearing that. I'd be lying if I said I wasn't a little stressed right now, but I have a good feeling about this little venture."

His eyes danced and the edge of his top lip curled upward. "For whatever it's worth, so do I."

Feeling her control slipping with each second of his presence, she sighed when he stood, nodded, and left the room. Sinking into the chair, she began to relax. The air seemed lighter. Her heart skipped and she felt like singing.

She stood and raised her arms over her head. "Everything is going to be all right."

By noon, parents, appearing eager for freedom, had dropped off fourteen excited girls. Lacey welcomed them personally. One of the three eight-year-olds, Melissa, seemed the most eager to get started.

"Can I see the horses now? What kind are we going to ride? I hope you don't have those old nags that can't even get up a gallop. And trail horses are out. My dad said you would have spirited horses and a good instructor. Is that so, or was he just saying that to get rid or me?"

"I promise our horses are not nags, and we do have a wonderful riding instructor, but we're not going to get started today. We have to get everyone checked in and settled."

As she spoke, Monroe walked up from the stable.

"Is he your husband?"

The curious girl was unable to distinguish the flash of embarrassment that flowed from Lacey to Monroe.

"This is Mr. Faulkner, the riding instructor." She smiled at Monroe and he accepted the cue.

"Hello, young lady."

She took his outstretched hand. "Hi. My name is Melissa, and I already know how to ride. I go to Colorado Springs every summer with my parents. We stay at the Broadmore and my folks take me horseback riding at this stable close by. Their horses are just old trail nags. All they do is follow each other around the same path every time. I tried to make one of them run. I just kept kicking his sides, but the only way to make him trot was to hold back on the reins until the other horses got way ahead. When I let go, he galloped like crazy to catch up."

She looked from Monroe to Lacey, her eyes dancing with excitement. "I got in trouble for doing it. My mom was angry, but my dad started looking for a place to send me so I could learn to ride like a pro."

She placed her hands on her hips. "And that's why I'm here."

Monroe smiled at Lacey. "I think we've got your contestant for the Junior Roundup. Mind if I start with her right now?"

"You don't mind?" Lacey brightened.

"Not at all. I can't let all of this enthusiasm go to waste."

Lacey watched him take the girl's hand and noticed that his entire expression had changed. His face lit up, and when it did, he was irresistible.

She walked back to the main house, muttering sardonically. Glancing over her shoulder, she saw Monroe lead Melissa to the stand he had built next to the gate. "I've been hot and bothered since that man arrived, and I don't know what to do about it."

Lacey's day alternated between hectic and spurts of calm. By six o'clock she was exhausted. Pearl and Shale got an early start on the first dinner preparations. After coping with "Guess what I forgot to bring?" and "I'm bored," Lacey realized the enormity of her undertaking. Her biggest challenge so far were ten-year-old twins who appeared to have serious disdain for each other and were determined to share their feelings with everyone around them.

"What the heck did I get myself into?" She fell against the kitchen counter. "After we put those little monsters down for the night, let's retire to the fireplace with a bottle of booze—one apiece?"

Pearl and Shale laughed.

"Don't freak out. They could be teenagers," Shale said.

"Yeah. Then we'd all be in the nuthouse before the summer is over. I'm sure they'll be fine once they get settled," Pearl reassured her.

"One older girl did slip in," Lacey said. "Her father claimed not to have noticed the maximum age on the flyer, but I think he did. She has a sour disposition that might tempt a parent to break the rules."

"I saw one of them trailing Monroe around," Pearl said. "Since he's easily agitated, I hope he holds up."

"That's Representative Thomas Hodges's daughter, Melissa. Eight years old and full of questions and enthusiasm. Monroe's face lit up like a beacon when they started talking. I don't think he'll have a problem. He told me he usually works with adults, but he and that child took to each other."

"If you don't mind my opinion, I think he's good with kids," Shale offered. "Micah likes him a lot, and you know how selective he is. Maybe he's had a lot more practice than we know, or maybe he's just better with kids than with adults."

Yank came inside with Micah and Tedera trailing behind.

"Whew! What a day! I don't know about the kids, but I'm about to drop. What do they pack in those bags? I've hauled several tons of luggage out to that bunkhouse, and all I hear is what they forgot." Tedera shook his head. "Sure smells great in here and I'm damn near—"

"Watch your mouth!" Pearl yelled.

"Sorry. I mean darn near starved."

With the staggered arrivals, no one had much of a chance to eat lunch and they eagerly piled around the table. Monroe was the last to join them before Pearl rang the cowbell for dinner. The women sat in the middle of the gathering, and the men were next to the back door. Pearl asked for a moment of prayer, which started another rift.

"We aren't Christians." A gangly redhead stood and proclaimed her displeasure. "We don't pray. My father says it's unconstitutional to ask someone to do what they don't believe in."

Pearl's expression changed from motherly nurturing to calm tolerance. "That's just fine, dear. We will not make, or even ask, you to pray, but at my table, we say grace as a matter of respect, and no one eats until the proper respect has been given."

The redhead was further silenced by the fourteen-year-old whose father had not stayed long enough to hear Lacey's age restrictions policy. "I don't care if you pray or not, as long as you shut up so the rest of us can eat. I'm hungry and I'm bored. I don't know why my dad left me here with this bunch of babies."

The adults bowed and Pearl delivered her words of grace.

"The undertaking of opening Camp Noepe has been a great one, and I'm thankful for those who have worked diligently to make it happen. We bow in respect, if not reverence, to offer thanks for our progress, and blessings for the road yet to be traveled."

The rowdy bunch hastened through a pile of fried chicken, mashed potatoes, boiled corn, and fried okra, which the feuding twins used as weapons across the table after failing to reach a mutual understanding on who got the bed closest to the window. Pearl dished up bowls of homemade ice cream while Monroe passed out leaflets and gave a brief pep talk.

"I know all of you are anxious to get in the saddle, but before you ride a horse, there are a lot of thing you must learn. The first and most important is to understand horses. When you begin your lessons, I'll keep you on the same horse if possible, because the next step in good horsemanship is to learn about the horse you'll ride. Since I've learned a little about each of the horses, I'll go by ages, the younger girls to the gentler horses."

His voice commanded respect, even from the most restless of the group.

"I want each of you to look at the sheets I'm passing out. It is imperative that you study and learn this information, beginning with the parts of the horse and the parts of a saddle. I don't want to tell you to step in the stirrup and hold the horn and have you do the opposite."

Lacey chuckled along with the girls, but inside she felt a quake. Monroe's strength was obvious and his charm, at least when he wasn't angry, was overwhelming. His eyes sparkled like the stars that were emerging from the heavens, his hands moved flagrantly as he spoke.

"When we begin our lessons, I want each of you to tell me of your prior experience with horses, and I want you to be honest. It's not okay to pretend to know or understand the things we're going to discuss if you don't. That could get you hurt." He paused and looked around the room.

"The first thing we're going to learn before we learn about horses is safety, and I will not allow any of you near a horse until I'm sure you understand the many ways you could be hurt. Horses, like all animals, have certain methods of defense to use against their enemies, and they will not hesitate to use them if they feel threatened. I know you're not the enemy. You're all sweet, nice, pretty young ladies, but the horse may have other ideas." His head swirled as he spoke, and he waited for the giggling to cease.

"Horses can strike out with their hooves. If the horse feels threatened he will likely bite, and if you make a surprise approach from the rear, you could get kicked."

Pearl and Shale began clearing the table and Micah distributed the materials that Monroe and Lacey had complied. Monroe continued.

"Never stand behind the horses. A fly might bite and cause it to kick, and though they weren't aiming for you, if you're back there, you'll be hit. When you walk near the horses' hindquarters, pat them and speak softly so they'll know it's you and not some thirsty horsefly."

Lacey listened, becoming high on his words and the ease with which he spoke them. Having spent more money on insurance than on the livestock, she was appreciative of his strong emphasis on safety. When he finished speaking and the kids finished dessert, Lacey and Jennifer escorted them to the bunkhouse, answered questions, provided toothpaste, soap, and other essentials, and settled a final argument between the twins.

Lacey returned to the main house and helped Pearl and Shale load the mammoth dishwasher that health regulations required. Micah and Jennifer helped as well, and when they finished, the five of them sprawled in chairs before the fire. Yank and Monroe, already enjoying a glass of wine, rushed to pour for the ladies.

"How was your evening with Melissa?" Lacey asked after Monroe took the seat across the checkerboard from Yank.

"Amazing. The kid is a natural. I gave her a ride on that bay and she loved it."

"Champion?" Lacey was concerned. "Don't you think that was a bit much?"

Monroe shook his head. "Not at all. I led Champion around and then gave her the reins and allowed her to walk him. She's a bright young lady. Just might be the contestant you're looking for."

"I don't know." Lacey shook her head. "She's only eight."

I've never taught kids, but in my observations, teaching is just half the battle. There has to be a longing, a hunger to learn. There also has to be a rapport with the animal. A bonding. I saw that with Melissa. Being younger is not necessarily a bad thing, either. It means she's more pliable and, in her case, very willing." He shrugged his shoulders. "Of course, I'm just making suggestions. It's your decision."

"No, I welcome your input." She was amazed at how quickly his demeanor could change. "I need all the help I can get. Look over this activity grid when you get a chance and feel free to make suggestions."

She smiled, thinking how different he was now, compared to his angry arrival. She hoped to keep it that way.

Lacey checked on the girls, had one last look at the following day's schedule, showered, and lay across her bed in the bunkhouse. Soft sounds from the radio flowed around her, turning exhaustion into relaxation. Thoughts of Mason prevailed, mainly because of the sexual craving that surfaced when she was around Monroe. Mason had been a zealous, though selfish, lover. His willingness to meet her needs was prompted by his own desires.

She substituted Monroe for Mason and silently narrated their lovemaking sessions, placing Monroe's hands in the spots where Mason's hands had caressed and massaged until she screamed with pleasure. She closed her eyes and relaxed.

The room became light and airy. She floated on blankets of soft, white clouds and inhaled arousing aromas. A kaleidoscope of brilliantly blinding colors passed before her.

Suddenly the scene changed. The brightness faded to soft lights that cast wavy shadows where the brilliance had been. Puffs of smoke emerged from the shadows. He emerged slowly and came to her in a haze of yellow radiance, his face glowing and alive. Her heart sang with unexpected pleasure. Her body came alive in lilting sensations too numerous to count. Immobilized, she tried to speak, but felt words were not needed. The longing in his eyes told a story, and the thirst in her body spewed a passionate reply.

She tore her gaze from his and careened down the bare muscular body, nude from the waist up. He stood next to her, touching her, pressing his warm skin against her until she burned from his touch. With his hands on her breasts, she realized that she was completely nude. Overcome with caution, she tried to run away.

He held her in place and scolded her with a weakening stare. Feeling chastened, she relented. His mouth crushed hers and she accepted his demanding kisses. Her reciprocal tongue dueled in an erotic battle with his. Every erogenous nerve in her body stood at full attention as he deftly slid her body beneath his.

Lurking over her, his eyes cut the bonds of her restraint. She felt brazen. Free of inhibitions. She wrapped herself in his closeness and begged for his torturous touch.

His lips curled into a menacing scowl and took her mouth in urgent kisses that heightened her passion higher and higher, until she was delirious with desire. She knew he wanted her to beg, and she shamelessly did, but he continued nibbling her face and neck. Painfully. Deliciously.

Writhing against his assault, she felt his hot palms skimming down her body, cupping her cheeks and pulling her close. His tongue made invasive sweeps inside her mouth, tasting until she was weak and faint. Every trace of precaution melted, she surrendered and wept with ecstasy as he filled her with delight. He made her world a place of perfection. He made her whole.

A noise cut through the night, slicing her dream in half. She jumped upright, still hovering on the cusp of sensuous fantasy and the brink of painful realism. After identifying the buzzing sound, she sat up, disoriented, and pushed the "Off" button on the radio. The static ceased, and her dream came back in vivid slides of unfulfilled lust. Her hands shook from the memories.

She showered and dressed, waiting for the rush to pass, but the touch of a man's hands on her soul, even in slumber, would not go away.

"This is ridiculous!"

She made her bed, snatched her hat from the rack, and headed out to the ocean. The fresh briny air brought goosebumps to her still moist skin. A chill seeped to her bones. She began running to generate heat. Faster and faster. The weight of her boots created resistance and soon tired her legs, until she slowed near the thicket where she had interrupted Monroe's solitude. The ocean was usually calming, but now caused pain in the part of her soul that longed for more than she had been able to find.

She walked over the sand, thinking and enjoying the privacy. Her eyes fell on the vines that had meandered across the smaller bushes on the side of the thicket facing the ocean. The wandering limbs formed a natural hutch between two tall pines. She ducked her head and looked around inside. It was as if nature had purposely constructed the shelter. Sitting on the dried grass, her head bowed and her hair fell forward, like a thatch of black silk, around her face. She thought of her father, her grandfather, and the dream she had left to finish.

She heard a whistle and knew it was Monroe, probably making noise to keep from scaring her. He whistled louder, but she still jumped when she saw his face.

"Good morning. I hope I didn't startle you. The air feels great this morning. Invigorating."

She stood and raised her shoulder to her cheek and rubbed. "Good morning. No, you didn't startle me. I heard your whistle. Up early, aren't you?"

"Yeah. I decided to walk off some of my thoughts and work up an appetite at the same time. You know how difficult it is to finish off the day with a great dinner and still awaken hungry, but I have to acquire an appetite for breakfast. I'd hate to miss one of Pearl's feasts."

"No, you wouldn't want to do that. Might hurt her feelings."

"What about you? After yesterday, I thought you'd be sleeping off the strain of that raving herd of young fillies."

She plunged her hands in her pockets. "I was tired, but I also came out to walk off some unpleasant thoughts." She looked up at his face. "I suppose we all have our ghosts."

"Is there anything I can do to help? I'm a good listener."

"Thanks. I would like to unload, but I'm afraid if I start, I wouldn't be able to stop, and I'm sure you have better things to do than listen to my babble. Just having a moment of weakness. It will pass."

"Was your breakup with the man you were engaged to very painful?"

She smiled in thoughtful remembrance. "No, not really. Marrying him would have been a big mistake and I had already recognized that. In many ways the breakup was a relief."

He looked out at the ocean. "I suppose I'd better head back. I didn't mean to disturb you."

"You didn't. Wait, I'll join you. I'm dreading that bunch of yakking girls, but I might as well gear up for the blitz." She walked fast to keep pace with his long strides. "I want to thank you for everything you've done. You seem to have a lot of patience with the girls."

"I love kids, but I have to admit, I did not imagine so many of them." He laughed. "I can't wait to hear more of those questions. 'Where do the horses sleep? Do they ever lie down? Can I hug this one?' That baby goat was almost hugged to death yesterday. I think it was a good idea to have the other animals here. What made you do it?"

"Actually, the ducks, two goats, and chickens came with the camp. Yank and I delivered the baby goat, Shags, and, I have to admit, I've hugged him a few times, too, but I don't like chickens. Nasty little things!" She made a mock groan.

"I don't like chickens, either. I used to like baby chicks before the feathers developed until my mother bought me a painted one for Easter. He grew up to be a rooster with an attitude. I raised him, but he hated me. Wouldn't let me near him. He'd spread his wings and charge as soon as I went into the chicken yard."

She laughed energetically. "You're making that up. A painted chicken?"

"No. Honest. They paint the baby chicks' fuzz yellow or pink, just like the stuffed ones you see in Easter baskets, but that thing grew to be a mean-ass rooster. A big one. My parents finally got rid of it. We probably had him for dinner."

Lacey threw her head back in laughter and he stepped in front of her. When she lowered her face, he traced the lines of her lips with his finger.

"You have a wonderful laugh. You should use it more."

"Thanks to you and the others, I have something to laugh about." She looked into his eyes and found the strength that had been missing in Mason. "You have no idea how excited I've been over this opening. I'm still flying high, which is one of the reasons I couldn't sleep."

"One of the reasons?"

"Yeah, and I'm not telling the others. You wouldn't want me to bare my soul, now would you?"

His mouth spread into a slow smile. "Touché."

They both laughed while a marvelous chord of happiness played softly in her heart.

CHAPTER 7

The day began with two tummy aches and a bad case of poison ivy, and that was all before breakfast. By the time Lacey made it to the stables, Monroe was well into his lesson.

"Okay Shelly, I'm going to use you to demonstrate the dismount. Take the reins in your left hand and hold them short to prevent the horse from moving. Take your right foot from the stirrup and put your left hand on the horse's withers. No, not there. You must learn the horse's anatomy. Here, put your right hand on the pommel. Now push."

Lacey backed away, the touch of his fingers still tingling on her face. She knew he wanted to kiss her and wondered why he didn't. Her face blanched each time she thought of her body's reaction.

Back in her office, she struggled with the mound of paperwork that resulted from one mail delivery. After sorting out the junk mail and dropping it in the trash, the remaining pile still appeared insurmountable. She was halfway though the stack when Pearl came in behind Tedera, who was carrying a large box.

"Lacey, this package just arrived. Did you order anything in the mail?"

"No." Lacey inspected the label on the box. "The only return is a post office box." She looked at Pearl. "It's from Texas." She ripped away the wrap and opened the large cardboard box. "Books. They're books."

Taking each of the volumes from the box, she read the titles aloud. *"Bill Pickett; Bulldogger."* She inspected the book while Pearl took another one from the box.

"Black Cowboys," Pearl read.

"Black Heroes of the Wild West." Lacey pulled the volume from the box. "I'm sure Monroe ordered them. He told me about the black cowboys, past and present, and I said I would like to have that information here at Camp Noepe to teach the youngsters, but I didn't expect him to do this. What a great start for our library."

She continued reading the titles and passing the books to Pearl. *"Reflections of a Black Cowboy,"* she read. "What a wonderful collection. I can't believe his generosity."

"It's easy to be generous when you're in love," Tedera, half hidden behind Pearl, mumbled softly.

"I heard that." Lacey's face blanched. "Would you please take these books to the activity room?" She wanted very much to let it drop, but curiosity prevailed. "Why do you keep saying he's in love with me? Did he tell you that?"

"Didn't have to," Tedera said over his shoulder. "I'm not stupid. I don't know this man's story, but I don't think money is his objective for working here. I think he needed to get away from something. Camp Noepe is his hideout, and a beautiful woman just happened to be part of the package. He's attracted to you. Don't take a genius to figure that out."

After the evening meal, Micah entertained the girls with his guitar, and the rest of the adults relaxed in front of the fire. Monroe smiled easily and Lacey felt self-conscious, wondering if Tedera had been correct. If he was attracted to her, what would happen next? She wondered if he wanted to hold her as badly as she wanted to be in his arms. Embarrassed by erotic thoughts, she took her coffee to the end of the sofa and nudged his elbow.

"Federal Express dropped off a box of books on black cowboys. It's quite an impressive collection. Do you know anything about it?"

Monroe shrugged his shoulders and slowly shook his head. "I can't say that I do."

"It came from Texas," she said.

He sipped his coffee and shrugged. "It is a big state, you know."

"Yes, I'm aware of that." She focused on the dimple in his chin and smiled. "In either case, it was a nice thing for someone to do, and I'm very grateful."

His head tilted and his upturned lips spread in a smile. There was so much she wanted to say to him, and two things holding her back. In spite of everyone's assertion of his feelings for her, she wasn't sure that he wanted to become involved. Fighting the tugs on her heart, she didn't either.

She had spent many sleepless nights mulling over the possibilities of a relationship with him. Everything would be fine as long as they were at Camp Noepe, but what would happen in the winter when they both had to leave? Would he want to live in New York? What would he do there? He was obviously educated, but what were his skills?

She took her thoughts to bed early, awakened after a hard sleep, dressed, and went to the main house. The kitchen was dark. Pearl had not started coffee, which was very unusual. When it occurred to her that Pearl might be ill, she went down the narrow hallway, tapped on the door and pushed it open.

The room was dark. Lacey had started across the floor when she saw movement from the other side of the bed. She tiptoed backwards, saw male clothing thrown haphazardly across the chair, and the scent of Tedera's tobacco filled her nostrils. Her heart danced for joy. Creeping soundlessly, she backed from the room and closed the door.

She went back to the kitchen, started the coffeemaker, and went in the storage area for a sack of oranges. On her way out, she saw Tedera making a hasty retreat through the front door.

Working as quietly as she could, Lacey filled the juicer continuously until she had extracted three large pitchers of juice. Just as she consulted the menu scribbled on the chalkboard to determine what was next, Pearl appeared, her face askew with embarrassment.

"I'm sorry. I guess I overslept. How long have you been in here?"

Lacey passed her a mug of coffee. "Long enough to make coffee and orange juice." She smiled, enjoying Pearl's discomfort.

"I must have been more exhausted than I thought. I slept right through the alarm." With her head down, she glanced upward and saw Lacey's slight smile. "You don't think I'm a loose woman, do you?" Her dark eyes glowed with humiliation.

Lacey laughed. "Mother Pearl, you're a woman, he's a man. What's wrong with that? I think it's wonderful."

"I don't know how it happened. I must have had too much to drink last night." She dropped her head. "And so did he."

"No one deserves to be loved more than you. All I can say is that I hope you enjoyed it."

"I should be ashamed to say this but, the truth is, I enjoyed it immensely." She stared in silent remembrance. "Your grandfather was gentle and loving. I miss that, and I always will. I never planned for this to happen, especially now."

"I'm sure Gramps would have wanted you to continue living, and Tedera is a nice man." She thought of Pearl's addendum, and the sadness with which the words were spoken. "Why did you say especially now?"

"Oh, it's just a little too late in life to begin a relationship. I allowed myself to enjoy the attention without thinking ahead to intimacy. Tedera is not your grandfather, but he's not all bad. I had almost forgotten how special a man could make a woman feel." She took a sip of coffee and stared into Lacey's eyes. "You should try it sometimes. It's good for what ails you."

Lacey threw her head back in a big laugh. "I'll keep that in mind."

"How long do you intend to hold out on Monroe? If your feelings for each other were any more obvious, we'd have to label you X-rated and keep you away from the children. The man is dying to get next to you."

"Okay. I'll admit to having feelings for him. So far they all fall under the category of lust, but I think I could love him."

"What are you waiting for?"

"It's not that simple."

"And we tend to make things more complicated than they really are. As you just said, he's a man and you're a woman. In case you haven't taken it any further, he's an intelligent, handsome, and very desirable man, and you're a beautiful, capable, intelligent woman. You know I don't advocate loose morality or indiscriminate sex, but when the lid is tightly clamped, pressure builds." She shook her head. "The two of you must be ready to explode."

"There are so many reasons for my hesitation, beginning with his very apparent hesitancy, and the fact that I know absolutely nothing about this man. Camp Noepe is my priority, and I don't want to engage in a personal relationship that might sour and leave me without a riding instructor. Besides, I don't know that he's interested."

"Yes, you do," Pearl answered, shaking her head and frowning.

"I know that he appears to be, but everyone can see he has his own demons. Don't worry about me. I'm just happy that you found someone to love."

"It's so strange." Pearl gave her head a thoughtful shake. "No one could have convinced me that I would ever become attracted to another man. I've loved your grandfather all of my life, since age twelve. No one can take his place in my heart."

"I know, and so does he."

She hugged Lacey's shoulders. "Having male companionship after so long is wonderful. I'm happy to have Tedera in my life, and I want that same happiness for you."

When Lacey didn't answer, Pearl pressed harder. "Honey, I realize your reluctance to get involved, but if life is to be enjoyed, you have to take chances. There are no guarantees. You might get hurt but you might also find something wonderful. Caution is fine. I'm not saying you should rush blindly into a relationship with Monroe, or anyone else. Just remember, though a coward has no scars, he also has no fun."

Lacey had been listening to Pearl and to the urgings in her heart. She knew she was being a coward for not opening her heart to the possibilities, but she had Camp Noepe to think about. She replayed Pearl's words and decided to watch for a sign from Monroe, something that would compel her to lower the barrier around her heart. She spent most of the day outside, watching his tenderness with the children and his calm, quick thinking after their first casualty.

Being a physician's daughter had not made Lacey comfortable with blood. She ran to a youthful scream and found one of the girls bleeding all over the walkway. She had sliced her foot on the sharp edge of a feeding trough. Monroe also answered the scream. He yelled for Shale, who had been a nurse's assistant, to apply pressure, instructed Lacey to get the Jeep, lifted the child into the back seat, and took over the steering wheel.

"You sit with her. Hold the towel around her foot. I'll drive."

She was glad he took over and hoped he had not noticed the tremor in her hands that remained until she called the girl's mother and was told that with six children, including four boys, cut feet rarely raised an eyebrow.

Monroe's actions and calmness under stress were more appealing than his killer good looks. She thanked him with words while holding back a crushing longing to show, not tell. She made it through the rest of the week and was scrolling over the budget spreadsheets on her computer when Monroe rapped on the door.

"Excuse me. Was wondering if I could borrow the Jeep this evening—that is, if you won't be using it."

His face was soft and her heart began to melt. "Sure. I've finished my errands. If I have to go out, I'll just use Yank's truck." She unhooked the keys from her large ring and passed them across the table.

"Thanks. I want to drive around and explore the island." He rattled the keys in his palm but did not move.

Lacey's first thought was that he needed an advance on his salary, but remembered that his payroll checks had not been cashed, a matter she wanted to inquire about but didn't know how.

"Actually, I wanted to know…that is, if you're not doing anything, if you'd accompany me. Maybe you could show me the hot spots in this wonderful old place."

Her heart leaped forward, and she cautioned herself about seeming overeager. "I would love to, and I do need a break."

She watched Pearl's sly smile as she relayed her plans for the evening. Selecting a nautical outfit from the closet, she applied makeup with shaky hands and went to wait for him in the main house. Pearl noticed her nervousness.

"Come on, honey, he's only a man. A damn fine man, but still only a man." She and Shale laughed together. "Relax and enjoy the evening."

"I think he's mighty handsome and you're beautiful." Shale giggled. "You make a nice couple. You will have beautiful children."

"For goodness sakes, you two. We're going to tour the island, not get married, or anything else, for that matter."

"Yank says Monroe can't keep his eyes off you. I'll bet he's more nervous than you are," Shale said.

Lacey smiled just as Monroe appeared in the window. "He's here. Please keep quiet, you two." She locked a demure smile in place and waited for him to open the door. "Ready?"

"I'm ready." He took her arm. "Since I don't know my way around, why don't you show me some of your favorite spots?"

"That's an easy one, the lighthouses." She glanced at Pearl. "We'll see you guys after dinner. Keep an eye on the kids."

"They're with Jennifer, Micah, and Tedera now, swimming. Don't worry, we'll keep the little darlings in line," Shale promised.

"Little darlings, my foot," Pearl scoffed. "Little devils is more like it. If those twins come whining to me one more time, I'm going to pack their little butts up and send them to their parents." Her frown turned into a smile. "You two have a good evening, and don't worry about a thing. We'll hold down the fort."

Lacey followed Monroe to the Jeep. "Just head up Old County Road. We'll visit the West Chop first, the island's last manned lighthouse, and make our way back to East Chop."

"That's exactly what I had in mind. I find the lighthouses fascinating. I've seen the one in Aquinnah. How many are there?"

"Five altogether, situated around the perimeter of the island. The one we won't see today is Cape Poge. It's in Chappaquiddick, the isolated island."

They talked easily about nothing in particular. He drove and she narrated as they made their way up to the West Chop lighthouse in Vineyard Haven Harbor and Edgartown Light. When they drove back to East Chop in Oak Bluffs, they saw a wedding in progress.

"Oh, look!" She ran from the Jeep to the edge of the crowd. "Isn't this romantic? I would love to be married here…that is, if I ever marry."

They stood back and watched the ceremony. When the bride and groom kissed, Monroe took Lacey's hand.

"I'm getting hungry. What about you?"

"Very. Let's go to the Navigator. They have wonderful lobster."

She directed him to the restaurant overlooking Edgartown Harbor.

"It's not crowded. We can get a table outside."

The hostess escorted them to a table for two above a flickering lantern. He ordered expensive champagne. "This was a special day, and special days always end with champagne."

"So what did you think of the tour?" She smiled.

"It was great. Thanks for showing me around. After stumbling through this first session at Camp Noepe, I can finally relax enough to enjoy an evening out. I want you to relax as well. I've seen the nonstop pace you keep. I know you must be exhausted."

"That's what Mother Pearl keeps saying." She brushed stray hair from her forehead. "Do I look that bad?"

"You look great. Pearl worries about you, and from the way you drive yourself, I can understand why. Were you always this ambitious?"

"I thought you were going to say obsessed. In a way, yes. Mother Pearl has worried about me since the day I was born, but I would think she might be a little distracted right now."

"You mean with Tedera?" When she nodded, he laughed. "It's great, isn't it? He acts like a schoolboy around Pearl. He's mindful of his language and doesn't smoke that awful pipe in her presence."

"He probably doesn't smoke because he doesn't want her to yell at him. Pearl can get plenty ticked off at times."

They both laughed.

"Mother Pearl is an amazing woman and a true romantic. She fell in love with my grandfather when she was a child, right here on the island, and he never knew. No one did. He married her first cousin, my grandmother, Hannah, but Pearl remained in love with him. She left the island and moved to New York to be near him."

"You mean after he was married?"

Lacey nodded. "She never told anyone and she never loved anyone else. She had other relationships. There was a serious one, some high-ranking military man, that everyone thought would end in marriage, but she couldn't go through with it. She kept loving my grandfather from a distance."

"How did he find out?"

"My grandmother told him. When she realized she was dying, she left him a letter saying she suspected that Pearl had always been in love with him. She told him Pearl would take good care of him and help him raise the children. My grandmother and Pearl were very close."

"That's amazing. It must have been difficult for Pearl. I mean watching him with your grandmother and still loving him. Did they marry right away?"

"No. Pearl would not admit her feelings, even after my grandmother died. She sort of eased into his life through the children—my father and my aunts. She was dating someone at the time of my grandmother's death, the man they all thought she would marry. My grandfather didn't mention my grandmother's letter. Pearl told me that she intended to marry the other man, but when my grandmother died, she decided to wait. My aunt says that when the two of them first got together, Pearl went nuts. It happened to her at Powan House. They said Pearl started laughing for no reason, singing all of the time, just happy, giddy like a kid."

"That's a very sweet story." The champagne arrived and he clicked his glass to hers. "Here's to sweet stories and to love."

"It is a sweet story. I think of it a lot now, seeing her with Tedera."

"She's certainly in better spirits now than when I first arrived." He paused and stared into her eyes. "What about you? What happened with this guy you were engaged to marry, if you don't mind talking about it?"

"I don't mind. He's an attorney. We had a good relationship before he became part of the family, so to speak. I think my mother pushed it forward. She kept saying I was lucky that such a handsome, ambitious man was in love with me, and I did enjoy his company at first. Looking back, I think most of it was fantasy, and not even my own."

"I'll bet he's still in love with you."

"Why would you think that?"

"Because." He shrugged. "Men sometimes have a hard time letting go, and an even harder time communicating their reasons for holding on."

"I don't want him to be. He's sweet but…I'm trying to think of a nice way to describe him. He's as stiff as a cadaver, and more selfish than anyone I know. Our relationship officially ended because he constantly criticized my decision to quit my job and come here. We were having dinner at Scola's one night and I just couldn't take it anymore. While he was gone to the restroom, I wrapped the engagement ring in a napkin and left it next to his plate."

He laughed. "I don't know how nice that description is, but I get the picture. Do you two keep in touch?"

"He e-mails me every day."

His face filled with frowns. "So is there a possibility that you—"

"Not a chance in hell," she interrupted. "I seldom answer, and when I do, it's always a brief assurance that I'm okay and that's it. I know if I didn't answer, my dear mother would swim here, give a stellar performance about how misguided I am, and blame Mother Pearl for corrupting me."

"Why did your mother find this guy so special?"

"Oh, no one can answer that better than Mason himself. Mason Phipps, the grandson of Franklin Phipps, Sr., attorney and right-hand man to Adam Clayton Powell. His father, Franklin Jr., made a name as legal counsel for ACLU. They merged their thriving law firm with one owned by a Jewish family, and now it's one of the busiest in New York."

She watched his eyebrow rise during her conversation and wondered if he was impressed or apathetic at the Phipps family's accomplishments. When he seemingly slipped into a silent reverie, she took a chance and ventured into sacred waters. "What about you? Never married? Divorced?"

His smile dimmed. "I was married. She died."

"I'm sorry." She understood why he might have been drifting around. "Any children?"

"She was pregnant when she died."

The pain in his voice twisted her heart. "I'm so sorry. I'm sure she was a very special person."

"She was beautiful and bright, witty and sometimes brash. Strong, but still childlike. My world lit up when she walked into the room." His eyes lifted to her face. "She was a lot like you."

They ordered dinner but she had gorged on his nearness until there was no room for food. They talked about music, wine, political awareness, and New York—he shared a visitor's observations. He told stories of Texas, his favorite horse, and spending Christmas in the country after a snow. When dinner was over and the conversation waned, he stood and took her hand.

"I had better get you back before Pearl comes looking for us. She scares the hell out of me." He squeezed her hand and chuckled. "It was a wonderful evening and this is a great place. Almost magical. Thanks for showing me around."

"Thank you. You and Mother Pearl were right. I needed to get away and relax."

The moon followed them on the drive back, brilliant and dreamy. The evening together, champagne, and three martinis had eased her into relaxation, but being alone with him now, in the twilight, tension moved in. He smiled at her and she felt warm all over. Their hands touched accidentally and she shivered.

"When we first met, I was awed that you came out here and began this adventure, but I don't blame you for leaving the city and settling on this little piece of heaven." He looked up at the moon. "Isn't it fascinating?"

"Yes, it is. Surrounded by something so beautiful makes it hard to imagine anything bad happening. I would like to stay here forever." Remembering Pearl's key ring in her purse, she pointed to Powan House.

"Stop over here. Right here in front of this house. I'd like to show you something."

He stopped and she took the keys from her purse. "I told you we had owned property here. This is it. Come on. I want you to see it." She walked ahead of him to where a dim light over the front porch lit the way.

"My family had owned this property since forever. They built a small house here and kept adding to it with each new generation. My dad had it remodeled when my brother and I were young. We came out every summer. Mom said it's too far from town, but everyone else loved it, especially my grandfather."

He followed her inside. "Wow. It's big. Who owns it now? Why do you still have the key?"

"Ramsey Treadwell owns it now." She found a light switch on the wall. "My Wampanoag ancestors owned that land long before the Pilgrims arrived. My West African ancestors married into the Wampanoag Tribe, and built Powan House. My grandfather, Asa Daigle, was born there. He moved to Harlem to practice dentistry, married Mother Pearl after my grandmother died, and maintained the family home. My brother and I played here as children, just as my father and his sisters had done. Papa's mental health failed while he was being treated for cancer. My father knew of Papa's condition, but didn't tell anyone else. Papa was a very proud man."

Her voice faltered at the memory of her grandfather's courageous fight. She cleared her throat and continued. "Daddy took over Papa's business and personal affairs. My dad was killed in a plane crash a couple of years ago. Papa was still coherent enough to fool everyone into believing he had everything under control."

"But the county served notices of the foreclosure, didn't they?"

"Yes, they did," she answered. "We found the notices and several other important documents, unopened, in Papa's desk. We immediately took care of every obligation, but it was too late to save this property. They didn't waste any time starting foreclosure proceedings for a small amount of back taxes. I suppose Treadwell really wanted that land."

She walked through the room and heard her childhood echo in the stillness. "I offered to buy it from him at market value plus ten percent, but he wouldn't budge, even after I asked him to name his price. When I mentioned training a contestant for the Junior Equestrian Roundup, he sneered and said he'd deed the property to me if I produced a winner. Now you know why it's so important to me."

"Bastard. We'll have to make him eat his words."

His arms wrapped around her like a warm blanket. She hesitated a moment, and then lifted her face to his. His lips gently sealed over hers, but the message they delivered sent a surge of heat from her fingertips to her toes. She remembered what Pearl had said about first being kissed and held there, and her heart took a perilous leap. She pulled away.

"I just wanted you to understand."

Neither of them spoke during the short drive to Camp Noepe. Monroe parked under the carport and walked Lacey to the bunkhouse.

"I really did have a good time. Sometimes we fail to see what's so clear to those around us. I really needed a break and I appreciate your thoughtfulness in taking me away from all of this." She gestured and smiled. "I had better get to bed. Tomorrow is a new day, and, as you said, a new experience."

His arms went around her. "I like the one I had today."

She melted against him and held onto his arm. When his head bent down towards her, she pursed her lips in anticipation. The kiss was light and very sweet. Still holding her, he whispered softly.

"Sleep tight."

She floated inside, dizzy with delight. It was less than she wanted but more than she had expected. She snuggled under the covers, still filled with his presence, and settled into a peaceful sleep.

CHAPTER 8

Lacey awakened holding a pillow tightly against her chest. She could not remember the dream, but felt sure that Monroe was in it. She put on a white bathrobe and sat in the open window, looking at Camp Noepe and feeling proud of her accomplishments. Her life was now perfect, except for someone to share it with, and if last night's kisses were any indication, that situation could change very soon. Monroe was the kind of man she needed. He was strong yet tender, and he appreciated the land as much as she did. She hugged herself and inhaled fresh morning air. "We're here, Papa. Pearl and me. We made it happen."

She showered, dressed, and walked to the main house, anxious to greet the morning and the man she hoped would fill the empty crevices of her heart. The morning air felt warmer than usual, like a protective cocoon. She smiled and savored the wonderful new feeling.

Pearl was in the kitchen making breakfast.

"Good morning." There was a new lilt in Lacey's voice. "Are you making fresh bread, Mother Pearl?"

"Yes, Teddy, I mean Tedera, likes my rolls." She looked up from her pan of yeast dough.

Lacey tucked her lips in to hide her smile.

"Go ahead, laugh. I'm being a silly old woman, but I'm having fun. We never know the extent of our time on this earth, and I intend to make good use of the time I have left. I want no regrets, so I'll give you a little piece of advice."

Lacey scooted back on the stool. "Okay. Shoot."

"Whenever you love, make it the best you can. You're an intense person, and I know you love hard, but I want you to take it one step further. Love better."

Lacey frowned. "What exactly does that mean?"

"Sometimes we forget to fully appreciate what we have. We take the ones we love for granted. Even when we love hard, we still do it halfway. You have a tight rein on your heart and I understand why, but when you let go, let go all the way. I'm not saying you should fall in love easily, but if you keep that rein too tight, it'll squeeze out the joy."

"I understand what you're saying, but isn't that what you did? I mean with Gramps?"

"Oh, yes. I loved that man so. I couldn't be happy with anyone else, and never thought I would have him. What I'm saying is don't play those coy games of bait and retreat. Let go. Enjoy. Tedera might just be interested in me for one reason, but as long as I'm going to indulge, I'm going to make his favorite foods, fuss over him, and let him know that I think he's special."

"Ah-h-h, that is so sweet." Lacey hugged her. "I'm not amused by your relationship. I think it's great. Seeing you this way makes me happy. I'm glad you found Tedera. I'm glad he makes you happy."

"Enough about me. What about you and the cowboy? I heard you come in last night. Did you have fun?"

"I had a great time. Monroe is so…so intelligent. He told me his wife died. I didn't ask details but the hurt in his eyes provided a clear message. I showed him Powan House. He kissed me there."

"And you wanted more, didn't you?"

"Mother Pearl, I wanted him to put his arms around me and keep them there forever. I want to go to sleep next to him and wake up in his arms, but I'm glad we've moving slowly."

"He didn't say how his wife died?"

"No. Why?" Lacey could see the skepticism on Pearl's face.

"I was just wondering."

Lacey firmly believed in Pearl's sixth sense; her telescope trained on the future had predicted a lot of things, including the death of Lacey's father. "You've had a vision, haven't you? Tell me what you saw."

"Let's wait before we start looking ahead," she said with a soft smile. "Just enjoy the moment."

"Come on in, Monroe. Sit down." Pearl stretched behind Lacey's desk and pulled herself upright. "Lacey went to a board meeting in town this evening and probably won't be back for supper. I just wanted to take a few minutes to talk to you, if you don't mind."

His reply was a quizzical stare.

"Lacey doesn't know about this conversation, and I'd like to keep it that way."

"Sounds serious." He removed his hat and toyed with it as he spoke. "Have I done something wrong?"

Her gaze intensified. She saw what was happening, even if he and Lacey were too stubborn to admit it. She knew they would be together. Leaning over the desk, her stare was strong enough to lift him from the chair. "You tell me."

"I'm sorry. I'm afraid I don't know what you're talking about." He twirled the hat around his fingers. His voice registered only curiosity, but his heart was filled with knowing throbs.

"I think you do." She smiled slowly, her lips pressed together. "Some folks call me a seer, a psychic. Of course others have used less flattering adjectives, but we won't go there." She smiled at his deepening frown.

"I wasn't aware of this."

"It's nothing that you should have known. I'm no psychic, a seer maybe, I don't know. But sometimes I can see into the future. Sometimes into the soul." Her eyes had not lifted from his face. She chuckled softly. "Don't look so frightened. I'm not dangerous."

"I'm not frightened. I guess I'm just wondering where this is going."

"I see something behind you, in your past. Not dangerous, just a little dark and shady. I don't know what it is. I'm not that good, but from the time you arrived here, I knew there was a lot about you that you've kept hidden. Whatever it is, you keep it close to the surface."

He shook his head. "You'll have to explain that one."

"I mean this thing is not buried way back in your mind. It's with you at all times. Sometimes I think you want to talk about it, but you're fearful of doing so. I'm not going to ask specifics, but I have to know whether this secret is something that will hurt my baby." She turned her head sideways and watched him fidget.

"Lacey is the daughter I never had. She's the closest person to my heart, and if anything happened to her, I don't know what I would do."

"I don't understand your concern. Have I not done a good job here at Camp Noepe? Are you afraid I'll do something to wreck Lacey's business?"

"Let's not play games, Monroe. I'm afraid you'll do something to wreck her heart. I know how you feel about her. It doesn't take special powers to see that. She's a strong woman, but she's also fragile in that she's intense. She loves deeply and she hurts the same way."

"Are you asking me to keep our relationship strictly business?"

"No." She repositioned herself in the chair and leaned forward to look into his eyes. "I'm asking you to consider her feelings, to tell her the truth about yourself and let her go into this with her eyes wide open. I'm asking that you not deceive her, and if there is something in your past that would cause her harm, please don't bring it into her life. She deserves better."

He looked at her without blinking. "There is something that I have not told anyone here. It would probably make Lacey see me differently, but believe me, it is not something that can harm her in any way. My past, my baggage, is strictly emotional, and you're right, I do see in Lacey all of the things I would like to have in a woman. Did have before my wife died."

He laid his hat on the desk. "I never dreamed of finding someone like Lacey here at Camp Noepe. The first time I saw her, I wanted to run away. I had planned to leave the day after I arrived."

"Why didn't you?"

"When I realized she was doing this by herself, that this is her operation, I knew she needed me. I was angry with her for needing me and with myself for finding her so irresistible. I found it hard to stay here. I just couldn't leave. I'd never do anything to hurt her."

"Are you afraid to love her? Is it because of the differences in your financial standing?"

He dropped his eyes. "I am afraid to love, not because of my secret but because…" he stammered before looking into Pearl's eyes. "My past, more precisely, the death of my wife, took a great toll on me emotionally. I'm not sure I can give Lacey, or any woman, the love she deserves. Our financial differences are not a factor."

"I've lived a lifetime, and with my above-average intuition I can see that you are no more a cowboy drifter than I am." She straightened her shoulder. "Lacey senses it, but I know it to be a fact, and that's what worries me. I saw the blisters on your hands the first week you were here. I'll stake my life that you hadn't taken a lick at a snake before coming here. That makes me wonder what you did in Texas, and why you left? What are you running from?"

"From myself, mostly. From pain, from a hurt I can't deal with." The words stuck, like a thorn branch, in his throat. He could not tell Pearl or Lacey just how shallow he felt inside. "Please don't worry about me hurting her. That is not something I want to do. If you think it's best, I'll keep my distance."

"I didn't say that. Lacey is not only beautiful, she's high-spirited. She's confident and independent. She intimidates most men, but not you. If you can love her the way she deserves to be loved, and if this secret is something she can deal with, you just might be perfect for her."

His eyebrows arched and he moved uncomfortably about in the chair, hefting the hat on his fingertips. "So are you giving me your blessings? Is that it?"

"You don't really need my blessings, but as long as you tell her about yourself, about this secret. As long as you're honest with her, I think you should go with your heart, and I'm sure she'll do the same."

"For you to think I could hurt Lacey, you must believe she could love me. Are you afraid I'll hurt her by leaving, or by staying?"

"That's a good question." She smiled mirthlessly. "I see that the pain you speak of has twisted your heart. You said you're not sure you can love her the way she deserves, so go or stay, if she falls in love with you, and I think that she is, you can hurt her. That's what I want you to avoid. Lacey is clear-headed, but I don't think she's ever been in love, really in love, the way she could be with you. There is too much fear in both of you. You're guarding your heart right now. She sees that in you, so tell her why. That's all I ask."

In many ways, he felt a burden lifted. "I'll tell her everything."

"This kid is fantastic." Monroe stood next to Lacey and watched Melissa take Champion through the obstacle course he had helped construct. "I can't believe she's learned so much in such a short time. She's great on the vertical, hasn't made a mistake in the last two weeks. She loves Champion. He likes her, too, especially since she started making him oats and molasses cakes."

"Bravo!" Lacey and Pearl yelled in unison.

"That was great, Melissa." His chest puffed with pride. "Remember, tilt forward and raise your body out of the saddle. Push your weight back into your heels and give Champion enough slack to move, but make sure he knows you're in charge."

He helped her down and passed the reins to Micah. "Rub him down. He's worked hard today."

"And I'll take Melissa in for something cold before she heads to the shower." Pearl escorted the child away, leaving Monroe and Lacey alone.

"You've done a marvelous job of getting her ready for the competition. I think Camp Noepe has a great chance of winning the young girl's division at the roundup." She tucked her chin into her chest, looked up, and smiled. "Melissa has a crush on you. Did you know that?"

"No." Embarrassment shrouded his face. "You're just teasing me, aren't you?"

"I am not. That little girl gets all gaga when she's around you." She watched Pearl and Melissa going into the bunkhouse. "I've learned a lot about kids this summer. Did you notice how each of the girls gravitated to one of the males here at camp? The older ones moon over Micah, some hang onto Yank, and the other two eight-year-olds seem to like Tedera, but Melissa only has eyes for you."

"Cut it out. You're making me feel like a dirty old man." He grunted.

"Her father is a politician. From what I understand, he doesn't spend much time with her. Her mother is a big corporate attorney, and Melissa is an only child. She's starved for attention, and you're giving her what she needs, Big Papa." She crossed her arms and watched him roar with laughter.

"In that case, I had better not upset her until this competition is over. You know how you women get when you're crossed."

She rapped him on the arm with her hat. "Yes, I do, and right now this woman is hot and sweaty. I'm going in to take a shower. See you at dinner."

"Wait. Don't ask any questions, but I have a surprise. Meet me in at the main house in about an hour."

"What kind—"

"Ah, don't ask questions, just follow instructions. Wear something comfortable. Something you wouldn't mind getting wet or dirty." He removed his hat in a sweeping bow. "Please, ma'am?"

"Okay. I'll see you in an hour." She smiled over her shoulder and ran off across the grass.

He watched her with the excitement that only love can bring. Their time alone had been marvelous, and he wanted more. After months of longing to touch her, he now knew how she felt in his arms, and it was a feeling he didn't want to lose. Realizing he had nothing planned, he hurried up the main house. "Excuse me."

Pearl looked up from her dinner preparations. "Come on in, Monroe. Dinner will be ready in about forty minutes. If you're hungry now, grab some of that fruit salad. That should hold you."

"Actually, I need a favor. A big one."

Lacey relaxed into the pounding shower and tried to think. Monroe's playful and very fetching invitation had both intrigued and frightened her. She wanted him to make a move, and, now that he had, she feared the worse. She feared loving a stranger, but knew she had to allow her heart to feel or she would dry up inside, just as Pearl had cautioned.

She hurried from the shower, toweled down, and smoothed her body with scented lotion. Feeling a tingle of excitement travel to her sensitive areas, she fumbled in the dresser drawer for an appropriate outfit. She wanted to be comfortable, but needed to feel seductive. She found just the thing. Smiling, she slipped into the white bathing suit with three red hearts interlaced across the right breast and pulled on a matching pair of shorts.

With the blow dryer humming in her ear, she mentally prepared a few lines of dialogue beginning with an appropriate reaction to the surprise. A hint of lip gloss and spritz of cologne later, her heart skipped as she walked up to the kitchen. Monroe hadn't mentioned using the Jeep, so she anticipated the surprise being within walking distance.

She walked into the kitchen. "Something smells good."

Pearl, Shale, and Tedera were busily shaking, stirring, and frying.

"Fried chicken. The kids liked it so much the last time, we decided to have a rerun." Pearl laughed.

"Yeah, the only things they liked better were pizza and hamburgers, and we can't have those every day. Of course, Pearl can make anything taste good," Tedera bragged.

"Where are Micah and Yank?" Lacey continued, looking around.

"Is that why you were looking around the kitchen?" Pearl flashed Lacey a quick glance. "You're looking for Micah and Yank?"

"I have a feeling you've been cooking up more than fried chicken, Mother Pearl. What have you and Monroe put together, and don't tell me you're innocent. I know that look."

Pearl panned toward the window. "You'll know soon enough. Have a good evening." She smiled as Monroe came rushing through the door.

"Sorry to keep you waiting. The surprise took longer than I anticipated. Shall we go?"

"After you." She followed close behind his powerful strides. "Are you going to tell me where we're going?"

"It's only a little further." He reached back and took her hand.

He wore khaki shorts and a faded orange shirt that played off his chocolate skin. Unexplained images of adorable little boys and little girls giggling under sun-bleached ringlets fogged her mind. She had never before thought of having children because, even after accepting Mason's ring, she had not pictured being them together as a couple.

They reached the thicket and he led her into the middle of the thatched den. Nature's shelter. Sun rays filtered softly through green overhang and a relaxing ocean breeze stirred the land. One of Pearl's old table-cloths covered an air mattress, candle lamps were embedded in the sand, and a covered picnic basket was set off to one side.

"If we were back in Texas, I'd invite you out to a nice restaurant with soft music and candlelight, but somehow I think this suits you better. I hope you like it."

There was no arrogance in his voice now, only compelling softness that melted her soul. "I like it very much. No Texas restaurant could compare with this. Thank you for such a wonderful diversion."

"Don't thank me yet." He uncovered the basket and took out two plastic champagne flutes. "I sent Micah and Tedera into town for the wine, and this is what they brought back. If it tastes like those bitter weeds we try and keep from the cows, don't be afraid to dislike it. I'm sure the meal is fabulous. Pearl made that."

"What's going on with you and Mother Pearl? You two have been conspiring behind my back a lot. I'll have to check this out." She smiled and took the glass.

"I had to enlist Pearl's help. I don't have much time left. We're beginning the second session of Camp Noepe." He cupped her chin in his free hand and hoped she could not hear his heart beat.

"I haven't dated much recently, so please forgive my ineptness." He filled the glasses, passed one to her, and held the other one up in his hand.

"Here's to you, Lacey Daigle. I've never seen a more graceful and competent lady, and in the short time we have left, I'd really like to know you better."

They touched glasses and drank the foaming liquid. "Uh, this isn't bad. Give old Teddy credit. The man probably knows more about alcohol than the two of us together."

"And many other things." His smile turned reflective. "This has been one of the most remarkable summers of my life, Lacey. Working here with the Whitefeathers, finding someone close to the grandmother that I sorely miss. And you." He raised his glass again.

"You certainly don't sound like a novice in romancing women, Mr. Faulkner. I would guess you're much better at this than you think." She lifted her glass and looked into his eyes. "Now tell me, just how well do you propose getting to know me in the short time until the camp closes?"

"Nothing has to end when the camp closes." What he felt with Lacey at his side was pleasure beyond all imagination.

"I know you're going back to New York and I'm going home to Texas, but that doesn't mean our relationship has to end. There are planes, trains, and, of course, telephones, faxes, and e-mails. This could be the beginning." He shrugged his shoulders and looked up. "The sky is the limit. Forever, even."

"Forever is a long time, Monroe. It's been my experience that long-distance relationships never work."

"But that's not what happened to you and the guy you were engaged to marry, is it? Weren't you both in New York?"

"Oh, yeah, we were in the same city, but we were distances apart in other ways. I wasn't speaking of that relationship, but I can see that each time one ends, it makes trusting the next one a lot harder."

"I respect your openness and honesty, so I'll try and be honest as well." He refilled their glasses. "Losing my wife was more painful than I care to express, so I'll only say that I've been reluctant to take a chance again, with anyone, but I would like to take that chance with you. I don't have any answers yet to overcoming bicoastal hurdles, I only know how I feel. If you feel half as much, I don't think we should allow what we have to fade away. Not at the end of the session, not ever."

She surrendered to his kiss. She moaned at the insistent exploration of his lips and fingers.

"You're everything that's been missing from my life. You're strong and gritty, yet so soft and sweet," he said. "Hope I don't sound too intense. It's just that I'm sorry to have wasted so much of the summer, and I really need to let you know how I feel before we close the camp." Feelings of longing penetrated every bone in his body. Every inch of him throbbed. He could love again, and he so wanted to love her.

She lay against him. She did not want to attack and retreat. She wanted to stay in his arms until the torrential flow of lust inside of her had been quenched. He let go and moved away, vacating the passion he had unearthed, leaving her shamefully exposed.

"I don't want to move too fast," he said in a voice husky with passion, and pulled his shirt down over the obvious protrusion in his pants. "I don't want to hurt you, and I don't want to be hurt. I want very much to act on my feelings, but that might not be good for either of us." He toyed with the wanton tendril of hair that curved around her ear. "I'm baring my soul here. Tell me how you feel."

"I'm willing to take that chance you spoke of, but I have to admit, I'm a little afraid. I don't really know you. We have been together here for months, but I don't know you at all."

"Would you like to?"

She looked into his eyes. "Very much." He reached for her again and she pressed her body against his.

"That's all I needed to hear," he said.

His kiss triggered more painful yearning. She became small in his arms and, there in the breathtaking vista of the shaded glen, she took Pearl's advice and loosened the strings of her heart.

It was difficult to think straight, and she did not want to say the wrong thing. Lacey moved away from his arms and studied his face. "I'm sure your wife was a wonderful person and I can understand your reluctance to become involved. I would like to hear about her when you're ready to talk, to get to know her through you."

"Are you saying it wouldn't bother you if I talked about her?"

"I don't think I could trust a man who stopped loving his wife simply because she died."

He kissed her again, softly and passionately. "I know you are an amazing woman, but I never thought you'd say that."

"I have a little experience with pain. After my grandfather and father died, I kept feeling that I would never be whole again because the memories were too painful, but I learned a lot from my suffering. The pain of losing them will always be with me, but I don't try to forget them. That would be wrong. I am not selfish enough to ask you to forget your wife, but I am selfish enough to ask to share your memories. That is, whenever you're ready."

"I'll be happy to share my memories with you."

They kissed again and he took her hand. "I don't mind hearing about that old boy whose heart must be shattered because you returned his ring. In fact, I want to know what he did, so I won't make the same mistake. When I give you a ring, I want it to be forever."

Alone in his cabin, Monroe kicked his boots under the bed in frustration. He had every intention of telling her everything, but each time he had tried, the words stuck in his throat. He could not tell her when every seductive inch of her face was before him, her eyes half closed and lips slightly parted. Burnished skin glistening with water from their romp in the ocean. Her breasts trembling under his touch. He started to speak, but their lips met and a radiant glow mushroomed around them. He knew he could love her.

He had sensed the urgency in her hot breath. Telling her his story would destroy the moment he wanted to last forever. Instead, he had moved down her body, rubbing his face on her thighs. Her delightful blend of innocence and passion had been overwhelming. In the misty veil of lust that surrounded them, his heart began to mend. He touched her body in all the right places, not stopping until the temptation became overpowering. He could not go on without honoring Pearl's request, but could not force the truth from his lips.

Now he sighed with regret because he had not been able to interrupt their evening of bliss with revelations of truth. He was unfulfilled in more ways than one. He held the phone to his head and contemplated his next move before dialing.

"Hi, Pop. How is everything going?"

"Good. It's good to hear from you. How are things on the island?"

He hesitated, knowing his father would hear the happiness in his voice. "The season is almost over, so I'll be home soon. I just hope I haven't put too much of a burden on you. I worry about your heart."

"As long as my children are okay, my heart will keep ticking. I worry about you and your sisters. I've mostly quit worrying about your little brother and, as Natty would say, put him in God's hand."

"Has he been acting crazy again?"

"No more than usual. Lorraine is the one causing problems now, but I won't bore you with that. How are you and boss lady getting on?"

"Progressing. She's done a magnificent job here this summer. I never would have believed it. I thought I should stick around and wait to bail her out, but she's first rate all the way."

"In bed, too?"

"Pop! I'm beginning to think your mind is locked on sex." He smiled to himself, the thought of her taking him back to an evening he would never forget. "My feelings for her are pretty strong, and I finally told her so."

"And how did she respond?"

"Very favorably."

"And how did she react when you told her who you are?"

He hesitated. He had been so out of touch with life, there seemed little need to worry about revealing his identity, but now he was falling in love. "I didn't tell her, Pop, and before you go off, let me say that I know I have to, and I will. As soon as possible."

"You're playing with fire, son. Everything is fine if you want a roll in the hay, but if you want a relationship, you have to tell her now. Lies just don't make a good foundation."

"I'm going to tell her, Pop, even if we don't get together. Do you remember the attorney who came down from New York on that Marsh deal?"

"You mean the obnoxious stick-in-the-mud we took to dinner?"

"One in the same. Mason Phipps. He's Lacey's ex-fiancée."

"Come on in here, baby, and tell Mother Pearl how your evening went." Pearl gazed up from her comfortable position on the sofa, her head resting on Tedera's shoulder.

Lacey half smiled. "It was nice and very relaxing."

"I'll leave if you two ladies need to discuss this in private." Tedera smiled.

"There's no need for you to leave. We're a close family here, Tedera. Nothing happened that I couldn't say in front of you. It was a wonderful evening." Lacey shook her head. "He wants to get to know me better, and I like everything I know about him so far."

"You two are young. You can afford to take your time. I'm making use of what I have left." Pearl's hand reached over to grip the arm of the sofa. "Did he say anything about his past?"

"Just that his wife's death was very painful and that he's been afraid to take a chance with anyone else. I suppose I should feel special."

"You are special and this man knows it, but I do think that before you go any further, you should find out as much as you can about this situation with his wife."

"I think he's a nice man, but very troubled," Tedera added. "There's a lot of pain in his eyes, even when he smiles."

"I know. I've seen it." Lacey thought of the way he looked when he spoke of his wife's death.

"Did the two of them have children?" Pearl asked.

"She was pregnant when she died. I'm sure that's a big part of his pain. He lost his wife and unborn child. If he didn't have pain from something like that, he's certainly not the man for me."

Pearl did not speak right away, and, when she did, the words came forward in carefully phrased monotones. "I think Mr. Monroe Faulkner has lost a battle with his heart. He's fallen in love with you, and I think the feeling is mutual. I know I encouraged you to act on your feelings, and I'll feel like the witch your mother accused me of being if this man hurts you."

"I'm a big girl. You're not responsible for my actions. You didn't force me to do anything I didn't want to do, and neither did Monroe." She turned at the sound of Pearl's amused chuckle. "What's so funny?"

"Oh, nothing." Pearl chuckled. "I just got a vision of Amanda's face when you bring home Mr. Monroe Faulkner, cowboy from Texas."

"Do you think Monroe would feel out of place in New York?" Lacey frowned.

"Not at all. I also think he's more than a match for your mother and her pious society friends." She tapped her forefinger to her chin. "You know, I think Mr. Monroe Faulkner might be just the man to take your mother down a few notches."

CHAPTER 9

Camp Noepe's premier session ended with a big celebration. The first campers to leave were the twins, who had finally come to terms with each other. The twins were followed by all of the eight-year-olds except Melissa. Lacey glowed when they all asked to come back next season. Her world seemed to be turning in the right direction. She felt proud, anxious, and apprehensive, all at the same time.

She and Monroe had spent their evenings together since the night of the picnic, a week of talking but finding no answers to the questions that plagued her mind. They had moved dangerously close to intimacy and, each time, he halted just as she surrendered. He seemed ready to share, but abruptly suspended the conversation each time, leaving her baffled and frustrated. She didn't want to pry, but the continued suspense and her growing needs were becoming unbearable.

After planning a full day of practice for Melissa, with Yank and Micah handling the other children, rain interrupted their afternoon. The season had been unusually dry, and they anticipated uninterrupted time to fine-tune Melissa's techniques. The morning session had gone without a hitch. The kids rode, swam, and ate lunch. Now, at the decisive period of Melissa's training, evening squalls began.

She walked down the hallway, assuring the kids that Shale would have some kind of rainy day activities to keep them busy. She spent extra time with Melissa, who had been shuffled to another room after her roommate left, and then headed to the main house. Monroe was there when she arrived.

"Bummer, isn't it? I just left Melissa. She's disappointed."

"I don't think the rain will last all day, but it is coming down now," Pearl said from behind the counter. "I've got some cookie dough here for the ones who want to play around in the kitchen, and Shale is over in the activity room digging out everything she can find to keep them occupied. I would suggest a movie, but I'm sure we'd have to listen to them bicker over what to watch."

"If the rain doesn't let up soon, I'll go into town and get a variety of movies and we can make popcorn, sing songs, whatever makes them happy," Lacey said as she set the table for dinner. "I have something for the older ones. I found some little travel makeup cases with sample-size cosmetics. They can paint toes and color their eyes."

"Well, I know where I'm spending my afternoon. I'll just give Yank and Tedera a chance to pick my bones in poker. Maybe if I keep playing, I'll win."

Monroe made a face and nodded to Yank and Tedera as they came into the room.

"Why don't you go into town with Lacey and bring back the lemons that you and Yank forgot yesterday?" Pearl fussed.

"I'm sorry, Pearl. I did forget," Yank confessed. "Do you want me to go in now?"

"Don't worry about it, Yank," Lacey told him. "Even if the rain lets up, I have to go in for office supplies. I'll bring them back. Is that all you need, Mother Pearl?"

"Lemons and onions. That's all I can think of right now."

Lacey looked at Monroe. "You're welcome to ride with me. That way you'll be able to finish the evening in possession of your shirt, because I don't think you'll ever win a hand with Yank and Tedera."

"Thanks." He looked around. "Maybe I would be safer with you."

The rain slowed to a menacing drizzle with no hint of stopping. Lacey and Shale had kept the kids entertained, but after snacks their restlessness turned to squabbles and whines. Lacey pulled on her rain slicker and dragged Monroe away from Tedera's rotating checker game.

"I think we'd better find some entertainment before Shale makes sushi from Kelley's hide. That kid won't stop complaining."

Monroe followed her to the truck, offered to drive, and then helped her inside. The windshield wipers worked hard against the downpour and Lacey wanted very much to snuggle next to him, but didn't. They stopped at Greenup's for the onions and lemons and were besieged with questions from Dave Greenup about his daughter's relationship with Micah. Lacey assured him that Micah was an upstanding young man and that he and Jennifer made a cute couple.

"Do you think you should speak with Micah?" Monroe asked when they were back in the Jeep. "Greenup seemed pretty riled."

"They're both sweet kids, but Jennifer is clearly the aggressor. Once she bared her claws, that boy didn't stand a chance. After overhearing a conversation where she was inviting herself to his cabin, I had a long conversation with her, simply because they're both in my employ."

Monroe gave her an amused glance. "What did you say?"

"I told her to cool it. Yank and Shale aren't ready to be grandparents."

"Come on," Monroe said laughingly. "You sound like an overprotective mother."

"I am very fond of Micah. He's a strong-willed young man with his head on straight. He plans to attend medical school next year and, if money is his only drawback, I'll make sure he goes. I like Jennifer and I like her father, but I didn't like the way Greenup referred to Micah. 'That boy' is already more of a man than most, and if he doesn't like Micah because he's

Native American, I'm sure he's hates me more. I'm all the minorities rolled in one."

"Now, now." Monroe shook his finger. "You were obviously privileged."

"Being one of the chosen few had many drawbacks, especially in my mother's house. When I turned sixteen she made me attend a yearlong chain of parties. So many parties they ran out of names for them. Teas, biscuits, lunches, brunches. My official presentation to society was the annual Smart Set Ball. I changed dresses three times. Mom imported everything she could have easily purchased at home, including tulips from Holland. I wore the white gown and gloves, changed to a persimmon dress with matching shoes, and finally a white pantsuit for dinner on her friend's boat. I'm sorry, make that yacht."

He laughed and agreed. "It wasn't much better in Texas. I escorted so many girls to cotillions, I started to feel like a teenage pimp in top hat and tails. I was even exported to New York to escort two of my mother's friend's daughters. They were only trying to make us feel special. Mothers do those things, just like you're being protective of Micah."

"Micah is ambitious, and ambition is the path to success. I would fight as hard for him as I would my own son."

A flash of pain struck Monroe's heart. He became sober. The thought of losing a son, even one he never knew, was still mind-bending. "I believe you would, but there's no reason to be upset. I think Dave is just showing parental concern. All parents feel their children are superior to everyone else's children. I'm sure you'll feel the same way when you're a mother." He smiled. "I never asked. Do you want children?"

"I suppose so. I never really thought about it."

He stopped in front of the video store, held the umbrella, and followed her inside.

"You mean you and this Mason were engaged and you never discussed starting a family?"

She inspected several movie jackets as they walked between the rows of shelves. "I was a hotshot businesswoman when I accepted Mason's proposal and his mind was, and still is, focused on his career." She tucked two movie jackets under her arm. "What about you? Do you want children, and if so, how many?"

He stopped in the aisle, took the wrist of her free hand and gently pulled her into his arms. "I want children very much. And as many as you're willing to give me."

Their lips met, and for the first few seconds, she forgot they were in a public place. The kiss was deep and her response was urgent and immediate. He let go of her and she stepped back, embarrassed, not at the kiss but how it made her feel. She knew if he didn't make a move very soon, she would. He didn't speak until she had gathered an armload of movies. He was still browsing.

"Have you seen this one?" He held up the double jackets for *Giant*. "I don't care what Rock Hudson was, he was all man in this one, and Liz Taylor is the prettiest woman ever to grace the movie screen." He held her wrist again, but the kiss was no more than a slight brush of her lips. "Of course, you could put them all to shame."

Her body tingled, from his kiss, his touch, but mainly from the promise of heaven she found in his arms. "It's a very long movie. I've watched bits and pieces," she said when she was finally able to speak. "But I would like to watch it." She slipped her arm under his jacket and felt the overwhelming need to be loved. "With you, Mr. Texas Cowboy."

The drive back was filled with tension and little conversation. "A million dollars for your thoughts." He finally spoke as they neared Camp Noepe, touched her thigh, and smiled.

"Why so much? I thought it was a penny?"

"It's a penny for most thoughts, but from the look on your face, I can tell the ones you're having now are very important."

"It's funny you should mention money," she replied in a lusty voice. "I was just wondering how you plan to support all of those children you want me to have. I was also thinking of where I'll stay when I return to New York. I gave up my apartment and placed my things in storage when I came here."

He thought it was a perfect time to tell her the truth. "Don't worry, I'll take care of that. You and our children will be—"

"Look out!"

She yelled and he braked in time to avoid a young fawn that loped across the road. He brought the Jeep to a stop near the ditch and they watched the fawn's white tail until it disappeared into the brush.

"Oh, isn't he beautiful? I hope he doesn't get hit. I'll bet there's a whole herd of them around here. We awful humans keep clearing the land and taking their homes. I'll bet the poor things are searching for food. I'll have to refill the trough down by the thicket. I love to sit and watch them feed."

"It's more of an overpopulation problem than anything else. We have a nice way of solving that problem back home."

"If you tell me you condone the senseless slaughter of those poor animals, I'll hit you," she scoffed.

"I would never tell a lie like that. It isn't senseless at all. We dine on them, feed all those children we keep having, which leaves fewer of them to dine on nature. It's a simple matter—"

She whacked his shoulder with her open hand. "How could you shoot those defenseless little things? That's horrible!"

"I didn't see you protesting the slaughter of that cow we had for dinner last night." He chuckled.

"That was different!"

"Oh? How is eating old Bessie different from eating Bambi?"

"It's just different. Cows aren't cute."

He laughed. "Only ugly animals should be eaten?" He parked with her still scuffling for a reply. "That's okay. Don't answer, and I promise to never invite you to dinner when we barbeque old Bambi."

"You're impossible, you know that?" She went inside ahead of him, pretending to be angry.

Pearl was making popcorn when they returned, some with butter and some with nuts and molasses. Shale took a batch of fresh cookies from the oven for Jennifer to serve, and everyone settled down in front of the television. It was three o'clock and the rain was still coming down.

"According to the weather report, this is an all-day rainstorm," Pearl announced when the adults gathered in the kitchen for coffee. "Have the horses been fed?"

"Horses, chickens, goats, and ducks. All fed," Tedera answered in the voice he reserved just for Pearl. "The only things left to feed are the *homo sapiens*. What's for dinner?"

"Your tapeworm has all cylinders purring today. You've been eating since you got up this morning." Pearl perched on her stool and tapped Tedera's head with her balled fist. "We're having ham, carrots, and potatoes, pound cake for the kids, and my chocolate chiffon cake for us later. Though after eating six batches of cookies, I doubt that anyone is going to be hungry for sweets, except maybe you."

"It's the weather. I need to keep busy. When I sit around, I get hungry and sleepy." Tedera yawned and poured a mug of coffee.

"Go take a nap," Lacey said. "Jennifer and Micah are babysitting, and I think Mother Pearl and Shale have dinner all mapped out."

"In that case, why don't we go to my cabin and watch our movie?" Monroe asked shyly.

"Yeah, go ahead. We've got everything under control," Pearl assured them before giving Monroe a menacing scowl.

Pearl's warning glance had not gone unnoticed. Monroe held the umbrella and ran alongside Lacey down the path to his cabin. He knew he had to tell her the truth, even if it drove her away.

He adjusted the television, popped in the tape and closed the lower curtains. "I'm going to get out of these wet clothes and I suggest you do the same. Your pant legs are soaked."

"Are you proposing that we watch TV in the nude?"

"I'm proposing that we not die of pneumonia." He reached behind the bathroom door and pulled out a madras plaid robe and a smile. "Here, cover your nudity."

"Thanks." She crossed her leg and yanked on her boot. "I believe these boots are permanently stuck to my feet."

"Here, let me help you." He turned his back, took hold of her foot, and worked the damp leather away from her sock. Instead of letting go, he removed the sock and stroked her toes. "Do you have any idea how much I want you, Lacey Daigle? I'm in love with you. Can you handle that?"

"I don't know." The other boot slipped easily over her sock. She stood and cupped his face in her hands. "But I do want to try."

He turned back the denim spread and made a stack of softness with the pillows. "The floor is cold. Sit here."

When she was seated on the edge of the bed, he removed the other sock. "You have beautiful feet." He stroked her legs. "Everything about you is beautiful."

Their eyes locked when he spoke, and she heard more than his words. He leaned over her, his hot breath fanning the flames that had already begun to soar. The explosion began before their lips met, and before the kiss ended, she knew she could wait no longer. His eyes searched hers while his hands tugged at her shirt, but as before, he stopped abruptly and pulled away.

"There is something I need to tell you before we go any further."

"Don't do this, Monroe," she pleaded. "It can wait until later."

"It's something I should have told you sooner, and I have to do it now. It might change the way you feel about me. About us."

"What?" she demanded in a voice filled with the urgency that raged within her. "Is this something awful? Are you wanted by the law? A moral degenerate? What?" She pulled at his belt until the buckle came undone.

"Nothing like that, but I am a liar and I need to set the record straight. Before I came here—"

Lacey ran her hand down the ridge of his arousal and felt him shudder.

"I can't tell you if you keep doing that." His eyes were glazed with lust.

"Then tell me later."

He sighed and brought his full attention to the thrill of her hands. The rain had increased. Sheets of water washed over the windowpanes, and the sharp crackle of thunder accompanied zigzags of silver. Rock Hudson was talking business and trying to ignore the lively brunette who had caught his eye the moment they met.

"Talk to me, Monroe." She unbuttoned his shirt.

"I tried, but you—"

"I don't mean that. Don't make me feel like a desperate woman. Tell me this is what you want. Tell me you're as eager as I am."

She watched as he removed his shirt and then his pants. Never had she seen a body so sculptured and so tempting. When she began removing her shirt, he took her hands in his.

"Let me." He unhooked her bra and kissed her hard nipples before sucking them, alternately, into his mouth. He trailed wet kisses up to her neck and whispered softly, "I want you more than I thought I could ever want a woman. I want you now. I want you forever." His hand reached down and peeled away her underwear.

She shivered involuntarily as his eyes raked over her nakedness.

"You're beautiful. I want you so badly, but I have something to say that you should hear—"

She covered his lips with her fingers and wiggled her body against his iron need. "Words can't help me now. Nothing you can say will make me want you any less. Just make love to me. I can't wait any longer."

His mouth was close to her ear and his hot breath chased away all rational thoughts. She welcomed his arms around her and the invasion of his tongue between her lips. His mouth traveled down the side of her face, close to her ear, his tongue burned her skin. She stroked the coarse hairs on his chest and slid her palms down the slope of his back and over the rise of his hips.

He teased her with his mouth and his hands. Every move carried her closer to the edge of her restraint. When his hand traveled down to the junction of her thighs, she parted her legs invitingly, wanting him to touch her everywhere.

He moved around on the bed and crouched above her, his head dipping down between her breasts. She moaned when his lips touched their sensitive buds, wanting him to linger and at the same time ease the painful longing that continued rising within her. He continued his sweet torture, caressing and kissing her body and loitering near her most feminine of places.

His hands were gentle but demanding and his mouth was filled with fire. He left no spot unloved.

When he left the bed, she moaned insistently. "Don't leave me now."

He came back to the bed amid the rustle of latex. "I don't want to leave you, ever."

Monroe welcomed the merger of her body heat with his and felt his breath coming in short gasps that allowed barely enough oxygen to fill his lungs. Wave after wave of sensation raked down into his lower regions, where the pressure of her hands shocked his nerve endings. After almost two years of needing a woman's touch and months of agonizing over his feelings for Lacey, his converging desires were being fulfilled in the sweetest torment he could have imagined.

He turned her to him and settled his body over hers. Using the heel of her right hand, she planed down his knotted muscles in his shoulders, while her left hand moved down his body. The thrill of his mouth on her skin drove her to the peak of passion, leaving no place to go but over the edge.

She opened her treasures and struggled to retain consciousness as he gently plowed his body into hers. They moved in rhythm with the rain. Lacey gripped Monroe's back and held him in place, wanting to keep his life inside of her for as long as she could. Feeling his body tense, she released him, felt his convulsive thrust, and the storm long building inside of her erupted in a dizzying avalanche of pleasure. In the seconds that followed, she was sure of only one thing—she never wanted him to stop.

Streaks of lightning flashed above the gingham curtains and she tried to control her jagged breathing. There had been nothing in her life to prepare her for the overwhelming delight of a man like Monroe Faulkner. Her first time had been quick and largely forgettable, the second time, with her history professor, had been a learning experience. Mason had filled her world with romantic evenings and bouquets of love, but needed constant reminders that sex should be a matter of mutual enjoyment.

Now, with all of the reasons she had to doubt a future with Monroe, lying in his arms, she felt fulfilled, breathlessly replete. He raised her hand to his mouth and kissed each fingertip. With no words between them, she nested in his arms and fell into a childlike slumber.

Monroe watched her, felt her body move slightly with each breath. Everything that he missed, everything he needed was right there in his arms. He spooned his body around hers, nestled his head in her hair and fell fast asleep.

They awakened together. The rain had stopped, and James Dean, now a rich oil baron, was stinking drunk. Lacey looked at her watch and knew she had to leave. He was addictive, and, for the first time in her adult life, she felt whole.

He pulled her into his arms. "Tell me I didn't fall asleep and dream all of this. You're too wonderful to be true."

She pushed up on her elbows and kissed his eyelids. "I don't know how you happened into my life, Monroe Faulkner, but I've never felt so complete. I hate to leave all of this, but I should get back and·help with the kids."

He tightened his grip on her arm. "You can't leave now."

She slid back into his arms after he had dug a foil wrapper from his wallet. "I don't want to leave—ever." She straddled his body and took him inside of her.

Monroe relaxed and allowed her to take him with a fervor he did not think she possessed. She lifted and lowered her body, taking only as much as she wanted and watching his face, distorted with passion. He covered her breasts with his hands, allowed her nipples to rest between his knuckles, and squeezed until a sound escaped her lips that was more animal than human. The increased friction of her agile aggression elicited a throaty moan that raised several octaves and hushed to a satisfied whimper.

With her spent body draped across his, she weakly kissed his face. "You've got to help me get back to the house, or Mother Pearl is going to come.looking for both of us."

"And do you think she would be angry at what she found?" he whispered.

"I think she would be elated. Of course, she'll know when she sees me. Everyone will know. The glow on my face feels strong enough to light the Eastern Seaboard." Remembering his earlier attempts to talk, she asked, "What did you want to tell me?"

"We'll talk later, after the kids settle down."

They dressed and he walked her back to the main house, stopping behind the stable for one last kiss, but one led to another and he had to pry himself from her body. "We'd better stop before one of the kids gets loose and finds us here. Look!" He pointed upward. "A rainbow. Isn't that a sign of good luck?"

She pressed her body against his. "Unless I find out you're married, a criminal, or some kind of nut, I've got all the luck I need." She took his hand. "Come on, let's get up to the main house and see if the kids are all in one piece."

When they rounded the building, she pointed to a green Chrysler in the driveway.

"I wonder who that could be. I don't know anyone with a car like that, do you?"

"No, but other than the people at Camp Noepe, I don't know anyone here at all."

Her footsteps quickened and Monroe paced at her side. "It's a rental car." She hung back. "Oh, God! If it's my mother, I'll just scream."

"Come on," he coaxed. "Just remember I'm with you, no matter what. The two of us can handle your mother."

She rushed ahead of him and into the kitchen, stopped short just inside the door, and gasped. "Mason! What are you doing here?"

He looked past her. "I came to Boston to help a client with a bad situation and promised your mother I'd come out here and see if you were okay. I think the big questions right now is, what are you doing here?" The sarcasm in his voice matched the anger in his eyes.

Lacey felt relieved. She had almost forgotten Mason's undesirable side. "What are you talking about?"

"Pearl was just telling me how well the camp is doing. She said you were checking the horses with one of your employees, but I suppose she was misinformed. Is that what this has been about?" He pointed to the yard. "You've been hiding here with John Tobias?"

"I don't know what you mean. Who is John Tobias?" This was new anger, she thought, vicious and cruel.

Pearl, Yank, and Tedera gathered around, each one staring in surprised perplexity.

"I heard so much about this sainted mission of yours, how you came here to fulfill your grandfather's dream and find the deeper meaning of life. Why didn't you just say there was another man? How long have you known him? Where did you meet?" Mason fumed, his fingers curved into fists.

She frowned and moved closer. "One of us is crazy and I really don't think it's me. Who the hell is John Tobias?"

"The man you were just with. The one who came in with you and then backed out the door when he saw me."

She looked around. Monroe was no longer there. "That was Monroe Faulkner. Tell me who this Tobias is, if you don't mind."

"As if you don't know. John Jacob, J.J. Tobias. He was just featured in *Business Monthly*, *Minority Millionaires*, and half a dozen other magazines. He's ones of the wealthiest minorities in Texas. Maybe in the country."

Lacey thought for a second. While she could believe this man might not be Monroe Faulkner, she knew he was not a millionaire. "The man you just saw is Monroe Faulkner, my riding instructor. I don't know any John Jacob Tobias. Maybe Monroe bears a resemblance to this man. In a hat maybe all cowboys look alike. How can you be so sure from just seeing this Tobias in a magazine?"

"I didn't just see him in a magazine. I met him, had dinner with him. If you recall my trip to Fort Worth last May, I closed a land deal for a client with Tobias and his father. We dined at a country club. Tobias came in late with a bandage over his right eye, some kind of freak accident involving a horse. If you don't believe me, just check around his right eyebrow and see if there's a scar."

She didn't have to check. Every fear she had of becoming involved rushed over her. She looked at Pearl, who quickly dropped her gaze to the floor. Everything fell into place, even the name Tobias. Monroe listed Tobias Ranch as his place of employment.

"He did leave in a hurry." Yank came to Lacey's side. "I'll go see if I can find him. Maybe you should let him explain."

"Go ahead." Pearl motioned him to the door. "Come in the kitchen, Mason. Let's have some coffee."

John Jacob Tobias walked hurriedly toward the ocean. Jumbled emotions ran, in erratic patterns, through his consciousness. His heart pounded and his hands were cold with fear. He should have told her sooner.

He knew Mason had recognized him. "I had my chance and didn't take it."

He could only imagine what they were talking about. Knowing Lacey as he did, he knew she would be much angrier having learned his identity from Mason than from him.

Less than an hour ago, she was lying next to him. Making love to her had been one of the greatest pleasures in his life. Her presence in his life had allowed him to look past his pain and into the future.

He walked along the sandy debris, looking at the water and wondering if she would forgive him. Pearl had warned him. Yank and Tedera swore Pearl had great visionary powers. Everyone knew he had a secret, simply because he never spoke of his past, but only Pearl had known that continuing to hold back could destroy any future relationship with Lacey.

In the maze of pain, he thought of Monroe Faulkner and felt his lies had smudged a great man's name.

He went to the thicket where he had first held her, wanting to go back to that sunbaked afternoon and rid his soul of the painful burden. The one person who could make it difficult for Lacey to forgive him had exposed his lie. He pounded the ground, wanting very much to weep.

"Monroe."

He turned slowly and stared, ruefully, into the eyes of a friend. "Yank, I've really screwed up."

"I don't have much time. I have a plane to catch back to New York, but I'm not leaving here without you," Mason said as he took Lacey's arm. "I know this man is Tobias, and if he's lied about his identity, there's no telling what kind of danger you could be in. Let me do some checking and find out what's going on. In the meantime, you need to return to New York until this is settled."

Lacey was silent. Monroe's scent on her body reminded her that she was just in his arms, in his bed, and though she had no reason to feel accountable, she did.

"We were about to have dinner. Can I fix you a plate?" Pearl's face was also plastered with weary frustration.

"No, thank you. I had lunch in Boston. When I found out I was coming here, I decided to try and understand the attraction Lacey felt for this place. Now I see that maybe it wasn't the place at all."

Tedera stood between Lacey and Mason, and Shale stole glances while filling the coffeepot. Lacey was trying to digest the news and formulate suitable responses to Mason's peppered jabs.

"You've always liked my chocolate chiffon cake," Pearl said, placing a large slice on a plate. "At least sit down and have some cake and coffee."

"Thank you, Pearl." He held the chair for Lacey. "I don't know if you're trying to pull something on me or if that's what he's done to you, but I know this man is John Tobias. If you lied to me, that probably means you came here with him and the two of you have been playing house. If he lied to you—"

"All right! Stop it. I don't care who this man is, I'm not going to sit here and listen to a lecture from you. I'd never met Monroe Faulkner before March. He answered my ad for a riding instructor, sent his résumé, and I hired him." She lowered her eyes. "I never laid eyes on this man before he showed up here at Camp Noepe. He's worked very hard to help get the camp ready, and he's done an excellent job of teaching the kids."

Yank ran in the door. He looked from Lacey to Pearl before dropping his head. "He's not in his cabin or on the grounds around the camp."

"He no doubt ran away when he saw me. That also tells me that you should leave here now. Do you have some kind of relationship with this man?"

"I'm not answering your inquisition. I returned your ring before I left New York. Our engagement is off and my relationship with this, or any other man, is not your concern."

"It's not just the relationship. This man is John Tobias. Doesn't that make you wonder why he's here posing as a riding instructor? You have to come back with me."

"Okay, let's say this man is a millionaire rancher from Texas." Saying the words was hard enough, but digesting the thought of being deceived and having Mason discover the deception was too much to comprehend. She wanted Mason to go back to his world and leave the one she had built in place. "Maybe he had business or personal reasons for wanting to hide out here. What possible reason could he have to harm any of us?"

"Oh, grow up, Lacey! There are a million reasons a man would want to conceal his identity, and none of them spells safe for you. You just can't admit that you've made a big mistake. A big error in judgment. Been mislead. Swindled! I don't have answers, but you need to be alert enough to ask the questions, and, until the mystery is solved, I think you would be safer back in New York."

Mason reached for her arms and Yank blocked his move. "There's no need for that." He stood between Lacey and Mason with one arm crooked and poised close to Mason's neck. The other arm swept back to hold Lacey in place. "Lacey owns this ranch. She doesn't have to go anywhere or do anything she doesn't want to do. There are three men here with Lacey. Besides, if this man is an imposter, he's been here for months and we're almost at the end of the season. If he wanted to do harm, I'm sure he would have made a move by now."

"Yank is right. There's nothing for you to worry about. I'm very safe here with Yank, Tedera, Shale, and Micah, not to mention Mother Pearl's shotgun. You go on back to your important life in New York and let me handle Camp Noepe. We'll learn this man's true identity and, I can assure you, I will take whatever action I feel is appropriate."

The kids started to swarm the kitchen, and Pearl left, with Shale, to get dinner on the table. Yank and Tedera sat with Lacey and watched in silence as Mason picked at his cake.

"Your mother is very worried about you, and so am I, especially now. When are you coming home?"

"The camp closes in a few weeks. I'll be home shortly after that. Tell my mother not to worry. And don't you go back to New York and share your suspicions about my riding instructor. Why would a wealthy man come here and pretend to be someone else? I can see the reverse, but what you're suggesting is ludicrous."

She said one thing, but her mind was inundated with wonder. She tried to steer Mason away from the subject with stories of the campers and questions about her brother. Relief took over when he announced he had to leave.

"As much as I'd like to stick around and find out what's going on, I have a plane to catch back to New York. Don't worry, I'm not going to mention this to your mother, but I am glad I came. Now I know I was right about this whole thing being a mistake."

Yank walked him outside, assured him that Lacey was in no danger, and took off toward the water. With his head thrown back and his chest pushed forward, he made a noise, an old Algonquin signal for all clear, before reaching the thicket. "He's gone. He tried to get Lacey to leave with him, but of course she wouldn't do it."

John rubbed his fingers across the ache in his temple. "How did she take it?"

"I'm not sure. I think she's still shocked. I know I am. I guess we all questioned you being a modern-day saddle tramp, but a millionaire rancher would have never crossed my mind. I'm sure it didn't cross Lacey's, either. Now Pearl…" He nodded and smiled. "I'm sure she knows. Pearl knows everything."

"I apologize for deceiving you. I'm sorry. My reasons for coming here, for using an alias, are personal. I never meant to cause trouble for anyone here. I hope you can forgive me."

"Don't worry about me. I forgive you, but then I'm not in love with you." Yank laid his hand on John's shoulder. "Lacey is the one you'll have to convince. I don't like that Mason guy, and from what I've heard, I doubt I would like Lacey's mother or that she would like me. They didn't want her to come here, and I know her mother has been bugging her to come back to New York and marry that bozo. Pearl said they both went nuts when Lacey quit her job. She told Mason over dinner in some fancy restaurant. He went off, Lacey got mad, took off her ring, and threw it in his soup." He chuckled. "Wish I'd been there."

John was still stuck on Yank's first words. "You really think Lacey is in love with me?"

"I would say she's about as much in love with you as you are with her, and it's no secret to any of us. It's on your face, man, in your voice, and in hers."

"If that's how she felt before, I hope that love hasn't turned to hate. How did Pearl seem?"

"Not angry or surprised. As I said, she knew all along. In any case, you don't have to tell me or anyone else why you lied about your identity, but you should tell Lacey. She'll understand. Maybe not right away, but she'll forgive you. I know she cares for you, and that not something you should take lightly."

Pearl rang the dinner bell and the campers piled in the kitchen. Blue glasses filled with lemonade, large bowls of boiled corn, fish, Pearl's secret recipe slaw, and buttered rolls filled the table. The campers all talked at once, relaying the events of the evening and showing off their latest craft creation.

No one voiced concerns in front of the children, not even when Monroe came in, silent and guarded, and sat down to dinner. Lacey was glad that Micah and Jennifer kept the kids busy with talk of singers, movie stars, and fashion. Her silence and the embarrassed anger in her eyes would have roused their suspicions. She could not eat, and the look on Pearl and Yank's face was more unnerving. Monroe's weak smile when she looked his way also did not help. By the time the kids finished eating, her head was pounding and she wanted very much to scream.

Pearl looked from Lacey to Monroe and back. "We'll finish in here, honey. You go and rest."

"Thanks, Mother Pearl." She turned to Monroe. "Can we finish the conversation we started earlier, Monroe? I believe you had something to tell me."

"Sure." He stared at the floor.

She followed him from the room and forced back the urge to speak until they were in his cabin.

He closed the door and hurried to straighten the bedcovers. "You want to finish the movie?"

"No." She moved quickly behind him, slipped her arm around his waist and forced him back on the bed. Her smile was filled with malice.

Straddling his body, she traced the outline of his right eyebrow. "You've healed quite nicely from your accident. Last May, I believe. There's barely a scar." She slid off the bed and spoke quickly. "Is that what you wanted to tell me, Mr. John Jacob Tobias, millionaire from Texas?"

He nodded slowly. "Yes. That's what I wanted to tell you. Should have told you. I'm sorry you found out this way."

"Well, since I did, at least tell me why." Lacey took a deep breath and exhaled slowly. "The truth this time, please."

"I know this sounds like a tired cliché, but I didn't mean to cause you or anyone else any problems or pain. I should've told you before anything happened between us. I tried earlier. I wanted to long before then, but there just didn't seem to be a good time to say it. I had made up my mind to tell you for sure today, but other things became more immediate."

"Don't bring the fact that we just slept together into this. You should have told the truth in the beginning, that is, if you're capable of telling the truth. And how the hell do I know you're telling the truth now? Do you know the kind of embarrassment you caused me? That pretentious asshole that I was daft enough to agree to marry, the same blowhard who's been telling me I didn't know what I was doing, just identified the man I hired." She threw her hands into the air. "Now I'm the one standing here with egg on my face. How could you?"

"I don't blame you for being angry. Please believe me, everything I said about my feelings for you was the truth. I fell in love with you the first moment I laid eyes on you. I just couldn't deal with it at the time."

"Don't bullshit me any longer, Monroe, or John, whatever the hell your name is. Just tell me what's going on. Who is Monroe Faulkner, and why the hell are you here?"

"I knew your fiancé would tell you, and I've been trying to find the words to try and make this right." He looked into her eyes. "I'm sorry I lied. It certainly wasn't meant to harm anyone."

"Then answer my questions." She felt dizzy and disoriented. After all of the precautions she had taken, this man had successfully stolen her heart, betrayed her trust, and made her feel like an utter fool.

"Monroe Faulkner is dead." He reached in his shirt pocket and fished out a letter, tri-folded and stained with sweat. "I found this in his possessions. Your check is inside."

Grief for a man she never met momentarily overtook her anger. "How did he die?"

"Heart attack. He was one of our most loved and trusted employees. I guess sort of like an uncle to me. His life was filled with more heartache than any man should know. His only child, his daughter, was murdered by her estranged husband. His wife died two years later, probably from a broken heart. Monroe suffered his fate without losing his compassion or his smile. He had a number of health problems, but nothing kept him down. He was diagnosed with cancer two years ago. That's when he started talking about seeing the world. He'd lived his whole life in the same place. Never left the state of Texas except to travel with the rodeo.

"I offered to send him anywhere in the world, but that wasn't what he wanted. He saw your ad and loved the pictures. Said this seemed like a peaceful place to die. We tried to talk him out of it, but his mind was set. He died just before he was scheduled to come here."

"I see."

He opened his wallet and took out a tattered photograph. "That's Monroe with me at last year's big barbeque."

Lacey stared at the weathered face that reminded her of Willie Nelson before turning her anguished eyes to John Jacob Tobias. "Why do you have his picture in your wallet? Were you that close?"

"My brother snapped the photo, and I don't really know why, but I kept it. Monroe was special to me. He had no one." His voice faltered. He took a deep breath. "We shared a lot. He was in my life for as long as I can remember. I don't even remember who hired him. Probably my grandfather. He never changed. Never complained. Just accepted whatever hand life dealt. I admired him a great deal."

After a pause to acknowledge his grief, she rebounded with anger. "You've only answered one of my questions. I still want to know why you're here. Why are you posing as this man you say is dead?"

John shook his head. "Can we just let it be? You know who I am. Why take it any further?"

"How could you ask that? We were together, Mon…Mr. Tobias." She stamped her feet. "I can't do this! I was lied to. Misled. Allowed to fall in love with an illusion. Don't you think I deserve to know the truth?"

"You fell in love with John Tobias. What difference does a name make?" He reached for her arm.

"Don't you dare touch me." Hearing happy chuckles from the children near the stable, she lowered her voice, but spoke through clenched teeth. "I'll ask you one more time. Why did you pose as this man? Why did you come here?"

"Okay, but it's a long story, so please sit down. My name is John Jacob Tobias, and according to most of the people in my world, I'm a very lucky fellow." He sat on the trunk at the foot of the bed.

"My whole life is a fairy tale. My grandfather, Nathaniel Tobias Sr., had a piece of seemingly worthless land down in Denham Wells, Texas. One day he learned there was a small but very fertile vein of oil on that land. Natty—that's what we call him—didn't have a formal education, but he's a very crafty man. He was able to parlay that little well into a tidy sum, and he used the money wisely. He kept his land, built a nice, but unpretentious, home for his family, and bought some livestock. My father, Nathaniel Jr., took the ranching thing a little further."

Lacey moved closer to the edge of the bed. The pain she saw when he arrived had resurfaced.

"My dad married my mom, a schoolteacher, and they had four children. I'm the third child. My two sisters married jerks, my younger brother is a crackhead, and I guess I'm a living, breathing coward. Not a strong man like Monroe Faulkner. I had everything I ever wanted. Love. Security. College. Nice cars. Nice clothes. Probably much like your life before your father and grandfather passed away."

He reached for her hand.

She pulled away. "Continue the story, please."

"I met my wife in college. I was a grad student. She was a freshman from a military family in New Jersey. I was not naïve or innocent, but I fell in love so hard I couldn't see straight. We married less than a year later. I returned to Texas to help my father with the business as planned, and she went along. I don't think she really liked it there, but she didn't complain. I built a home for us on a spot by a little brook. In the middle of construction, she learned she was pregnant. It was the happiest day of my life.

"She never got the hang of horseback riding. Horses seemed to frighten her, but she was determined to fit into my world. Determined to convince me that she was happy living in our little town. I gave her a horse for Christmas. He was gentle, and she started getting the hang of it. She was with him out by the barn, waiting for me to turn in the driveway so she could show me how well she had learned to ride. The horse had been pastured far away from the house. He'd never been close to a car. She tried to ride out to meet me, the horse bolted, and she took a spill."

Emotion crowded his voice. His eyes became misty. "That's when my world fell apart. Everything around me, the wealth of it all, became tainted by the pain it caused. I begged the doctors to save her. Save my baby. There was nothing they could do. Money, everything I had, was useless." He squeezed his hands into fists. "I watched life drain from her beautiful face. I guess that's when I really started admiring Monroe. Life had robbed him of everyone he loved and he just kept pushing. Kept smiling."

He kept his face turned away from hers. "Family and friends tried to help. After a year, they started fixing me up with different women, but it didn't work. I wanted Debra, and she was gone."

"I'm sorry. I know it's very painful."

"Everyone in and around Denham Wells knew me and knew of my loss. The outreach was tremendous. I started to hate the condolences. Resent their pity. My grandmother's sister had a home here on the island, and my family vacationed here until my grandmother's death years ago. When I found your letter in Monroe's possessions, I remembered how much I once loved it here. I also remembered what Monroe had said. I wanted to come here, not to die, but to find life in a place where no one knew me. Where no one pitied me. I wanted to be a stranger. I wanted to see life, to be happy, to see past the pain. I truly wanted to emulate a man who accepted loss as part of living. I wanted to smile like Monroe Faulkner."

"I'm sorry for your pain." That's was all she could think to say. The hurt on his face was not pretense. He had loved his wife.

"Oh, the story gets really good now." He chuckled, mirthlessly. "I mentally matched the name Lacey Daigle with a crusty, saddle-weary, middle-aged woman. I figured she was the owner's wife or whatever. Then I came here and found you. The first time I saw you, walking down the path from the stables, your blue-black hair glistening in the sun, I couldn't believe my eyes. I looked at your face and thought I might faint. Something told me to turn and run, not walk away. Something even stronger made me stand there and listen to your briefing on the island and Camp Noepe."

Lacey felt her face turning red. His next statement made her sway in even greater surprise.

"You couldn't look more like Debra if you tried. Each glance, each toss of your head, brought her back to me. I felt I had been tricked by fate. I was running away from painful memories, only to find them here, ready to pounce on a heart I never thought would heal. You never said you owned Camp Noepe, so I assumed you were in charge of running the place for someone else. That's why I reacted the way I did when you

started describing the situation. You were counting on
Monroe Faulkner to help you get this place going and
along comes J.J. Tobias, thinking only of his own
selfish needs. I knew I had to stay. I wanted to tell you
the truth, but I thought it was too late. I saw your
pride. You wouldn't have accepted my help if you'd
known the truth."

"So you lied to help me?"

"No, I stayed to help you. Then I lied to myself
about living here and not falling in love with you."

She looked at him and quickly turned away. She
knew the feelings inside her chest were love, but that
was not what she wanted to feel. She could imagine
Mason and Amanda questioning her every move and
reminding her of the poor judgment she used in hiring
a man who could have been a serial killer.

"I started comparing you to Debra. I saw your
difference and your sameness. You're stronger, more
stubborn. More determined. A demon in denim."

"Don't flatter me, Mr. Tobias."

"That wasn't flattery. I noticed your speech. Perfect
diction. No trace of an accent. I was fascinated and
mad as hell. I felt trapped. I also felt something I
thought I would never feel again. I was angry with you
for arousing those feelings, and at myself for letting it
happen."

"Is that the flattery part?"

"Can't let it go, can you?" He flashed a tight-lipped
smile. "Everything about you screams sophistication.
You're beautiful. You're amazing, and I'm in love with

you. I'm sorry I lied about my name. Everything else is all me. What I can't understand is how you ever hooked up with that prancing pansy, Mason Phipps."

"Mason was not right for me. I recognized that and broke off our engagement. You're not right, either. I can't love a man I can't trust. Stay and finish the season, or leave. It's your choice, John Jacob Tobias. What do your friends call you?"

"J.J.," he said solemnly.

She stood without looking at him and walked to the door. "In that case," she said, glancing over her shoulder. "I'd better call you Mr. Tobias."

"Lacey, please believe me, I'm so terribly sorry for having lied to you. I love you."

"As they say, one lie ruins a thousand truths."

She hurried away from the cabin, but not before he saw the pain in her eyes.

CHAPTER 10

"I can't believe this!" Lacey paced the kitchen. "Why me? Why the hell me, and why was Mason the one to let me know what a fool I've been? I'll never live this down. Mason will tell my mother, even though he swore not to, and that woman will hound me with this for the rest of my life."

Everyone had gathered around to hear her story and, one by one, gave her looks and words of sympathy and left the room. She was now alone with Pearl.

"Don't you think you're taking this a little too seriously? Are you angry that he's not a poor drifter?"

"I'm angry that he lied. He made me look like a fool in front of Mason." She stopped pacing and looked at Pearl. "Did you know? Did you see this?"

"I knew he was no down-and-out drifter, but it didn't take any special insight to see that. You knew it, too. You said his hands were too soft, he was too refined, too educated to be a run-of-the-mill cowboy. He said he loves you, and that I believe."

Pearl took hold of Lacey's shoulders. "He didn't lie to promote himself. He was just a man, hurting and needing relief. I know he should have told you and

I'm sure he knows it, too, but please don't beat yourself up over this. I think you're mostly angry that Mason was the one to discover the truth, but you need to get past this and get on with loving and being loved."

"How can I, Mother Pearl? He made me feel like a fool, and in front of the one person I—"

"Lacey," Pearl sternly cut her off. "I know your pride has been hurt, and I know that Monroe, John, has not been honest about his identity, but honey, this man loves you. He's not lying about that, and I, for one, am damn glad he's not a penniless cowboy. He's a real man, Lacey. The kind you need. The millions only make him a better catch. Give him a chance."

Lacey couldn't sleep and she didn't go outside for fear of running into John Tobias. With the moon still resting on the treetops, she dressed and walked up to the main house. The smell of freshly ground coffee helped her eyes open, and she smiled after seeing Tedera tiptoe down the hallway and reenter through the kitchen door.

"Good morning." His smile softened the hard lines of his copper skin. "What did you do to Monroe, I mean John? I saw him walking around the camp late last night, and now he's dressed and sitting on his back step. I don't think he got any sleep."

"Good. I can't say I got much sleep myself."

"Pearl doesn't think you should be angry, and neither do I. He's a wealthy man. That's better, right?"

"He's a lying son of a bitch, and I don't understand why Mother Pearl is taking his side."

"Pearl would never take anyone's side against you. She loves you more than anything. This man came here because he was having trouble with his past. He came to find a future, and he found you. Bitterness is poison to the heart, Lacey. Don't let it kill the love inside of you. The love you feel for John. Don't hold the lie against him. It was a harmless lie." He saw her frown and quickly added, "I know it made you angry, but he loves you. He wants to make you happy, and I think he can if you let him."

"That's what I say." Pearl yawned, hugged Tedera and then Lacey. "Good morning, baby. I know you didn't sleep last night, and I'm sorry. I wish you would try and look at this more objectively. Monroe Faulkner is really John Tobias, that's the man you know. He lied, but he had good reason. He helped make Camp Noepe a success. Don't you think it's better to have a rich man posing as a poor man than the other way around? You've got someone who loves you and can offer you the things you deserve. Look at all the things you have in common."

"That's true," Tedera agreed. "No one could have worked harder than John here at Camp Noepe."

"He lost his wife and child. I'm sure you can imagine how that must have hurt." Pearl smoothed Lacey's hair.

"I don't think there is a good reason to lie."

"Come on, honey. Don't be so rigid." Pearl hugged her and kissed the top of her head. "You're judging him without mercy. He didn't do that to you."

"You might be right, but I'm still angry. Maybe I'll get over it, and maybe I won't." She knew they were right and could feel the anger draining away. She felt John's love, right next to her love for him.

"I don't want your pride to deprive you of the chance to be loved by this man. You know he's special. You knew it all along. The two of you belong together."

"I love you, Mother Pearl. I'm glad you're here with me." She sunk her face into the comfort of Pearl's shoulder. "I think I'll take my coffee and go back to the bunkhouse. The girls should be up by now. I know Melissa is raring to get back to practice."

She left the main house but was back before Pearl and Shale had finished the biscuits.

"Something's wrong with Melissa. She won't get out of bed."

"Is she ill?" Shale asked. "I'll go take her temperature."

"She doesn't want you to check her temperature. She says she's not riding in the contest and she wants to go home. From what I heard, she seemed more angry than ill, but I couldn't determine why."

"That's strange." Shale frowned. "Maybe it isn't. Come to think of it, Melissa hardly said a word during dinner last night. Before that she was fine. Let's see if

Micah knows anything. He and Jennifer were with the children all evening."

"Don't worry, honey. She'll be okay," Pearl assured her. "One of the other kids probably said something to hurt her feelings. I'm just thankful we haven't had more of this. After the initial round of grumbling, they've been a fairly carefree bunch. I think having Micah and Jennifer here made a big difference."

"I agree, but I'm still worried. She is so mature and determined. There hasn't been one cross word from her since she's been here. She's never complained or whined about anything, and she has worked so hard for this contest. It doesn't make sense that she would give up."

The kids came to breakfast without Melissa. No one seemed to know why she was upset. There was another empty place at the breakfast table. John did not make an appearance. Consumed with anger, pain, and worry, Lacey barely touched her meal and was too lost in thought to hear the breakfast conversation. She stood to leave the table long before the meal concluded.

"I'm going back to the bunkhouse to check on Melissa."

"Ask John if he knows anything," Yank suggested. "He's been sitting on the back steps all morning."

"Could I speak to you in the kitchen, please?"

Lacey nodded and Yank followed her. "Have you spoken with John, or whatever his name is? Is he planning to leave now?"

"I don't think so. He apologized for not telling the truth and said his family was all over him to date and get on with his life, and the more they insisted, the greater his pain became. That's why he used that other man's name and came here. He said he wanted to see what life was like as Monroe Faulkner because, with all of his problems, Monroe Faulkner was a happy man, even as he took his last breath."

"Thanks for telling me. I'll go check on Melissa now."

"Lacey," Yank spoke softly. "I don't mean to butt in." He grunted a laugh. "We all say that, don't we? And then we go ahead and butt in anyway. It's just that Monroe, John, was so sad when he first came here, but he's been a different person lately. The change happened when he fell in love with you. Don't give up just yet."

She smiled at Yank and headed down to the bunkhouse. Melissa was still in bed and insisted that she wanted to go home. When Lacey tried to comfort her, she angrily jerked away.

"Leave me alone! I don't want you to touch me."

Startled, Lacey left the room and, hoping John had an answer, forced her feet to walk down the little dirt trail to the row of cabins. The sun was turning the previous day's rain into stifling condensation, but the grass was verdant and the rosebushes around the cabins were filled with aromatic blooms. She stood on the steps, going back to yesterday, when she thought Monroe Faulkner was the greatest thing to ever enter her life. Disappointment rose high enough to push her fears aside. She took a deep breath and knocked softly on the doorframe.

"I was about to go to the stables and begin my day. Don't worry, I'm not goofing off this morning," John said, answering her knock with a rushed defense.

"It's not about that." Looking at him, scrubbed clean but with red-rimmed eyes, she wanted to run to his arms. "It's Melissa. She won't get out of bed, but I don't think she's ill. Says she wants to go home. I thought you might know why."

"No, I don't, but I'll go with you to speak to her. She's a brave little girl, so I don't think she's getting nervous about the competition. Yesterday she was raring to go. She had trouble with one of the jumps and was upset that the rain prevented her from practicing."

"Lots of things were different yesterday."

"Lacey, don't do this."

"I'm sorry. I shouldn't have said that. I want to get past this, but it keeps eating at me, John." She shook her head. "I don't think I can get used to calling you John. I know it shouldn't make that much of a difference, but it does. I feel betrayed by someone I was just starting to really trust, and it hurts. Pearl thinks I'm making mountains out of sand dunes, and maybe I am. Right now, I just feel confused."

He gently wrapped his arms around her. "I'm so sorry I didn't tell you sooner. It seemed pointless in the beginning. Later, it kept getting harder and harder. Don't judge me without giving me a chance to prove that I'm in love with you."

He kissed her forehead and she clung to him, feeling the anguish drain away. Their lips met and she leaned her body into his. She heard her name and looked over her shoulder to the window.

"Lacey! Lacey!" Micah ran down the path. "Lacey, come quick! It's Pearl. Something's wrong!"

Lacey ran with him, and John followed close behind. Shale and Tedera were on the floor next to the sofa when Pearl lay, her eyes closed and her hands folded across her chest. Yank was on the phone.

"What is it? What's wrong with Mother Pearl?"

"I'm not sure," Shale answered. "She said she was feeling a little faint, and I told her to come in here and lie down. Thinking it might be the heat, I got some ice in a cold towel and found her here, gasping for breath. I loosened her clothes and she just passed out."

Yank joined them. "The paramedics were just down the road at the Fincher place. They'll be here in a few minutes."

"Her pulse is still strong." Shale moved aside as Lacey knelt on the floor.

"Mother Pearl." She stroked Pearl's face. "Mother Pearl, can you hear me? Help is on the way. Please try to hold on. I love you so much."

The siren sent Yank and Micah running down the walk. Everyone moved aside as one of the paramedics

ran to Pearl's side, while the other two secured the
stretcher next to the sofa.

"I can't be certain, but I think she may have had a
heart attack," the female attendant announced as they
lifted her to the stretcher. "We've alerted the hospital."

"Can I ride with her?"

The male attendant started to speak, but the
female cut him off. "Sure, come on."

"We'll follow you." John was next to her, helping
her into the back of the ambulance. "Micah and
Jennifer can take the kids to the beach. We'll be here
for her and for you." He kissed her hand before the
attendant closed the doors.

Numbness had taken hold of Lacey's body and
would not let go. Within a span of twenty-four hours
her world had turned upside down, and the one
person who had provided emotional stability was
gone. She held the phone to her ear for a long time
before she was able to dial. "Mom, I've got—"

"Lacey! I'm glad you finally decided to return my
call. Mason came back from Massachusetts with all
kinds of stories about you and some man. How could
you—"

"Mom, listen—"

"Sometimes you're just too trusting, and that
makes you blind. I don't know what's going on, but
from what Mason said, it doesn't sound good. You've

got to stop, Lacey. You can't see the bad in some people or the good in—"

"Mom! Will you please shut up for a second?" Lacey waited for silence. "It's Mother Pearl. She had a heart attack this morning. She died about three hours ago."

She spent the next hour on the phone, calling family and friends from Pearl's address book. Reality sunk in when she finally finished and slumped back in her desk chair.

The blow of Pearl's death reopened the tender wounds of loss in her heart. She moved in a trance and spoke in a measured monotone. Barely aware of her surroundings, she watched Tedera, Shale, Micah, and Jennifer cry, and heard John Tobias tell Yank that they would have to make sure the camp ran smoothly until the kids left. She sat in her office, listening to the normal sounds: kids' laughter, Shale clanking around in the kitchen, and the large clock that she had placed outside of her door, ticking away the seconds just as before. It was all the same, yet everything had changed.

"Lacey." Tedera poked his head in the door. "Can I come in?"

"Sure." She dried her eyes.

Grief tilted the tan face toward the floor. "I didn't know if you're aware of this, but she told me she wanted to remain on the island after it happened."

"You mean she told you she wanted to be buried here? When did she do that?"

"Right after you came here. She said she was born here, would die here." He held a sealed brown envelope out to Lacey as his eyes leaked onto his cheeks. "She showed me this about two weeks ago, before she sealed it. Everything is in here."

She took the envelope and held it against her chest, then steadied her hands and pulled the glued edge apart. She stared down at the curvy handwriting.

"I don't understand. Why did she do this? Did she know?"

"She just said it was something she felt she should make clear. I don't know why she told me. I asked if she was ill, and she said you insisted she get a complete physical before she came here, and the doctor said she had the body of a thirty-year-old."

"Excuse me, Tedera. I have one more phone call to make." With Pearl's will and instructions that her body should be cremated and spread over the cliffs of Aquinnah in her hand, Lacey held on until the soft voice on the other end spoke her name.

"I don't understand, Uncle Max." Max Steinberg had been her father's associate and best friend. "You said she was healthy. How could this have happened?"

"I had the same thought. When your mother called, I went back to the office and reviewed Pearl's file. Lacey, there was nothing to indicate a heart problem. I checked every test result, every gauge that we use to diagnose problems, and nothing was amiss. I'm so sorry. You've been through so much lately. I wish there was something I could do."

"We're all powerless, aren't we, Uncle Max? We can't help those we love. Freak accidents, unexplained illness. I don't think I can take another loss." She placed her head on the desk and allowed the numbness to take over.

"Lacey." John stood over her. "Tedera told me about Pearl's wishes. Will you please let me help with the arrangements? I can get a plane here if you need transportation. I'll make phone calls if you need me to, and there's no need to worry about the camp. Shale and Tedera will handle the cooking, and the rest of us will take care of the kids."

"I appreciate that. Most of the kids are leaving before next Friday. I'll alert Melissa's parents—"

"I've already called them and, after much persuasion, they agreed to come to the show."

"What are you talking about? I meant call them to pick her up. She's not going to ride, and it's just as well. As soon as the kids leave, I can close the camp and go back to New York."

"Melissa wants very much to compete." He hung his head. "I learned why she was upset, and you were right. I guess she did have a crush on me. She apparently saw the two of us kissing. We talked and she's okay. She wants to compete. Says she wants to do it for Pearl."

"There's no need to do it now. I don't care about the competition or Ramsey Treadwell."

He came around the desk. "But you do care about Powan House. You did it, Lacey. You made your grandfather's dream come true. You can reclaim your family homestead. Where I come from, that means a lot, and I know it means a lot to you. Don't you think it's what Pearl would have wanted?"

When she didn't answer, he took her in his arms. "I know how you must feel. I'm so sorry, and I'm here for you. Anything you need. Anytime. I love you."

"Please. I'm having enough trouble keeping my head on straight. I can't do this alone. I need Mother Pearl."

"You're not alone." He held her closer. "I'm here for you. I'll be here for you, no matter what. I love you so much."

She didn't know how long she was in his arms. He held her tightly against him and she tried to think ahead. His lips were on her face when she recovered, and though she protested, she very much wanted them there.

She forced her body to move. "Don't feel that you have to babysit me. I'll be all right."

"Why do you do this, Lacey? You just suffered a devastating loss. Don't feel that you have to be brave. I've been here long enough to see the closeness between you and Pearl. You have every right to fall apart. It would be unnatural if you didn't. Don't be afraid to reach out, to lean on the people around you. We all love you. I love you."

She moved away from him. "And just why shouldn't I be afraid to lean? Everyone I've ever leaned on has left me. My father, my grandfather, and now

Mother Pearl. I could have leaned on Monroe, but he doesn't exist, and I'm sure John Tobias will disappear as suddenly as he arrived. With everything I've been through, I've learned one lesson. The only person who is sure to be there for me is me."

Without eating or sleeping very much, Lacey stumbled through the next three days. John made most of the arrangements for the memorial service, and everyone worked to keep the camp running smoothly. Yank told her he had never seen his father so upset and that Tedera had loved Pearl very much. No matter how hard they tried to get her to lie down, to rest, Lacey continued working in the office, afraid that if she stopped, she would surely fall apart.

John was constantly at her side, offering his services and forcing her to eat. Minneola, and Pearl's other sister, Andretta, stayed at the camp to be with Lacey. Amanda, Nicholas, and Mason, along with Lacey's aunts, Gwenneth and Lynda, called at least twice a day. Wanting to get everything taken care of as soon as possible, Lacey and Andretta cleaned out Pearl's room. Each time Lacey touched something that Pearl had cherished, her heart found a new place to break.

Mason, the first to arrive, found Lacey and John in Lacey's office, going over Pearl's final arrangements. He lashed out before the hellos were said.

"Well, well, well, Mr. John Tobias." He walked around John. "Don't tell me. Let me guess. You're broke, lost everything, the creditors are after you, and you're hiding out at a girl's camp."

"I'll be glad to address your concerns, but later." He looked at Lacey. "This is neither the time nor the place, Mason."

"It may not be the time, but it is the perfect place. It's the place where you pretended to be someone else to run some kind of sick scam on an unsuspecting woman. Why are you still here? I'm on to you. Maybe Lacey's not, but I sure am."

"Mason, please." Lacey held up her hand. "John is right. We're planning Pearl's memorial service, and though nothing would give me greater pleasure than watching the two of you have a showdown at the Camp Noepe corral, please don't do it now."

"Say whatever you will, but I'm not leaving."

"Fine. I'll have Shale prepare one of the vacated rooms in the bunkhouse. You can sleep there."

John hovered over Lacey with Mason nearby for the rest of the evening. When John was not around, Tedera acted as Lacey's bodyguard until the rest of the family arrived.

As directed, Pearl's memorial service was short and dignified. There were many plants and flowers that would later go to the Tashmoo Retirement Home. A childhood friend, who was also a minister, read the lines that Pearl had written, concluding with: "Weep not, for I have lived a good life. I have known love. I now rest in peaceful radiance, somewhere between the sun and moon. My spirit will follow you always. My soul is with the wind."

Lacey stared straight ahead, hearing wails of sadness from every corner of the room. She clutched her brother's arm as Pearl's niece, Camarilla, sang The Lord's Prayer. The funerals of her father and grandfather merged with Pearl's for one heartbreaking loss. John sat with the Whitefeathers, solemn throughout the service. She knew that he was also feeling the pain of another loss. She watched Amanda holding onto Mr. Rydell with the same calm façade that was her trademark.

The Whitefeathers and the Greenups cluttered around Tedera, who sat still and quiet like a statue. Micah and Jennifer stayed at Camp Noepe with the remaining campers.

John hung back, but Lacey's every move brought him to attention. He wanted to be her comfort. He directed Yank and Shale to consult him rather than Lacey when there was a problem, and swore to take responsibility for the results. He also arranged for food and drink back at the camp after the service. Everything was set. Pearl's ashes had been placed in a bronze urn, and after the company departed, Lacey and Tedera would drive to the cliffs and carry out her last wishes.

Amanda let go of Mr. Rydell's arm long enough to question Lacey when she spotted John back at Camp Noepe. "Honey, who is that adorable man in the Armani suit?"

"John Jacob Tobias, formerly known as Monroe Faulkner, my riding instructor. The one Mason told you about." She had avoided him as much as she could and hoped there would be no outburst of temper from Mason, which she now realized, along with his insatiable appetite for sex, had been the only thing that made him appear alive. A look of gleeful condescension remained on his face, but never a speck of sadness.

Nicholas and Lacey clung to each other, but this time Lacey knew her pain was much greater than her brother's. Her closeness to Pearl had existed for as long as Lacey could remember. She had always gone to Pearl with her problems as well as her joys.

As soon as they arrived back at the camp, Pearl's niece, Elfie, and Elfie's husband, Peter, besieged Lacey with questions about Pearl's estate. Elfie and Peter had helped Pearl with the bakery since Lacey's grandfather died and had been in full charge after Pearl left for the island. Their feral insistence made Lacey angry, and during her struggle to avoid lashing out, she saw her mother and John together. Amanda was all smiles and, in spite of Lacey's grief, she was amused at her mother's fascination with the millionaire.

Monroe Faulkner, even with his undeniable charm and good looks, would have been dismissed with a wave of the hand, but John Jacob Tobias, wealthy Texan in an Armani suit, took immediate hold of Amanda's attention.

When Mason approached her, Lacey chose the lesser of two evils. Leaving Elfie and Peter to ponder their fate, she joined him in the yard.

"Thanks for rescuing me."

"Who are those people? They've been following you around since we arrived here."

"Mother Pearl's niece, Elfie, the one who runs the bakery, and Peter, the idiot she married. Mother Pearl's ashes aren't cold yet and they're hounding me about ownership of the bakery. I will have to remember to call Mr. Chambers, the accountant who handles Mother Pearl's affairs. She said more than once that Peter would steal the comb off a rooster."

"An amusing colloquialism. You have to get away from these people. All of them, including Tobias."

His snobbish retort made Lacey wonder how she could have thought she loved him. "I'm not in the mood for your rancor, so tell me what you'd like to talk about. Anything that the two of us agree on, if there is such a topic."

"I love you. Let's talk about that. Let's talk about you coming back home, back to me and to the plans we made, unless you've made alternate plans with Tobias."

She ignored the last part of his statement. "I'll be home very soon. The last camper leaves next week." She made a mental note to ask John when Melissa's parents planned to pick her up. "I'll be home as soon as I can close the camp." She looked at him and tried to feel something. "It's pretty obvious that we have different views of life. We would never get along, Mason. I'm surprised we remained together as long as we did."

"That's not true. There are lots of things we can agree on, and I hope one of them is the date of our wedding. I love you and I'm not letting you go. I do want to know about your relationship with Tobias. I saw the two of you walking back to the kitchen the day I was here. You looked like more than boss and employee. Don't you think I have the right to know if the woman I love is involved with another man?"

"Mason, for all I know, you could have screwed half the female population of New York by now, but I'm not questioning you."

When she tried to walk away, he caught her arm. "I guess I should have, since you obviously haven't been suffering for companionship. Have the two of you been sleeping together the whole time you've been here?"

"Let go of my arm." She spoke through clenched teeth, trying to deliver a forceful message without alerting those around her. She did not see John until he had spoken.

"Lacey?" He moved between her and Mason. "Can I help you with anything?"

"I think you've already done enough, don't you?" Mason let go of Lacey's arm and faced John. "I want to know why you lied about your identity, why you came here and pretended to be a riding instructor. You may have gotten Lacey and the rest of the people here to believe whatever sick story you've told, but I want the truth."

"As I said before, some other time."

"Let's get something straight, Tobias." He reached for Lacey. "This is mine. Understand? If I find out you've—"

"Oh, whoopee!" Lacey threw her hands in the air in a disgusted scowl. "Why don't I find a couple of dueling pistols and you two can have a nice, civilized gunfight? On second thought, I'll get Mother Pearl's shotgun. The only problem I'll have is which one of you to shoot first."

She left them and went back to the guests. Nicholas had been pensive and withdrawn since arriving on the island.

"I know you loved Mother Pearl, but I sense something else is going on. Wanna tell me about it?"

His shoulders remained slumped in the tailored black suit. "Some other time. I don't want to dump my troubles on you now."

Lacey took his hand and guided him out to the stables. "This is the dumping ground, little brother, so let me have it. Is it work?"

"No." He shook his head. "Mom succeeded in driving a wedge between me and Greta. I love her, Lacey. It's really hurts to be in the middle."

"What did Mom do?"

"Greta's dad was married twice before he married her mother. Mom invited Greta's mom to lunch and started talking about wanting me to have a stable personal life so I can concentrate on my career. They discussed the possibility of the two of us marrying, and Mom voiced her concerns about Greta. She mentioned something about the sins of the father. Greta was in tears, her mom was livid, and our mom jubilantly admitted her deeds. I do admire what you've done here on the island, but I wish you'd come home," Nicholas pleaded. "I've missed you more than anyone has. You're the only person I can talk to who understands."

"I'll be home soon. Maybe I can talk to Greta's mother, at least let her know that everyone in the family isn't like Mom. I wish she'd just lay off."

She stayed close to him until the two limousines lined up to take them back to the airport. Knowing that Nicholas was weak when it came to Amanda, she promised to be home very soon, hugged them all, and waved goodbye.

When the last of the guests had gone, John drove Lacey and Tedera to the cliffs. Standing together, they bid a teary farewell and scattered Pearl's ashes down the jagged ridges of the historic terrain. Tedera lingered and Lacey walked back to the Jeep with John, leaving him to say a private farewell.

"Tedera and I talked last night," John said softly. "He really loved Pearl. Said she was the only woman, other than his late wife, who could make him laugh."

"I'm glad they had the past few months together. I know she was happy."

"She wanted you to be happy, too. She told me so." He took Lacey's hand. "Now that I think about it, Pearl spoke of your happiness almost as a last concern. I want to make you happy, Lacey. I can make you happy. Pearl thought so. We were so good together. That's what you should remember. I know I'll never forget it."

"For me either, but I can't think of that right now. I was so ready to love you, and I wish I could go back, but I can't. Not now."

"I can wait as long as it takes."

Tedera joined them. His sad eyes half smiled when he saw them holding hands.

Later, when the camp was quiet and the moon was high, Shale and Yank said goodnight, leaving Lacey and John alone on the deck.

"I want to thank you for all of your help. I don't know how I would have made it through the last few days without all of you."

"There is no need to thank me. Everyone here loved Pearl, and I was no exception." He moved next to her.

"I also want to thank you for your contribution to Camp Noepe. This summer meant a lot to Mother Pearl and to me. I'm glad she lived to see the success of her husband's dream."

"So am I. Melissa wants very much to win the trophy, for Pearl."

She turned quickly. "John, I withdrew from the competition. I told you that."

"I know." He looked away. "I reinstated the entry. I just didn't think you were in any spirit to make a decision."

"I did make a decision. I said I didn't want to compete. You just took it upon yourself to go ahead and do it anyway." The last emotion she wanted to feel was more anger, but once she crossed into that lane, she found a measure of relief.

"Please don't be upset, Lacey. I did it mostly for Melissa. She was so disappointed, and she's worked very hard for this. She also wants to do it for Pearl, and I thought that once you felt better, you would, too. The two of you did something wonderful here this summer. This is not about beating Ramsey Treadwell. Let's finish the season with a winner for Camp Noepe and for Pearl. You'll get your family land back and keep it for future generations."

"Fine. We'll do it your way." She wasn't angry anymore, but the alternate emotion was despair, and she didn't want to return to that.

Yank came to her and expressed his concern for Tedera. "He's done nothing but smoke cigarettes and drink since Pearl's death."

"I thought he only smoked a pipe."

"He quit cigarettes four years ago, right after the doctor showed him a picture of his lungs." He rubbed the back of his hands over his chin. "I'm sure you're aware of some of the superstitions of our people. My father is fundamentally old school. He placed his own meaning on the brief relationship he had with Pearl just as he is now placing his meaning on her loss. There's no way to know what's in his heart. He spends most of his time down by the water, looking over to the cliffs. I've never seen him this way."

Lacey promised to speak with Tedera, but noted that the entire mood at Camp Noepe had changed. There was no arguing among the remaining girls, but there was also no joy. It was over, she thought, wanting very much to close the doors and go home.

Two of the remaining campers left and Lacey learned that Melissa was afraid to sleep alone. Melissa's parents were scheduled to arrive the following day, so Lacey spent a miserable night pretending to be asleep in the bunk next to Melissa.

John met Mr. and Mrs. Hodges at the airport, got them settled in a suite at the Menemsha Inn, and hurried back to run through the jumps with Melissa.

Lacey admired his dedication, but had lost all enthusiasm for the competition and for Camp Noepe. The family homestead had been important because Pearl was there to share and love it with her.

She sat near the corral and watched the practices, trying to make the adjustment from Monroe Faulkner to John Tobias, but her heart was somewhere else.

When she learned the Hodges were spending their evening in town and would not see their daughter until the following day, she felt a tinge of sadness for the child and a little anger at having to spend another night in the bunk, pretending to sleep. She was exhausted the next morning, but tried to share the enthusiasm around her.

For the first time since Pearl's death, there was excitement at Camp Noepe. Shale made breakfast and they made orange juice toasts to Melissa, who enjoyed the attention. Lacey noticed that she did not appear the least bit nervous. She drank in John's every word. She wanted to win. Lacey was glad John had gone against her wishes, but would not give him the satisfaction of knowing this. Yank and Micah had also worked with Melissa and were equally excited about the competition. The child seemed glued to John, and he applauded her efforts.

"He'll be a wonderful father," Shale commented. "Have you noticed how he corrects Melissa? He never says a word when she makes a mistake. He waits until she does it right and then points out the prior error. I can't wait to see him with his own children."

"Write and tell me how it turns out," Lacey scoffed.

Shale stood back and gave Lacey a silent once-over. "Yank and I had a bet about the two of you. I said you would never fall for a poor drifter. Yank said when you looked at Monroe you saw the man, not his wallet. Let me tell you about hypocrisy. If this man had arrived here at Camp Noepe claiming to be wealthy and you found out he was poor, your conscience would not allow you to think less of him, so why do it now? I know he lied, but I'm glad he's a wealthy rancher and businessman. Now he can be a good father who also provides for his family."

"I hear what you're saying and technically I agree, but my heart is not in the relationship or anything else right now."

"It's not your heart that's causing the problem. It's your pride. Pearl was right about that."

"I can't think of that right now, Shale. My mind is plastered with too many things over which I have no control."

She drank three mugs of coffee and nervously paced the kitchen floor, watching from the window as Yank and Micah hitched the horse trailer to Yank's pickup. John worked calmly with Melissa, whose apprehension surfaced when Jennifer arrived with Mr. and Mrs. Hodges. The men loaded Champion in the trailer. Tedera joined them, but there was no excitement on his face. His eyes were red-rimmed and he did not speak a word.

John drove the Jeep with Lacey, Melissa, and her parents, and attempted to keep the conversation going. When Mr. Hodges thanked him for the "marvelous summer" that Melissa reported having, Lacey watched John beam.

"Your daughter has worked very hard. She's good with horses and determined to learn. Working with her was all pleasure."

"I hope I win. I just have to win," Melissa piped up.

"We all want you to do your best, and we know you will," Lacey added. Before she could say that winning wasn't everything, Mr. Hodges joined the conversation.

"Winning is important. Just concentrate on the fact that no one remembers the losers, no matter how hard they've worked. I was the runt on my little league team, but I did well because I refused to allow myself to do less."

Lacey flinched and studied the little girl's face in the rearview mirror as her father continued enumerating his many successes. With each word, Melissa's forlorn expression took on more gloom. Lacey and John exchanged concerned glances.

"I've watched Melissa practice," Lacey said. "I know how hard she's tried, and I will remember this event, no matter who wins. I'll remember it for the rest of my life."

"So will I," John agreed. "You'll always be a champ in my book, Melissa."

CHAPTER 11

The Middle Road Summer Festival commemorating the end of the season was the last major event, other than Labor Day celebrations, that drew full island participation. The campgrounds had been transformed into various configurations for competitions and displays.

Lacey watched the line of shiny new trailers bearing the lassoed "T" and the accompanying entourage of Treadwell employees swarming the campgrounds. Ramsey Treadwell smiled and nodded in his usual pompous manner, which was sufficient to bring Lacey back into the competition. In her mind, Treadwell was the face of everyone who had ever doubted her grandfather or doubted her ability to successfully operate Camp Noepe.

After a morning of listening to her father's lecture on the intrinsic worth of winning, Melissa became hesitant, and Lacey watched John coax her through the anxious moments and sit with her during the wait. There was no doubt in her mind that he would indeed be a great father. Her heart said she should make every effort to keep John Jacob Tobias in her life.

Lacey sat next to him and watched Melissa and Jennifer enjoying the clowns. "I think Mr. and Mrs. Hodges are terrible parents. The only attention they've given Melissa is to tell her how awful it will be if she doesn't win."

"I wanted to punch that man. He kept brow-beating her until that happy little smile turned upside down." He held his head down and continued talking. "For whatever reason, God didn't allow me to know my little boy, but I hope and pray to have that chance again, to have a little boy or a little girl to love. I know parenting is difficult. I can't swear that I'll win father of the year, but I damn sure would never do what he's been doing."

"I've watched you with Melissa, with all of the campers. I know God will give you that chance again, and when he does, I have no doubts that you'll be a wonderful father."

"Thank you." He lifted his head and took her hand. "I've thought of having children a lot lately. With you." When she started to withdraw her hand, he held it tightly in his. "Don't pull away from me, Lacey. I love you. I've only used those words sparingly in my relationships with women. When I've used them, it was because I meant them from the bottom of my heart."

She didn't reply until he let go of her hand. "I'm not doubting you on that."

She moved closer to the Whitefeathers and stayed there during the competition, with John rooting nearby. Lacey saw the pride on his face when he ran to help the winner of the Junior Equestrian Roundup Championship from her horse. Thinking of his pain at losing his wife and child, she felt the victory was his in more ways than one. He had discovered another part of himself, one that might make his life easier, and for that she was glad.

Lacey's heart swelled when Melissa dedicated the winning statue, a child atop a bucking stallion, to Pearl.

"She would be so proud of this," Shale said through her tears. "Pearl had the biggest heart of anyone I've ever known."

"She did at that," Tedera added. "She's smiling right now. I know she is."

"And you filled her heart with happiness during her last days." Lacey had noticed Tedera chugging beer from the cooler in the back of Yank's truck. "This was a great summer for her, Tedera, for all of us. Let's remember that happiness above all else. That's what she would have wanted."

Lacey and John dropped the Hodges off at the airport, and Melissa clung to John.

"I'll never forget you, Mr. Faulk...I mean Mr. Tobias. Will you be here again next summer?"

Lacey felt mixed emotions, knowing that Camp Noepe was now officially closed and there would be no next season.

John went back to his cabin and called his father.

"Nothing ever works out as planned. I don't know what to do. I'm afraid, Pop. Afraid that if I come home without her, I'll be right back where I started. I didn't think it was possible, but I'm in love with her. It's not just love. I connected. Our hearts connected. She belongs with me."

"I'm glad, but you have to convince her of that. Bring her home with you. A pretty woman is always welcome here."

"I'm serious, Pop."

"I know you are, son, that's why I'm trying not to be. I'm glad you found someone, but doesn't that let you know that life can be good again? No matter what happens with Lacey, you will know that you are capable of loving a woman again. Isn't that part of what your quest was all about? The knowledge that your life is not over, that you can feel all of those emotions again. That should take you well beyond where you were when you left here. Maybe Lacey was your stepping stone back on the right track."

"You're right, but I want her in my life. I have to make her understand." He said goodbye, grabbed his jacket, started back to the main house, and found Tedera sitting on the grass by the stables.

"It's a damn shame," Tedera mumbled. "A man my age thinks of women but he seldom thinks of love, not the kind I had with Pearl. In a few short months, she made my life rich again. I felt like a man. Now she's gone and I don't know if I want to go on without her."

John thought of his father and of his own pain. "I came here with those same feelings, Tedera. I had lost the only person I thought could ever make me happy. And then I met Lacey. You are very lucky to have had that feeling. Pearl would want you to remember her love for you and not dwell on sadness. In the months that I've been here, I never saw Pearl unhappy. That's what she would want for you."

He continued talking until Tedera stood and walked with him back to the main house. He listened to his own words and knew he had to heed the same advice. Debra was gone. He would love her forever, but could never hold her in his arms again. Lacey was there, and he knew if he lost her there would be a new hurt to overcome. He found her in the kitchen.

"Can I help with anything?"

"No, but thanks for asking."

"That was some competition, wasn't it? I don't think I've ever been so proud of anyone. I don't like to gloat, but I've always been competitive, and watching Treadwell eat dirt was very satisfying. I was only sorry we didn't have two or three contestants to wipe that smirk off his face."

"I'm no better. I gloated, too, but mostly I was just proud of Melissa." Lacey managed a smile. "She rode well. You did a great job. You should be proud."

"I'm proud of you, of what you and Pearl achieved here this summer. When I first arrived, I wouldn't have taken a bet on your chances of making this a success, but you did, in every way."

"Thank you." She put away a stack of blue willow dishes. Pearl's face was there in each one. Grief gnawed at one side of her heart, and her feelings for John shrouded the other.

"Your mother is a very beautiful woman." John drained the last of his coffee and poured another cup. "Of course, looking at you, one would have guessed as much. She was also very friendly, nothing like you described."

"She recognized your suit," Lacey sneered.

"Excuse me?"

"Your suit. Armani, wasn't it? My mother could stand on Fifth Avenue and spot designer labels in Rhode Island."

He chuckled. "She also referred to Mason Phipps as your fiancé. She thinks you're still engaged, and so does Mason. He wanted to know if I had taken advantage of you and when I asked what he meant, he asked if we had slept together."

"Referring to Mason as my fiancé is wishful thinking on my mother's part and stubborn pride for Mason. He and I are history. Mom will just have to accept that. Maybe she can find me another man with money or a promising future." She faced him. "How did you answer his question?"

John walked around the counter and stood next to her. "I told him it was none of his damn business. He said he's still in love with you. He's known you longer than I have, so I'm sure he knows what a special person you are."

"And I could get excited about that if I thought my definition of love applied to Mason, but it doesn't. The relationship we had was never about the kind of love I need. The kind I felt with you." She stopped and dropped her head. "Mason will find someone else and I will find a way to get my career back on track. I came, saw, and conquered, even made Ramsey Treadwell eat dirt, but now it's time to go home."

He set the coffee mug on the counter and leaned on his elbows. "I stood in an antiseptic room at St. Joseph's Hospital and watched my wife and my unborn son leave this world before they had a chance to really live. I was helpless to save the people I loved and I couldn't live with that. I left home, took the identity of a man who died with less than a thousand dollars to his name. I also tried to take his outlook on life, to see what I was missing.

"I came here with hopes of finding something that would give meaning to my life, and I found you. Beautiful, educated, cultured, wealthy, but totally unspoiled by material trappings." He took a photograph from his wallet and handed it to her. "I was shocked at your physical resemblance to Debra. I thought of how much Debra would have liked you, how well the two of you would have gotten along. It seemed like some kind of destiny—that I was meant to find you, to love you. I do love you, Lacey."

She stared in silence. "Your wife was beautiful."

"And so are you. Do you see the resemblance?"

She nodded and handed the photo back to him. "Let's not talk about this now."

"If not now, when? We'll be leaving soon, closing the camp. I can't walk away from here and leave my life hanging this way. I found someone to make me feel whole again. I don't want to lose you. Please come home with me."

"That's not possible." She wanted to say the thought had crossed her mind many times.

"Why not? What will you do back in New York?"

"For starters, I need to take care of Mother Pearl's business affairs, have her will probated, and figure out what to do with the bakery. All of that is now my responsibility, because that's what she wanted."

"Speaking of the bakery, the only people I met at the service that I really wanted to choke were those two relatives of Pearl's who run the bakery. They actually asked if I knew whether Pearl left the bakery to them."

"They should have known better. Mother Pearl said many times that if they had any snap, they could have purchased the bakery by now, but they are too busy waiting for a handout. She left my brother and my cousins a nice cash bequest. She left everything else to me."

"That's only right. You were the daughter she never had. She loved you very much. She told me so."

"She loved all of us, but she was closer to my father than to my aunts, and closer to me than to Nicholas. She remembered everyone in her will. Actually, she was a fairly wealthy woman. Her needs were simple, especially after my grandfather died. Whatever I decide to do with the bakery and the building it's in has to be a tribute to her, to the woman she was."

"You'll do the right thing." He moved closer to her. "I have to go home to Texas. I left my father to run things and I have to return soon, but if you need me, I'll come to New York as soon as I can. I want to be with you, to be there for you."

She stared into his eyes.

He prayed she would say what he wanted to hear.

"It's not going to work, John. I fell in love with Monroe Faulkner. I don't know how to transfer that love to John Tobias."

"Quit saying that. You never met Monroe Faulkner. You fell in love with me." He took her in his arms, stroked her hair, and spoke in soft whispers. "I love you so much. I don't want to lose you. You can't deny the impact we had on each other. I know you felt it."

"John, I'm too upset to think right now."

Having no further words of persuasion, he turned and walked away.

Lacey went to her office and stared into the silence of the evening. She thought of everything that had happened during the summer. "Oh, Mother Pearl. I can't make any decisions right now. I can't even think straight. I need you here with me."

"She is here with you."

She jumped about and found Tedera standing in the doorway.

"There was no one in this world more important to Pearl than you. Do you think she would just abandon you? Even death couldn't accomplish that. She'll always be with you. You lost someone you love, but you've gained a guardian angel."

She stood and walked into his arms. "I know. Her presence and her love will always be with me, and with you."

Feeling drained, she went to her room in the main house and climbed between the sheets that Pearl had placed on her bed. Holding the covers close and thinking only of the woman who would remain in her heart forever, she fell fast asleep.

The camp was too quiet the next morning. Lacey could not concentrate. Finishing the mug of coffee she had taken to her office, she went back to the kitchen for another and decided to finish packing Pearl's room instead of staring at the lined pages on her balance sheets. She had already given all of Pearl's clothing and jewelry to her sister, except for the small cross that Pearl always wore around her neck. That was now on Lacey's charm bracelet, the one her father had given her when she was sixteen.

She packed the remainder of Pearl's personal belongings in a box with the Bible on top. She planned to give that to Tedera. Thinking of her new family, she headed out to the barn where Yank and Micah were loading the animals for transport to his place in Aquinnah. She said good bye to the baby goat, who was now too old for hugs, and went to the bunkhouse, where she remained for the rest of the day, cleaning and packing.

She saw the truck and trailer return, watched John wander around the stables and then up to the house. He was looking for her and she did not want to face him. She had not stopped for lunch, but was still not hungry enough to walk into the gathering back in the main house. Finding an unopened bag of chips in the dresser, she wandered down to the thicket and sat in her favorite spot.

Memories flooded her head. Lying against John, their bodies drenched from the playful waves. He had held tight, sometimes in a desperate grip, as if he was afraid to let go.

Crow ran into the thicket and she knew he was not alone.

"Lacey?"

Outwardly she remained immobile, but her insides quivered, as they always did at the sound of his voice.

"I didn't know you were here, but I'm glad you are." He ducked the hanging vines and joined her in the clearing. "Yank said you wanted him to sell the animals and would start looking for a buyer for the camp. I don't understand. Your first year was a raving success. I don't know how profitable it was but —"

"This had never been about money. For someone who knows the pain of losing a loved one, you can be terribly insensitive. I can't return here next year. This was something I began with the person closest to me, the one who shared my dreams."

"I'm not being insensitive. I was thinking of Pearl. Running the camp in coming years would be a tribute to her, to her memory. You still have the contract with IMF for the winter. You can't just sell it, Lacey."

She stared ahead and he continued.

"I'll come back next spring. I'll help."

Lacey knew it was a crucial moment in her relationship with John, and with herself. This was more than a commitment to return to Camp Noepe, it was a commitment to their feelings for each other.

"How can you make that promise when you have no way of knowing what next year will hold? You have a business, a family in Texas. John, I don't know—"

His lips sealed over hers and she surrendered, weak in his arms, but strong in the feelings that made her come alive.

"I found my soul here on the island. I found you. I want to marry you, to be with you forever. Let me love you, Lacey. I won't let you down."

"I love you, too." She breathed the words. "I just can't seem to get to where we were. I'm not angry with you anymore. I'm just trying to fit the pieces together."

"It's easy."

He kissed her hard. His lips crushed hers. His tongue probed her mouth. She clung to him, feeling his strong arms around her just like the first time.

"Lacey." He shook his head. "You don't know how happy you've made me. I haven't worked out the logistics or anything else, but I know I don't want to live without you."

"Then hold me. Hold me tight, because I don't know how long I can keep it together."

He held her against him and they kissed again and again.

"You're not alone, baby. I'll be here for you." He tugged the tail of her shirt from the waist of her jeans and slid his hand up her back. "I haven't seen you cry since it happened. Let go if you need to. I'm here for you. I plan to make that the pleasure of my life."

She melted into his arms. Needing him. Needing to be loved. He moved away and eased her down on the warm ground. "I love you, John Jacob Tobias," she whispered when he nestled next to her. "Mother Pearl taught me so much, and I do believe in powers greater than our own. We're here together for a reason. She said that, and I believe her."

He hovered over her, just as he had in her dream. His hands were hot on her skin. Hunger washed over her.

He removed his shirt, folded it, and placed it under her head. "I believe her, too. You've made me whole again. I never want to lose you."

His lips covered hers in a natural fit. The surroundings, the feelings in her heart, having his body close to hers, everything seemed perfectly natural. She slipped out of her top. He unhooked her bra and kissed the valley between her breasts. His lips trailed up her neck and sealed over her mouth. She held on in fitful passion. In the recesses of her soul, she felt that making love in the natural splendor of a world she had come to love would bond them together forever.

Crow, who was lying on the grass nearby, sat up and barked as a resounding boom split the silence around them. Lacey pulled from John's grasp in time to see an orange ball shoot into the air above Camp Noepe. They scuffled into their clothes and sprinted across the sand. A crackling blaze over the main house was fully visible and horrifying. Lacey saw Yank and Micah running from the stables. Fearing that Shale had been in the kitchen when the explosion and fire began, Lacey's knees buckled.

"Shale! Where is Shale?"

John let go of her hand and ran faster, almost colliding with Shale, who ran around from the bunkhouse. Everyone was accounted for but Tedera.

"I called the fire department!" Micah yelled. "When I told them it was an explosion, they said to stay completely clear of the area."

"It's my fault! It's all my fault!" Shale's scream was as deafening as the blast had been.

"I left a pot on the stove. I know it's my fault!" Shale continued screaming as Lacey and John held her arms and Yank rushed to her side. "Where is Grandpa? Grandpa!" Micah ran toward the stables, his face glowing like the crackling embers.

No one noticed when Lacey slipped away and entered the side door of the building leading to Pearl's quarters and to the office. John glimpsed her blue top disappearing through the door. He yelled and ran after her.

"Lacey! Don't go in there!"

She was gone, disappeared through the door.

"Everyone stay back! I'm going in to find her!" John ran past the others and into the side door. "Lacey! Lacey, get out of the building! Lacey!"

She came towards him, pushing her leather desk chair loaded with a large cardboard box balanced on top of her computer. Pearl's personal belongings and Lacey's purse sat atop the Bible that she planned to give to Tedera. The other items in the box were Lacey's accounting records and the trophy from the Junior Equestrian Roundup.

"Give it to me! Run out of here! We don't know what caused the explosion and it could happen again, in another part of the building. Run!"

They moved quickly, together, with the chair in front of them, to the door. John lifted the chair into the yard and pushed it to the grass bordering the garage. With enormous speed, he hosted the box and the computer into the Jeep, grabbed the keys that protruded from the pocket of Lacey's jeans, and backed the Jeep down the driveway to the gravel road.

The fire truck arrived just as the kitchen roof collapsed. Dry timbers cracked and folded while water sprayed over the blaze. Lacey stood, transfixed at the sight of the Camp Noepe sign standing proudly amid the ruins.

The fire was controlled within an hour, before the blaze reached the back end of the structure. Everything in the office was saved, but there was smoke damage throughout. Shale continued to sob that she had been at fault, while Yank and Micah roamed the area searching for Tedera. John held Lacey. Held her tight, almost painfully confining.

"That was a stupid thing to do! You scared me half to death!" He kissed her face over and over and held her to his chest. The concern in his eyes was both touching and frightening.

"I'm okay. I had to get the camp records. This place is still my responsibility."

"It's your responsibility to stay safe." He released her so suddenly that she almost lost her balance. "What am I doing? What the hell am I doing?"

He stormed off and joined the others to search for Tedera and left her more shaken by his desperate anxiety than she had been by the fire. Another siren sounded and a police cruiser pulled up to the end of the driveway. Deputy Cal Murdock got out, walked around the car, opened the back door and yelled at Lacey.

"Is this the one you're looking for?" He pulled a somber Tedera from the back of the car. "Found him up on the bluffs. He's unharmed, but it seems he did kill a few pints of whiskey. The empty bottles were scattered around him."

"Thank you very much, Deputy."

She hugged Tedera, led him to the side steps and began looking for a way to let the others know that he was all right. Sirens wouldn't get their attention at this point and since there was little work left at the camp, no one carried phones. They had spread out along the beach so she knew they could not hear her yell.

Trudging through the rubble of her dream, she stumbled over debris the firemen had hauled away from the kitchen wall. Stooping to the ground, she used a stick to dig through the charred boards and the remains of her sunflower curtains. She hit a solid object and heard a sound that brought tears to her eyes. Raising the old blackened cowbell from under a piece of window frame, she held it high above her head.

John was closest to the house and the first to arrive. He found her standing on the hill behind the kitchen, still shaking the bell, with tears streaming down her face.

CHAPTER 12

Neighbors and townspeople came to help clear the rubble once the insurance investigator determined that a faulty gas line into the kitchen caused the explosion. Lacey was sure John had been avoiding her, and even after his frightening display of emotions unearthed the reservations she had finally buried, she still wanted him near.

With most of her boxes packed for shipment back to New York, Lacey called a friend from her hotel days and arranged to stay at a hotel until she could determined her next move. She informed IMF about the fire, and they agreed to cancel the contract with no penalty. With a heavy heart, she sat down at her desk and wrote one final check on the green paper with the erect cross-timbers holding the Camp Noepe sign.

After a phone conference with the insurance adjustor and her attorney, she loaded her bags and laptop into the Jeep and called Yank and Micah, who had taken the remaining two horses to Aquinnah. She found Tedera in the stable and gave him Pearl's Bible.

"I'm glad she met you, Tedera." She kissed his weathered face and hurried back to the room for her briefcase and purse. John was waiting by the steps.

"I thought you had already gone." She stopped in front of him. "I noticed that you haven't cashed any of your paychecks." She stuffed the folded check into his shirt pocket. "I realized you couldn't do anything with checks made payable to Monroe, so I wrote your total earnings on one check. Give the money to charity if you want, but you earned every cent."

"I'll think of something." His eyes were red and his voice strained. "I need to apologize for my behavior after the fire."

"There is no need to explain. We were all over-wrought. It's okay." She tried to smile.

"Have you made any decisions regarding the camp?"

"Yes, I've contacted a realtor, and once the insurance claim is settled, Fran Gosling will list it for sale. Yank is going to dispose of the animals. He already knows someone who wants to purchase two of them."

"Please don't. You shouldn't make a decision right now. So much has happened, Lacey, and I don't believe you're thinking clearly. Wait and give yourself time to adjust."

"I've made my decision, John. I don't want the camp. I came here with Mother Pearl to finish what my grandfather started, and I did. We did. I'm very proud of what was accomplished here this summer, and I know I have you to thank for part of that success. I just can't come back next year."

"I'll buy Camp Noepe. Just name your price."

"Don't get involved in this. You were here on a mission, just as I was. Your mission is accomplished, so go home, complete your healing, and find someone to love. You deserve to be happy."

"Can you just forget what we had together? Are you thinking of marrying Mason?"

"Absolutely not. I'm going home, to New York, and no, I'll never forget what we had together. It was wonderful, all of it. I'm still grateful for your help with Camp Noepe and I wish you nothing but the best."

"When are you leaving for New York?"

"Right now."

He stared in disbelief. "Now? When now? Today?"

"I have a ferry to catch in an hour and a half. I'm driving to New York today."

"Were you planning to just leave without saying goodbye? I don't understand you at all. I love you, Lacey! Does that mean anything?"

She smiled and traced his upturned lips with the tips of her fingers. "I love you, too, John. I really do, but this can't work. You know it as well as I do. We're from different worlds. You were searching for peace and I for a deeper meaning to life. We both found what we needed, and just because I was there when you found it doesn't mean you owe me anything. I enjoyed the time we spent together."

"I saw an envelope from Treadwell Farms on the table. Is it what I think it is?"

She nodded. "He deeded the property back to me."

"And that means nothing to you now? I deceived you, and I know that was wrong, but surely you're not going to allow that to keep us apart. I didn't just find peace here in Oak Bluffs, I found the woman I want to spend my life with. That's also what Pearl wanted. Doesn't any of this matter to you, Lacey?"

"All of it matters more than you could know." She sat on the edge of the step. "All of my life, I've depended on Mother Pearl's advice, but contrary to my mother's beliefs, there was never any real advice. Mother Pearl said just enough to make me think, to help me find my own answers. That's what I have to do now. I have to think for myself, and, with all that's happened, I think I should leave the island. Maybe I never should have come."

"Is this what happened with Mason? When things got complicated, you just broke your engagement and ran away?" He took hold of her arm. "I felt something the moment I met you, and it deepened each second that I was here at Camp Noepe. It was wonderful and special, and I know you felt it, too. Love doesn't happen every day, Lacey. You can't just run away from relationships, leaving bits of yourself behind."

She moved past him, got her belongings, and locked the door. "I have to leave now, John."

"What about the camp? I'll buy it. Can't you at least stay and talk about that?"

"If I stay, I'll miss the ferry." She fished her hand around in the outside pocket of her bag and handed him a card that read Warren & Mitchell, LLP.

"Douglas Warren is my attorney. Work out the details on the camp with him."

She closed his fist around the card and held it to her face. "It was a wonderful summer. I'll never forget it, or you."

With only a call to her brother saying she was in New York and would contact them later, Lacey hid out at her hotel for over a week, dining alone at night and spending her days at a spa. The sights that had once inspired her were now inconsequential and the simplistic lifestyle of the island haunted her dreams. She read, watched every movie on cable, including the ones labeled "Adult Entertainment," and walked the streets of New York, people-watching and window-shopping.

Her time on the island had been dreamlike, surreal. Monroe Faulkner, aka John Jacob Tobias, was also a dream. With each new morning, she better understood John's desire to leave familiar surroundings, especially when the familiarity was a constant reminder of his loss. She missed the island, but here in the city, she was just a face in the crowd, lost in misery known only to her. She was back in her element, watching the continued excitement and joining in only when the mood struck.

She also better understood John's disappearance into the character of Monroe Faulkner, his need for anonymity, and his desire to keep his pain private.

There was no one she cared to speak with or share the feelings she hid inside. A chance meeting with Drayton Snow, the decorator for her last hotel, yielded a Saturday night dinner invitation, and she accepted.

Drayton was easy to be with, very sweet, and, because he was gay, there was no chance of relationship problems. They stopped in at an art exhibit, had a late dinner, and talked for hours about mutual friends. He was funny and for a brief period she was able to forget her pain. Back in her suite at The Palace, she was no longer content watching movies. The evening of conversation had whetted her appetite for company.

Draped in a caftan of Sunday loneliness, she wanted to hear a familiar voice. She had not kept in close touch with any of her friends since leaving, and knew she would feel like a hypocrite for inflicting her sadness on them now. She finally called Nicholas and invited him to dinner. They dined in the hotel and then went back to her room with a bottle of wine, talked, and watched a ballgame.

It turned out to be just the form of rejuvenation she needed. She was up early the next morning, had breakfast, and took a cab to Royal Street Bakery. Pearl had lived, with Lacey's grandfather, in an apartment above the bakery, which Lacey dreaded entering. There was also the sad chore of packing away Pearl's belongings.

Sitting on the floor of Pearl's bedroom, Lacey began stuffing the boxes she had purchased on her way over. When Elfie knocked on the door, Lacey was glad

to take a break until she learned the nature of the interruption.

"Lacey, Peter and I have been wondering what
Aunt Pearl wanted to do about the bakery. I'm sure
you know by now, and we are tired of the suspense. We
have to plan our lives, and it's unfair of you to keep us
in limbo."

She had given Pearl's will to the attorney with
instructions to delay opening probate until the books
had been audited and an evaluation of the property
had been made. "I'm sure Mother Pearl was tired of a
lot of things that she couldn't change, and so am I. Her
attorney is opening probate, but will need the
accountant to go over the books, as well as the bakery's
assets, to determine market value. I can't proceed
without some answers or the court's permission."

"Market value? So you're selling the bakery? Is that
what Aunt Pearl wanted?"

Lacey gave the persistent young woman a deep
sigh. "What would you suggest?"

"If you propose selling the bakery, that means Aunt
Pearl left it to you. Peter and I deserve to know what's
going on. If you plan to sell the bakery, I think we have
a right to protest. Peter and I are the one who kept this
place going. You rarely set foot in—"

Lacey slammed a handful of books to the floor.
"I've heard about this, about family members gathering after someone dies and bickering. I will not allow
you and Peter or anyone else to desecrate Mother
Pearl's memory this way, do you hear me?"

"She was my aunt, my blood aunt. She was related to you by marriage."

Lacey stood, walked up to Elfie, and used her body to push the short, stocky woman back to the door. "Didn't you hear me? Mother Pearl's possessions were hers to do with as she pleased. How dare you stand here and insinuate that you were closer to her than I was? I don't give a damn about blood relations. I loved her and she loved me. Do you even understand what that means?"

The force of her voice caused Elfie to duck as if he had been slapped. Lacey continued pushing her backwards toward the door.

"I know all about you and Peter, so don't try to snow me with that blood relative crap. Instead of worrying about an inheritance, be grateful for the things she's done for you thus far. Running the bakery is your job. You and Peter are paid to be there."

With Elfie bent backwards in the doorway, Lacey straightened up and began to speak in normal tones. "There will be a reading of the will, at which time everyone will learn how Mother Pearl's possessions were distributed. The court will also want to know the value of the bakery and the condition of the books. Is it too much to ask that you wait until then?"

"No, that's fine," she mumbled. "I just needed an answer."

She was as close to hating Elfie as anyone she had ever known, but knowing Pearl would have wanted all of her things put to good use, she asked if Elfie would like some of them once she sorted them out.

Pearl was a pack rat. Each room was stuffed with items she had collected over the years, and Lacey assumed they were valued at whatever sentiment Pearl attached. She went down to the bakery for coffee and returned to her position on the floor, the phone cradled between her legs. The first call was to her cousin, Amy, who ran a shelter for abused families, and the next was to her old friend Terri Vale, a real estate broker.

She looked around the apartment and decided to use one of the two bedrooms to stack all of the boxes and furniture that she planned to give to the shelter. Amy had been thrilled with the donation and promised to come right over with three men and a truck, but Terri arrived first.

"I remember your grandmother. I'm sorry about her death."

"Thank you." Lacey had met her downstairs in the bakery and escorted her up the back stairs. "There is so much here, Terri, I don't want to waste anything. I called my cousin who runs a shelter, and she's sending a truck. I just need to know what the real estate market is like in this area and what I can reasonably expect should I choose to sell."

Terri looked around the apartment. "Surely you're not thinking of giving this wonderful furniture away. Have you lost your mind? There's a fortune here."

She walked around pointing out significances that Lacey would never have known, and by the time she finished they had an estimated value of nearly half a million dollars in furniture and collectables alone. When Lacey asked Terri what she thought the building was worth, she went on another digression.

"A friend of mine just rented a place about two blocks from here. It costs a fortune and isn't nearly as nice as this. Why don't you just live here? This is a hot neighborhood, you know. I'm dating Brain Willis, a building contractor, who could make this place like heaven. Sell some of these things, but not the really valuable ones. Take the money and renovate."

After Terri passed on her ideas, Lacey saw the apartment in a new light. "What about the bakery?"

"Keep it there if you'd like. I'm sure Brian will know how to use the ambiance of the bakery to enhance the building's appeal."

Without meaning to, Lacey became excited. When Amy arrived, Terri stood guard over a sofa and table that she wanted to purchase on the spot.

"This is gilded bronze. I believe this piece is attributed to Gouthiere. That's Spanish marble on top." She leaned into Lacey's ear. "I'll give you ten thousand," she hissed. "Right now. Check."

Lacey figured if Terri, whose parents were antique dealers, was offering ten, the table was probably worth thirty, but because it was Terri who prevented her from giving the pieces to a shelter, she agreed to the price.

When the guys from the shelter removed a box of clothing, Terri gasped. "That's a secrétaire a abattant! Pewter and brass!" She inspected the piece and screeched in a voice that made Lacey and Amy jump. "The stamp of Philippe-Claude Montigny! No less than $75,000."

By the end of the day, Lacey came to realize what an astute businesswoman Pearl had been. In her preliminary assessment, Terri pointed out many things of value, not just furniture, but a lot of things that Lacey had considered junk, including a doll that she said was worth thousands.

"Pearl told me about some Frenchman who was madly in love with her. Maybe he gave her these things," Lacey mumbled in amazement.

Amy still found a truckload of things for her shelter and, according to Terri, Lacey was sitting on a gold mine. Exhausted and hungry after working late into the evening, Lacey stopped at Sorrell's Deli for a bite before returning to the hotel. She had barely begun her meal when a familiar voice drifted across from a table of diners. She turned slowly and peeked around her chair into Mason's smiling face.

Their table was between Lacey and the door, so she could not escape. Hoping he would not notice her, she finished her salad, skipped the cheesecake she hungered for, and started for the door. It occurred to her that the diners were paired, which meant Mason was with a date. She stared sideways and recognized the woman as a sister of one of Mason's friends.

She hedged around several tables but was unable to escape. Their eyes met and she had to speak. "Good evening, Mason." She lingered briefly, smiled, and continued to the door.

"Lacey!"

He ran after her. "Lacey! Wait!"

"I'm really in a hurry, Mason. You're on a date. Go back to your friends. We'll talk some other time."

"How long have you been in New York? Nicholas said something about a fire at the camp and that you wouldn't be returning as quickly as you thought. Why didn't you call?"

"I've been really busy, Mason." She casually removed the hand he placed on her arm. "It's good to see you. I'll call you when I get settled. Maybe we can have coffee or something."

"I was having dinner with friends. Join us. I think you already know everyone at the table."

"You have a date, Mason. Please stop pretending."

She hurried away, glad that he was with someone else, but angry that he played the jilted, lonely lover. She also hoped Mason's new status would finally halt her mother's attempts at matchmaking.

John Jacob Tobias shifted to fifth gear, and the red blur streaked down the quiet ribbons of highway leading from the small community of Denham Wells into a maze of Fort Worth skyscrapers. He fought against a heart full of agony, the aromatic fumes from his father's smoldering Macanudo cigar, and trail of singed Cosmoline from the Ferrari's powerful V12 engine.

Having led a life filled with wealth and privilege, John felt it was selfish to complain. Yet, his heart was hurting almost as much as it had been before he went to Martha's Vineyard. He looked to his right and felt admiration well in his eyes.

"Roars like a lion! Which model is this?" Nathaniel's hands grazed the leather upholstery.

"The 550 Maranello. The last one I had was the 348 Spider, but it was too hard to maneuver in city traffic. I wanted the F355 Berlinetta, but with no more than four thousand manufactured each year, I would have to wait forever. This one is loaded with extras, and because of that, it had been on the car lot for over two months, which is a rarity."

"I like this body style better than the others," Nathaniel said. "I watched you drive up. Those alloy wheels are something else."

The car leaned into a curve and he pulled himself upright. "Too bad it only has one passenger seat. Imagine the honeys you could pick up in this piece of machinery."

"Sure, Pop." He laughed and downshifted to avoid a slow-moving vehicle emerging from the crossover. "I like the aerodynamics and drivability, but this will probably be my last Ferrari. I think I'll get a Corvette next time."

"You had, how many, three 'Vettes? I'm all for buying American, but I have to admit, the horsepower on this baby is something else." He smoothed his hair, a thick mop of black with zigzagging strands of silver. "Times sure have changed. I remember when black men were hot to trot over the Pontiac Firebird, Grand Prix, and Trans Am. Just as we were prone to dress beyond our means, no self-respecting brother would have been caught dead in a Chevrolet, unless it was a 'Vette."

He chuckled in reflective merriment. "Most of my friends lived for the day they could buy a new car. Cadillac was at the top of everyone's wish list. We respected the Riv and the Deuce and a Quarter, the poor man's Cadillac, but you knew you had your stuff together when you could afford a Seville."

"I remember Natty talking about his first car, and what it was like to be one of only a handful of blacks who could afford that kind of luxury. At least it was a little better in your day."

"Not much. I was still a wealthy black man in a segregated society where most of my friends were too poor to pray, and in many cases, very resentful. I didn't complain about it then and I still can't, because no matter how many problems I had, my bank account afforded me one less than other blacks."

"You and Natty both have great attitudes about the whole thing."

"That's not hard to do, son. I've been blessed. Throughout my life I've always been able to load my problems on one side of the scale and have it tilt in my favor. Growing up with money when nearly everyone else was in dire poverty was lonely as hell, but I enjoyed my life. I drove nice cars loaded with pretty women." He leaned closer to his son. "Of course that changed after I met your mother."

Nathaniel was the source of John's strength, Natty provided inspiration, and his mother had added refinement and sensitivity. Having lost his own wife, John knew the look in his father's eyes.

Nathaniel stared straight ahead. "I was happy to be able to give her the things she wanted. Her family tried to make her feel guilty, but, after all was said and done, your mother and I were very happy." He stumped the fat cigar butt in the ashtray, removed another one from his breast pocket and rolled off the paper.

"I didn't have the years with Debra that you had with Mom, but I know how it feels to want happiness for the woman you love."

"Debra was happy, and she brought a lot of happiness to our home. She even made Natty smile. He loved her biscuits." He puffed out a curlicue of smoke. "You've got to stop feeling guilty for her death, John. It wasn't your fault."

"I know, but I can't help feeling that I never should have brought her here. It was obvious she felt out of place."

"She did not. She wasn't used to country living, but it's not like you took her to some shack in the wilderness. Debra had the best of everything, and she enjoyed her life with you. She would want you to be happy. She'd want you to get back with Lacey. Tell me about her. It's obvious you're hurting for her. Tell me what really happened up there."

"It all seems so unreal now, Pop. I went to that camp expecting some dowdy old woman and a very boring season in lovely country. What I found was not just a raving beauty, but also one that looked so much like Debra, she took my breath away. Worldly and windblown. Beautiful, even in denim and plaid. She's classy, confident, and cultured. When she gets mad, you'd better run like hell. I spent the first three months angry and giving her grief for making me feel guilty enough to stay. She was counting on Monroe. I couldn't let her down. I was more angry at myself for being so damn attracted to her."

He changed gears as the freeway became more congested. "It was so peaceful there. I guess I found my soul and lost my heart."

"So what do you plan to do about it?"

"She's grief stricken right now. She truly loved her grandmother. I think Pearl was one of the few people who accepted Lacey for who she is. Unpretentious. Unspoiled by the life she was given, and seemingly unaware of her tremendous beauty. I can't get her out of my mind."

"Well, I'm glad you're home, but I wish you'd brought her with you. Don't give up so easily. Let her adjust to her loss. I'm sure she wants you as much as you want her."

"I don't just want her, Pop. I love her. She's fresh, wholesome, and unpainted, with skin that invites a touch. Big black eyes that still sparkle with the wonder and anticipation of youth. Her hair is straight and black with the same luster as Pearl's and Yank's. When I met her, it was easy to spot the sadness in her smile. Now it's tripled, and I'm partly to blame."

They rode in silence to the Royal Hotel. John unfolded his tuxedo-clad frame from the leather seat, adjusted his tie, and held out his arm to prevent his father from walking ahead.

"Just a second, Pop. I'm not properly dressed." He pulled upright and forced a wide smile across his face. "Okay, let's go and accept this…what is it again?"

Nathaniel smiled back. "The Patron Saint Award."

Terri's mother came to appraise Pearl's collectables and informed Lacey that Terri's assessment had been quite accurate. She gave Lacey figures on all of the items, but chose almost half of them for her shop. The building contractor hurried together a computer sketch of his proposal for the renovation and immediately applied for a permit to begin the work. Just having an agenda brought orderliness to Lacey's life. She called her uncle, the judge, who used the owner's death as a reason to push through the paperwork for the permit.

Pearl had left all of her possessions to Lacey, but she could not legally sell anything from the apartment until after probate. She did allow Terri's mother to take the pieces she desired to purchase, just to gain space. Having cleared away a considerable amount of clutter, she found the apartment quite sufficient even without renovation and decided to move in right away. After all, there were only so many nights she could remain in a borrowed suite at The Palace.

Knowing Mason would tell Amanda of their meeting, she phoned her mother and listened to the sermon she knew was imminent.

"Darling, why are you living there? You know there's lots of room here, and this is your home. Pack your things and come back to your old room. In no time at all, you and Mason will be married, but until then you belong here with me."

"Thanks, but I'm quite comfortable here, and I wish you'd give up this notion of a marriage. Mason is dating, and that's what he should do. Didn't he tell you?"

"He was having dinner with friends, Lacey, not dating. Mason is in love with you, but I can't swear that will continue. Claim him now before someone else does, and come on home. I'll have your room freshened up, help you get settled, and we can spend a little time together. I don't complain to my children, but I get lonely sometimes, too."

Guilt eased into Lacey's heart. "I know, Mom, and I promise we'll spend more time together. Just let me get through the ordeal of sorting out Mother Pearl's estate, and sorting through my own problems. I promise we'll go shopping, dine together, and do all the fun things you like."

Lacey promised to attend her mother's dinner party as a way to halt the recriminations, and then worked diligently for the rest of the week to keep her head together. Anything to shut out thoughts of Camp Noepe, Pearl's death, and John Jacob Tobias. With a tentative plan of action, Lacey was able to rest better at night. Money was not a problem, and given the value of Pearl's collection, she could complete the renovations without touching the remainder of her savings. With no job in sight, that was a great comfort.

Douglas Warren called with John's offer for Camp Noepe. Lacey quickly agreed to the price. The proceeds of the sale, along with the insurance settlement, would be used to replenish her investment accounts and would conclude a chapter of her life that had been painful but wonderfully fulfilling.

After several full nights of sleep, Lacey felt rested enough to be lonely. John's last words continuously circled through her mind. She did love him and didn't want to give him up, but there were too many unknowns, and she was afraid. By the end of the week, she was restless enough to look forward to her mother's dinner party until a call from her brother quieted her excitement. Nicholas talked relentlessly about Amanda's interference in his love life.

"She cautioned me to dress for dinner Friday night, so I'm sure she's planning to push one of her society friends in my life. I've talked Greta into going out with me, but of course, Mom doesn't know. I can't imagine what will happen if the two of us marry. I'll probably be banned from the family altogether. Greta is afraid to be in the same room with Mom, and because she is my mother and I love her, I don't know a way around a confrontation."

"Don't let her do it," Lacey cautioned. "Be firm with her, Nicholas. This is your life."

Amanda called Friday morning with another wardrobe advisory, telling Lacey that the evening was not formal but to please look stunning because dignitaries would be in attendance.

Feeling the need for a perk, Lacey went to the little boutique she frequented on Fifth Avenue and bought a slinky blue dress, matching bag, and shoes. After taking a long bubble bath, she styled her hair in a sleek upsweep and called a cab. Even if she could have found a parking space, she didn't dare walk any long distances in new shoes. Months of wearing comfortable boots, sandals, or sneakers made the four-inch heels feel like twelve-inch stilts.

"Oh, darling, you look wonderful," Amanda gushed and leaned forward for an air kiss. "The bartender has not arrived, but Mr. Rydell will make you a drink."

Lacey flinched at the formality that had haunted her childhood. She and Nicholas were teased for wearing dress clothes to play and for never getting the soles of their shoes dirty. Even more frustrating was Amanda's continued reference to the man in her life as "Mr. Rydell."

"Nicholas will be here shortly. I wanted both of my children here when the guest of honor arrives."

Ignoring the strong urge to run away, Lacey glanced into the dining room and a table set for ten. "Who is this guest of honor, Mom, and who are the other dinner guests?"

"The four of us, Gwenneth and Tom, and Ambassador Sandoval and his family." She smiled. "He has a lovely daughter. I hope your brother will find her attractive."

"Mother! Why can't you allow Nicholas to make his own choices? He has a lovely woman in his life. Back off. Did anyone stand over you and Dad when you were dating? Think of the pressure you're placing on Nicholas. Don't even think about fixing me up. I won't stand for it."

"Honey, you have Mason." Amanda hooked her arm though Larry Rydell's and smiled. "You two are perfect for each other."

"I don't have Mason, and I don't want Mason. I saw him with Cleo Waters the other night. She might have something to say about me still having Mason, and don't tell me it was just dinner with friends. I saw them. That man is free to choose whomever he wants, and it seems he has. And what makes you think Nicholas and I need fixing up? Is there something wrong with us that prevents us from finding a mate on our own?"

"Both of my children are wonderful prospects for any man or woman, but you have to reconsider what you have with Mason. I'm sure what you saw in the restaurant was no more than friendship."

The fact that Amanda failed to press the issue warned Lacey that Amanda had already spoken with Mason about it and that she should proceed cautiously. Maurice, the caterer, and Nicholas arrived at the same time. Leaving Amanda to fuss over Maurice, Lacey pulled her brother into the bedroom.

"Do you know about this ambassador Mom invited to dinner?"

"No, but I know she's successfully derailed every relationship that has meant anything to me. I'm never bringing another girl here. She's also dead set on you and Mason getting together."

"You're around Mason a lot now. I'm sure you know he's dating. I ran into him the other night with Cleo Waters, his friend Charlie's 'little sister,' as he used to say. Miss Cleo is not so little anymore, and she and Mason were all over each other."

"I wondered how he knew you were back. He came in the next morning asking all kinds of questions about you, but he never told me this. Let him find someone else. I like Mason, but I don't think you love him enough for marriage, and the more I'm around him, the more I feel he's not right for you."

254

"He's not right for me, and he's a coward. Why not just tell the truth? He's dating other women. That's his prerogative. His face turned ashen when he saw me the other night. He has no numbers to call me, and I asked Mom not to give him my new cell number." Lacey squared her shoulders and placed her hand on her brother's shoulder. "Just watch out for Mom tonight. Don't let her railroad you into anything."

Her warning proved very timely. The ambassador arrived with his wife and daughter, a waif of a girl with large eyes and a nervous laugh. Before Lacey could digest that shock, Mason arrived and took his position next to her at the dinner table. Throughout the meal, Amanda bragged on her children's accomplishments, and Lacey watched Nicholas shrink into the chair's upholstery in embarrassment.

Mason spoke as if they were still engaged. Lacey raised a furious brow in her mother's direction when he said Amanda would be quite busy "planning our nuptials." She also knew that her mother was not fond of her Aunt Gwenneth, but had invited her to dinner because Gwenneth's husband was a district court judge, a fact that Amanda also mentioned more than twice.

Tired of the charade, Lacey moved to put an end to Mason's grandstanding. "I've been away for almost a year, so I have a lot of catching up to do." She smiled broadly. "Mason, I know you've done a lot of dating since I left, so tell me where the hot spots are in the city."

"She's referring to the fact that Mason entertains a lot of clients," Amanda said quickly. "Don't worry, dear, you and Mason will have ample chance to catch up on your socializing."

"That's so true." He pushed back from the table and stood next to her. "Our marriage plans were put on hold so that Lacey could open an upscale summer camp in Massachusetts. We do have a lot of catching up to do."

He knelt before her. "I know we've done this once, but because of the interruption, I would like to ask you again, in front of these distinguished guests, to be my wife." He took a box from his pocket and opened it to reveal a very large emerald-cut diamond.

"Oh, this is heavenly! Wonderful." Amanda beamed and looked across the table. "Since we have a judge here today, you could do it now."

Lacey reeled from the shock. "No, Mother. I don't think that would be a good idea. We'll discuss this later."

A waiter arrived on cue with a tray of champagne glasses.

"Let's toast this splendid occasion. Look at them. Don't they make a handsome couple?" Amanda beamed while failing to acknowledge her daughter's look of mystified disdain.

The gathering retreated to the living room for after-dinner coffee and Mason found his arm in Lacey's stern grip. She guided him away from the crowd and into her bedroom.

"What the hell was that all about? You know, you and my mother should be politicians. How are you going to explain this to Cleo, and I'm sure there were others. I know you better than you think."

"Lacey, you walked out on our engagement, not me. I loved you then and I love you now. I want to marry you. I want a life with you, only you. Yes, I've been socially active, but you're the woman I love."

He was charming and boyishly handsome and, in spite of herself, Lacey felt the warmth they had once shared. Had it not been for the strong memory of John's arms, and the feelings for him that occupied a large portion of her heart, she might have weakened. Those memories kept her awake at night, haunted her dreams, and followed her into consciousness. Mason could not compare with John. She knew no one could.

"I'm flattered with the proposal and the gorgeous ring, but we have been away from each other for a long time." She pushed him away. "I expected you to have other relationships, to have a commitment to someone else. There's no need to lie about it."

Before she could continue, his arms encircled her and his lips pressed against hers.

"I love you. I have no other commitments and I don't want any. All I want right now is us, back together. You have no idea how much I want you. Let's go to my place and celebrate. It'll be like old times. Good times. Making love all night. I'll prove how much I've missed you."

"I don't know what to say." She did, but refrained. "Give me time to think."

He pulled away. "Haven't you had enough of that already?"

She thought of John, back in Texas with his family, probably with another woman. "I don't mean months." She walked around to the other side the bed, away from his reach. There was no chance of a marriage with Mason, especially now. "I just need to sleep on it."

He moved in front of her and guided her hand to the ridge next to his zipper. "And I need you to sleep on this. How much torture can one man take?"

Amanda knocked on the door. "Come on out, you two," she whispered. "You have to say good night to our guests. You can catch up later."

Too torn to argue, Lacey took Mason's hand, smiled, and joined her mother and guests for a nightcap. Conversation whirled around her, but her mind was wandering around the great state of Texas, hoping that somewhere in the vastness, John Tobias was thinking of her.

CHAPTER 13

John drove the rental car onto the ferry without realizing he was gripping the steering wheel hard enough for his nails to gouge indentations in his palms. So much had happened during his months on the island. It had changed his life.

Back in Texas, he had tried unsuccessfully to accept yet another loss, telling himself it was better to have happened now than later. His family advised him to wait and give Lacey time, but waiting had become too painful. Feeling he had lost all connections with her, he pursued the purchase of Camp Noepe, the one thing they had in common.

Lacey was a beautiful, wonderful woman, and he was in love. No matter how he tried, he could not shake the thought of her. He had amused his father with stories of his first encounter with Lacey and the others at Camp Noepe in hopes that once he shared his feelings, they would subside. The only thing he achieved was letting his father know just how strong his feelings were.

"Son, you've been dealt some good hands in your life and a few bad ones, most of which you had no control over. This one is different. I'm sure this girl is in love with you. She's probably missing you the same as you're missing her. Now, I was a true womanizer in my early days, but when I met the right woman, I knew it. I was not about to let anything stand between the two of us. That's what you have to do with Lacey. Instead of trying to forget her, you should be trying to figure out ways to get her back in your life."

"And maybe I should just accept her decision to return home. If her mother had anything to say about it, she's probably already married to Mason Phipps."

"I don't know him well, but I do know that he was quite rigid. There is no way she could prefer him to you. You say you owe her, so go save the poor girl from a life of boredom."

"How can I do that, Pop? She doesn't want me."

"I don't think you believe that. Didn't you say the two of you were together when the fire started?"

For a second John was back on the beach and Lacey was in his arms. "We were together on the beach. I think I had convinced her that we should be together but later, when she ran into the burning building, I lost it. I suppose I saw Debra fading away and I couldn't hold on, expect this time, Lacey acted without thinking. I yelled at her when I got her out. I felt ashamed afterwards, so I avoided her until I could think of something to say. When I did, she was already packed for New York. The only connection we have now is Camp Noepe, and once I've purchased it, there will be no reason to see her."

"You're wrong." Nathaniel looked at his son. "You love her and that's a very good reason to see her. You want love. If Lacey is afraid, then you'll have to be brave enough for both of you, and I know you are."

John held onto the papers he received from Lacey's attorney. He had not signed them. It hurt to even think of breaking the link between them. With those papers tucked in his pocket, he was headed back to Oak Bluffs. There had to be a way, and he was determined to find it.

He drove off the ferry and felt his heart shatter. As much as he wanted the camp, he knew that just as Lacey could not face the area without Pearl, he could not spend any time there without Lacey. Each mile of the drive to Camp Noepe brought him more in touch with his feelings. He turned in the driveway and slowed down the stretch of gravel leading to the main house, thinking she should be there, her head held high and her dark hair blowing in the wind.

Before Lacey agreed to the sale, John had hired Yank to bring some people in and clean up the remaining debris and to secure the rest of the main house to prevent further damage. After inspecting the buildings, he walked out to the covered grove. It was there that he first realized just how much he wanted her. He remembered her touch, her smell, and the cute little laugh that caused her nose to crinkle. He remembered the passion in her eyes when he held her. She was vibrant, full of life, full of fire. A ripple of pleasure coursed his body and the emptiness that followed was overbearingly convincing. He had to get her back.

He inspected every inch of the remains of Camp Noepe, looked into each room of the main house, the cabin he had occupied, and the bunkhouse, as if he expected to find her there, hidden in the quiet wonders of the place she loved. He left Oak Bluffs and drove back into Chilmark and on up to the Aquinnah Cliffs.

He parked the car and walked down to the expanse of brilliant colors that attracted visitors and islanders each year. He understood Lacey's strong attraction to the area and why Pearl wanted the marvel of nature to serve as her final resting place.

He removed his hat and bowed his head in reverence, sadness, and in joy.

After calling ahead, he drove the short distance down State Road to where Yank and his family lived. The modest frame house was tucked into the landscape as if it was part of the natural setting. Yank met him at the door.

"Come in!" He pulled John into an embrace. "It's good to see you, old friend."

John immediately felt at home.

"Come in, John!" Shale smiled her crooked-toothed grin and held out her arms. "It's good to see you. Can I get you a cup of coffee?"

"No, thanks." He hugged her round shoulders. "I've missed all of you. Where is Micah?"

"Right here." Micah ran in and extended his hand. "Hi, John. I'm glad you came."

"I'm glad to be back on the island. It seems so long ago."

"We're going to talk business," Yank said, and led John out to the backyard, where a cooler of beer and two lawn chairs were positioned under the protective limbs of a large tree.

A dog ambled over and sniffed John's pant leg. "Crow!" He rubbed the scraggly mane around the dog's ears. "I wasn't sure what had happened to you."

"I promised Lacey I'd find him a good home, and I hope I did. None of us wanted to lose him. Something happened at Camp Noepe this summer for my family and me. It was much more than just a job."

John allowed Crow to lick his hand. "We were a family there at Camp Noepe. I miss it, too. I stopped by on my way out. Your guys did a good job of cleaning it up. It's hard to believe there was so much damage in such a short time."

"I think it was just luck and quick action by the fire department that kept the whole place from going up in flames. We had that one brief rainy spell, but the land was thirsty. Those old timbers were like kindling."

John remembered the rain.

"Have you spoken with Lacey?" Micah asked as he joined them under the tree.

"No, just her attorney. She agreed to sell me the camp, but her attorney will handle the transaction. He said she's living in Pearl's apartment on the second level of the bakery, and renovating the entire building."

"At least she's not with her mother and that man. He's a jerk," Micah said, rolling his dark eyes.

"That's not polite, son," Yank reminded him.

"It may not be polite, but it's true. I saw the way he looked at us at Camp Noepe, like he smelled something foul. I heard the way he talked to Lacey. I didn't like it and I didn't like him. Lacey loves John." He searched John's face. "I don't see why it's so difficult for two people to get together if they care for each other. Just seems like we always make mountains out of anthills with it comes to love."

"He's not just talking about you and Lacey now," Yank said. "Jennifer Greenup went off to spend her last year of high school abroad. Where did she go, Micah?"

"Florence, Italy. Some foreign exchange program."

"He called her all the way overseas. She was too busy to talk, and hasn't called him back or even sent a letter."

Micah hung his head. "We were together all summer and she didn't even tell me that she was going, only that she had a chance to go if she wanted to. She said she loved me, but I don't think she did. Love doesn't go away that easy." He looked at John. "Does it?"

John heard the pain in Micah's voice and felt the lump he could not swallow. He shook his head. Micah was young but had an honest passion for life. If the emptiness Micah felt was even close to his, John knew he was looking at a brokenhearted young man.

"Look at Grandpa. He hasn't forgotten Pearl," Micah reminded them.

"How is Tedera?" John asked.

"He spends most of his time down by the cliffs. I don't remember him mourning so much when my mother died. He never smiles anymore, John." Yank shook his head. "Papa was seventeen when he married my mother. She was sixteen. When she died a few years ago, he suddenly became an old man, but Pearl made him smile again. I wish it could have lasted."

"Where is he now, at the cliffs?"

"He was in his room watching television. Probably fell asleep," Micah answered John. "I'll go tell him you're here. That might make him feel better."

John talked about restoring the camp and Yank made notes. When Micah returned with his grandfather in tow, John saw the furrows pain had plowed in the proud old face.

"Tedera. It's good to see you." A thought popped into his head. "Come join us. I need your help with a project I'm trying to put together."

There was little emotion in the faded eyes, but Tedera shook John's hand and joined the little circle.

"I've decided to restore Camp Noepe, but I want to add a cultural center. I know there are a few here on the island already, but this one will be special. We will call it the Pearl Daigle Cultural Center, but I need your help in finding information and artifacts on your people—Pearl's people—to share with the visitors who are unfamiliar with your culture. You are the history of this country. Young people need to know that."

A gleam appeared on his face. "Tell me what you want. I'll be happy to help."

"In order to make it special, we will need some authentic works, not the things you can buy in stores. We also need to compile information on Pearl, her life here on the island and in New York. She seems to have led a very interesting life. Do you know where her sister lives?"

"Yes, I saw her last week." Tedera had come alive. "Lacey sent me out a box of things that belonged to Pearl. Do you want photographs, too?"

"I think that would be nice. We'll chronicle your people in the life of one of its own. If we can collect enough recipes, we'll do a cookbook with some of Pearl's favorite dishes. Hopefully, her sister can help with that."

"Is Lacey going to help?" Tedera asked.

"I haven't told her yet, but I hope she will." John quickly realized the innocent endeavor was yet another way to keep Lacey in his life.

"When are you two getting married?" Tedera asked in total sincerity.

John was silent. It wasn't just the question, it was the way Tedera spoke, as if it was the natural thing to do.

"I haven't spoken to her since she left Camp Noepe," he finally answered.

"But why? The two of you are going to marry. Pearl said so." His declaration was blunt and spoken with certainty. "She saw it."

John felt a tug at his heart. "Did Pearl tell you this?"

"Sure. I think she told Lacey, too. She said she would, but I don't know if she had a chance to tell her before...before it happened." He looked toward the cliffs. "She was a fine woman. She liked to cook for me."

"She was a fine woman," Yank agreed. "And she could see things. I know most people think it's nonsense, but she really could see the future."

John was not sure how to take this bit of optimism. "Did she tell you that she saw Lacey and me married?"

"She saw Lacey in white and you were there." Tedera looked at John. "You might as well accept it. It's going to happen, just like Pearl said."

John studied the face of a man convinced. "Well, if the lady is going to marry me, I had better make sure the two of us start talking, and I think I know just how to do it. Thank you, my friend." He shook Tedera's hand. "Somehow, I felt that coming here would tell me what I had to do, and it did. Thank you."

Yank and Micah walked John to his car.

"What are you going to do?" Micah asked.

"Don't ask questions like that," Yank scowled. "That's personal."

"It is, and it isn't," John said. "You two spent more time with her than I did, so I'm sure you've seen her angry."

They both nodded.

"I'm going to make her angry with me again. Hopefully I can make her angry enough to come to me, but I'll need your help."

"I'll do whatever I can, and I want to thank you for giving Papa something to live for. That's important with my people." Yank shook John's hand.

"I think having reasons to wake up each morning is important for everyone, and I'm glad I could help. This summer on the island gave me something to live for, and now I have to make it a reality. Do they have weddings at the lighthouse here in Aquinnah or the one in Oak Bluffs?"

"They sure do. Just contact Martha's Vineyard Historical Society and reserve your date. They open in June," Micah offered.

"That's a long ways off, but I may need that much time. First, I'll have to get Lacey to agree to marry me."

Shale came out to say goodbye. "Have you asked her to marry you?"

"No, not yet."

She leaned into the window of the rental car. "Then what are you waiting for? Pearl had planned to tell you that you might have to prod her a little. She said Lacey was stubborn as a mule sometimes."

"She's right," Yank said. "Lacey is just about the sweetest person I know, but she's got a stubborn streak a mile long." He smiled. "Of course, it was that stubborn streak that helped her get Camp Noepe up and running. A weaker woman would have just quit."

"A weaker woman never would have bought the place," Shale added.

John looked from one to the other. "Are all of you really convinced that Lacey and I will marry?" When they all nodded, he took his cell phone from his pocket and dialed. "Mr. Warren, this is John Tobias. I wonder if you might be able to spare a few minutes. I desperately need your help."

Before Lacey left her mother's dinner party, Amanda had ranted about the wedding, the honeymoon, and where they planned to live when they returned. Lacey answered each question with "we'll talk about it later," and then spent the weekend dodging Amanda and Mason's calls. When her phone rang on Saturday and Sunday, she knew it was either her mother wanting to talk about the wedding or Mason wanting to talk about sex, and neither subject appealed to her. She ignored it, but finally called

Drayton Snow and spent Sunday afternoon laughing at his jokes.

A friendly dinner was not what she wanted. She wanted John Tobias. His voice rang in her ear all weekend, she felt his hands on her skin, and remembered the warmth of his strong body next to her in bed. She knew that rain would always bring back memories of that day. She wanted to call him, to hear his voice once more.

"I'll just call Douglas and tell him I'll handle the sale of Camp Noepe myself." She changed her mind before finishing the sentence. One phone call would only intensify her longing.

Mason banged on her door at three p.m., making her wish she had answered the phone, lied, and said she was ill.

"What's going on? I've been calling for two days. Why don't you answer the phone? I thought something had happened to you." He looked down the hall toward the bedroom. "Are you alone?"

"No, I have a battalion of men stashed away in there," Lacey told him. "What do you want, Mason?"

"I want what I've always wanted. I want you." He encircled his arms around her waist. "I love you. I want you. I need you." When she didn't respond, he released her and stood back. "The big question is, who do you want? Is John Tobias here in New York?"

"I don't keep tabs on John Tobias. I have no idea where he is."

"You said he was buying your camp, so I assumed—"

"Don't assume, Mason." She stopped his words. "John is purchasing Camp Noepe through Doug. I have not seen or spoken with him since I left Oak Bluffs. Is that what you wanted to hear?"

"I want to hear you say you love me. I want you hear you moan and cry out when we make love. Is that too much to ask?"

"Excuse me, I'll be right back." She went to the chest in her bedroom and returned with the little blue box. "We broke up before I left here because you had no earthly clue as to what I'm all about. You see things through that little microscopic lens. I don't want to fight, Mason. Just take this ring back. I only accepted it because I didn't want to create a scene at Mom's dinner party, but of course, you knew that. And so did she."

"I asked you to marry me almost two years ago and you said yes. I haven't forgotten that, just as I haven't forgotten what we meant to each other, the good times we had together. Okay, so maybe I'm not as understanding of your needs as I should be." He took the hand that she held out and closed her fingers around the box. "I love you. I'll do whatever it takes to make you forget the problems we've had. I want to go back to the way it was before. Tell me that I mean nothing to you and I'll leave and never bother you again."

She saw a reflection of her own pain in his eyes. "I can't say you don't mean anything to me, but I can't say I'm ready to marry you, either. I'm not sure we could ever get back to where we were before."

"Can we try? Can we just date and see how things go?"

She did not pull away until after they had kissed. She hoped to feel at least some of what she had felt for John, but that did not happen. No one would make her feel the way he had.

When the construction crew arrived early Monday, Lacey retreated to the bakery to plan her day. First she would visit the storage facility to determine how she could use the furnishings she already had. Drayton had helped her choose most of the furniture, and had agreed to help her decorate. She sipped her coffee and waited for him to arrive. When he did, he became excited over the large living space Lacey would have once she had a wall removed. She planned to have the space that Pearl used for storage, which comprised a third of the floor space, converted to a large bedroom and bath. She and Drayton went shopping for everything that was needed to make a comfortable home.

She was exhausted when they finished but felt that much had been accomplished. Drayton arrived early the next morning, they dined in the bakery, had the antiques that Lacey chose to keep picked up for restoration, and tagged the others for sale as soon as probate was completed. After choosing material for drapes and spreads, they found suitable covering for the Empire carved mahogany sofa that Terri identified as neoclassical, probably New York, 1823-35. They also found upholstery for the seven Hepplewhite mahogany dining chairs, and a round contemporary table for the eclectic style that Lacey admired.

Drayton left for work and Lacey made final selections for the guest room draperies. Tired and hungry but not wanting to eat alone, she called Nicholas and they agreed to meet at Rothschild's.

"I had a long discussion with Mom yesterday," he said. "I told her to back off. I can't date that girl from the dinner party. I told her so, and I told her about my plans with Greta." He changed the subject. "What happened up in Massachusetts? You've never really talked about it."

She told him all about John. Her face burned at the memory of a perfect rainy evening.

"So what are you planning to do? Are you in love with this man?"

"I am, but I don't know if it would work."

"You can't marry Mason if you're in love with someone else. Does he know about John? I mean that you're in love with him?"

Lacey shrugged. "I wanted to tell him, but my relationship with John seems like something from a dream. I think of him and I know I love him, but it seems so unreal now. Mason came by Sunday night and we agreed to see each other, for dates, I guess you might say, and see what happens. You know, I look at him and see everything Mom sees. Good looks, stability, prosperity, but I don't see, or feel, what I had with John." She shook her head.

"You don't feel love," Nicholas added. "You don't feel for him what you felt for John Tobias, just as I'll never feel for another woman what I feel for Greta Lang. I've tried to do it Mom's way, and it doesn't work. Of course, I don't care what Mom says, I'm not dating that ambassador's daughter. No way in hell."

He made a face and Lacey laughed.

"It's a shame that we judge people by appearance, but we do. Mason is handsome in a pretty way while John is ruggedly handsome. He's tall and dark with powerful hands." She hugged herself and swooned. "I can't feel more wonderful with a man than I did with him."

"I only spoke with him briefly, but I know Mason quite well, and I can see the difference. Why don't you call him? Someone has to make the first move."

"I know. I keep telling myself that maybe I'm not in love, maybe it was just the moment, but I can't get him out of my mind."

"Do you love Mason?"

"I thought I did, but I left here, Nicholas, and Mason was not on my mind for one minute. Well, maybe four or five, during those lonely nights. I spent months with John, but we had only been romantically involved a few weeks, and I can't think of anything but him."

"I'm glad we had this talk because I've made a decision." Nicholas hefted his glass of white wine. "I'm going to Greta and ask her to marry me, and if Mom doesn't like it, tough."

Lacey raised her glass to his. "And I applaud you."

"Now, I want to hear you say you'll do the same with John Tobias."

"Oh, I don't know, Nicholas. You and Greta were together for two years in college. It's not the same. John was lost and lonely without his wife. I could have been just a filler."

"And it may be the greatest love you'll ever know. Can you afford not to pursue it?"

CHAPTER 14

Lacey left her brother, promised to think about her feelings for John, and took a cab home. Amanda was waiting in the bakery.

"Honey, where on earth have you been? I've waited for hours."

Lacey looked confused. "Was I supposed to meet you here?"

"No, no. I came over because I knew you wouldn't listen to what I have to say on the phone. I had to say this to your face, and I hope you take it seriously."

Lacey sighed. "Let's go upstairs." She led the way down the narrow hall that fed into the back staircase.

"I don't remember coming here at all. How long did Pearl live in this godforsaken place?"

"Don't start. There is another entrance, but this is the one that leads from the bakery. Eventually, this stairway will be replaced with an elevator. At least that's the plan."

The stairway ended on the stoop to the kitchen door. Amanda scowled as Lacey walked over the workmen's tools and into the living room, which was a lot smaller than it would be when the improvements were completed.

"Oh, honey! This place is too small and too…what's the word I'm searching for? It's just downright shabby. Even with renovations, it's still a dump. Besides, it's over a bakery, a place where food is prepared. Everything in your home will smell of food and grease. Ugh!"

"According to my realtor friend, this dump is worth a small fortune. I need a place to live. I own a building in a prime location. Doesn't it make sense to renovate this place and stay here? I'll show you the plans, Mom. It's going to be fabulous when they finish. I can't think of a better place to be."

"How about your home? Our home? Your room is as you left it, but if you want to update, to change the décor, we certainly can. I would love to have a project right now. I need something to keep me occupied."

"Mom, I'm a grown woman. I shouldn't live at home."

"And just why not? You'll only be there until you and Mason marry and then you'll have your own place. I'm sure you know Mason would never live here, which makes it even more ridiculous to spend good money on renovating this place." She gestured and made a face.

"I only took the ring because I didn't want to commit the unpardonable sin of making a stink in front of your guests, just as you knew I would. I don't love Mason."

"That's just what I came to talk about. Mason has been trying to reach you since Friday night and you will not answer his calls. Your little trek to Massachusetts is over, Lacey. You're back in New York without a job, and the place you sunk your money in is not even worth the effort you put into it. What are you planning to do?"

"Obviously you haven't spoken to Mason lately. He came by and we talked. We talked and agreed to wait and see what happens, but I can tell you now nothing will, because I don't love him. As for my financial status, I'm selling Camp Noepe to John. I have money. I have this building, and the junk that's in it. Junk that's worth a small fortune. Thanks to a very wise and thrifty woman, I'm far from broke."

"You're also far from thinking clearly. I don't understand why you left Mason in the first place or your reluctance to marry him now. Good men don't grow on trees, and this man is one you should be happy to have. He's a full partner in his father's law firm, he's overpoweringly handsome and—"

"I was there at the dinner, Mother." Lacey interrupted, swallowing her anger. "I heard you talk about Nicholas and me as if we were slaves on the auction block. 'Take this one, she can cook, sew and keep house.' Nicholas has a girl that he loves, or he did have until you fouled it up. What's wrong with Greta?"

"That girl hails from a family that wouldn't know class if it jumped on their backs. I don't understand why Nicholas would want to associate with people like that, just as I don't understand how you could feel so comfortable with those backwoods Indians. I just want the best for my children. Is that so wrong?"

"They prefer Native American, Mother, and they're not backwoods. An antique dealer took one look around this apartment and declared Mother Pearl a genius. In case you've forgotten, the man you married was part Native American and so are your children." Her face became a mass of frowns. "And what's best for your children is what your children want, what makes us happy, not what you see as fitting."

"Do you really think you're a better judge of class than I am?"

Lacey inhaled deeply. "Let's not have this discussion, Mother. It will only lead to more disagreements. You have your ways and neither Nicholas or I will ever try and change that. Why are you trying to change us?"

"I am a respected member of society in this city. There is nothing about me that needs changing." She stood and walked to the table where the case of fishing lure had been placed. "Look at this! Some kind of voodoo ritual, I'm sure. This woman, even in death, has a hold over you. Why can't you see that, Lacey? She was and still is—"

"Mother! I will not let you stand here and degrade Mother Pearl, not in her home."

"I didn't come here to discuss that woman, but looking around me, I find it odd that you would want to even visit this place. Pearl was clearly out of her mind."

"That's it! Please leave."

"Are you inviting your own mother to leave? Being in the company of such reprobates has taken a toll on your senses."

"Mother Pearl was a wonderful woman, and she was more of a mother to me than you've ever been." Lacey saw the damage her words had done, but could not stop the flow of anger. "Why do you have to have the deciding vote on everyone's life? Why do you think you know best? Your ambitions are not mine, and I don't give a damn about this so-called class you continue to rant about."

"I don't believe you just refuted all of the efforts I've made to give you the best life possible. How can you say that I was not a good mother?"

"You were a great mother, but you never stopped to listen to the things I wanted, and Mother Pearl did. You just have to make everyone what you want them to be. I have to wonder if all of those trips Daddy took, the way he pushed himself, were more for you than for him."

Amanda flailed her arms and tears appeared in her eyes. "Are you saying I drove your father to his death? If I'm a bad mother, you're certainly a horrible child. That woman has turned—"

"Don't say that! Don't ever say that again! I loved Mother Pearl! I loved her and I needed her. I need her now. She understood me, and, for your information, the things in that case are priceless fishing lures. The things here in this apartment that you see as junk are well-thought-out collectibles that, according to the appraisal I just paid for, could only have been assembled by an incredibly shrewd person."

"Fine, do what you will. I see that my word has no meaning, but let me tell you this, the only reason you even have this last chance with Mason is because of me, the horrible mother. That man is not going to wait another day for you, and only agreed to wait this long because I asked him to do so. He had written you off months ago and was dating someone else. I've convinced him to reconsider."

Amanda retaliated, her eyes moist with tears. "That man is the best you could hope for in this world of slim pickings, but if you're too stubborn to believe it, just live life your way. And I did not drive my husband to his death! Do you hear me? I did not!"

She stormed from the room and left Lacey simmering in anger and regret. She never wanted to cause Amanda pain, but her feelings for Pearl had always been a sore spot with her mother. When Lacey was younger, her father said Amanda reacted out of jealousy for the relationship she and Pearl had.

She poured from an amber decanter marked "bourbon" and drank the strong liquid in one big gulp. Feeling her heart pound against her chest, she took deep breaths and tried to calm down. Surrounded by reminders of the woman who had been there for her during every phase of her life, she tried but failed to understand why her mother was so against their relationship, especially now.

"Sorry, Daddy. Mom isn't jealous of Mother Pearl. Your wife is a snob. Always has been, and will probably never change."

She poured another drink, gulped it, and grabbed her jacket. Going back down the rear staircase, still fuming, she thought of Mason's condescending smile and became angry with her mother all over again. The cab ride allowed more than ample time to cool down before reaching Mason's apartment.

She finally arrived at the feeling she had when she saw Mason with another woman—a feeling of relief. He didn't love her any more than she loved him, but like Amanda, he wanted someone who would help him shine socially. Who better than the daughter of a socialite?

Her brief walk from the cab to his apartment gave her more time to think. This time, all of those thoughts were about John Jacob Tobias.

She heard a faint sound of music coming from the lavish apartment that Mason had rented after winning his first big case. She pounded her fist against the door and stood back from the peephole. After a long pause, he flung the door open and rushed toward her.

"Hello, Mason. Sorry to drop by unannounced, but this won't take long."

"Lacey. I can't believe you're here. I called you twice today to ask you to meet me for dinner tonight and once again, you refused to answer the phone or return my calls."

He was holding a drink and from the swagger in his otherwise staid step, Lacey knew this drink was not his first. His clothes were also disheveled and his eyes red-rimmed. She looked past him to the sofa where a woman with too much makeup and perceptibly fake breasts looked up in annoyance.

"I am interrupting your evening." She pushed past him. "Don't worry. I'm not planning to stay. I just need a few minutes of your time, and then you can get back to the business at hand." She raised an eyebrow as the blonde on the sofa straightened from her comfortable position and stared at the two of them.

"You didn't interrupt anything. This is Cindy, my next-door neighbor. She and I were just having a little drink. Come on in, I'll make one for you."

"No, thank you." She did not sit or remove her jacket. "I can say what I have to say in front of your guest, if it's okay with you."

Mason stared at the woman, who finally stood, gave him a disgusted nod, and walked past Lacey to the door.

"Will you call me later?" She passed her hand over Mason's face.

He ignored her and slammed the door. "I'm so glad you stopped by. I really wanted to see you tonight. I've had a bad day. A bad week. Lost an important case. I need the woman I love to cheer me up. Let me take your jacket and fix you a drink."

"I'm not staying. I'm just here to clear up some obvious misunderstandings between us."

"I'm glad you're here, baby. There are quite a few things I need to clear up, like the date of our wedding and how many years it will take to make up for the time we've been apart."

She brushed his hand from her thigh. "Don't bull-shit me, Mason. I just learned from my mother that you were dating someone in my absence and only agreed to give our relationship another try because she asked. Tell me about that."

"That's not exactly true. I was dating someone else because I didn't have you or think I ever would. Your mother made me see that you just had to work off the misery you suffered after your father and grandfather's death. I didn't give our relationship another try because of your mother." He grabbed her hand. "Just remember, I wasn't the one who walked out, and there's no reason for me to believe that you weren't having a thing with Tobias. In fact, I'd bet on it."

"I walked out on our relationship because of your unwillingness to understand my needs. Everything was and still is about what you want. When I wasn't around, you simply latched onto someone else, and that's fine. It's what I expected. What I didn't expect was to have you pull a hypocritical act of pretending to be lonely and waiting, and of still wanting to marry me."

He drained the glass. "I wanted to marry you before you left and I still do, but I wasn't about to sit around for a year while you were off at some riding camp." He swaggered to the sofa, grabbed her hand, and pulled her down with him. "And by the way, I know what kind of riding was going on up there."

When he tried to kiss her, she pulled away.

"I wasn't faithful and neither were you, but of all the women I've been with, you're the one I want to marry. You're the only one I wanted to marry, then and now. I had encouragement from your mother, but I bought the new ring and proposed because I want you to be my wife."

"And that's why you were here with this woman tonight? Come on, Mason." She took the jeweler's box from her purse and stood. "Here's your ring back, and don't do me any favors. Call your neighbor and resume your private party. You have every right to do so, and don't let my mother or anyone else convince you otherwise."

"Let's be real about this. I love you. I just got tired of waiting, but since you're here, everything is okay." Instead of taking the box, he grabbed the hand she held out, pulled her down to him, and forced his lips to hers. "Everything is fine now, baby. Just relax and let me show you how much I missed you."

"I don't think so, and I would appreciate it if you let go of me. In addition to being a whore, have you also become a drunk?" She tried to move away, but he gripped her arm tight enough for his fingernails to cause pain through her shirt and jacket.

"I'm a man trying to make the best of being jilted by the woman he loves. Yes, I do drink more now than before you left. This whole thing hasn't exactly been easy for me, especially when I learned that you were up there in the woods with Tobias."

"So you just started drinking and ending up in bed with whomever happened to be handy? I know you're selfish, but that doesn't sound at all like you." In spite of her anger, she wanted their parting to be one of mutual agreement and without rancor.

"Many things about our relationship will remain dear to me, but let's face it, Mason, it's over between us. You've moved on, and so have I. Let's just wish each other well."

He gripped her arm when she tried to stand. "Not this time, baby. I loved you enough to marry you, but you wanted to run off to the woods and spend a year sleeping with cowboys and Indians. Well, it's my turn now."

He slid his free hand under her shirt.

"Take your hands off me!" She slapped him hard, but he did not loosen his grip on her hand. "Let me go right now or you'll regret it."

"The only thing I regret right now is spending so much time trying to be a gentleman when you obviously prefer cave men, big tall Texans with boots and spurs. We've had some clock-stopping sex, and don't try and deny it. I'm not from Texas, baby, but I've got nothing to be ashamed of."

"You will if you don't let go of me. Think of how a rape conviction would look on your record." Anger flowed through her veins.

"Oh no, baby, I've got that covered. Thanks to your mother, a roomful of very distinguished people saw you accept my engagement ring, and I have at least one witness who saw you come here tonight of your own accord. Try to lay anything on me, and I make sure everyone knows that you spent the summer with John Tobias, except you thought he was some down-and-out cowboy. Your mother is right. Association has lowered your standards. You no longer have discriminating taste."

During his slurred attempt at degradation, Lacey was planning her next move. She relaxed against his hold and didn't flinch when he tugged her jacket from her shoulder. Mason was drunk and far from rational, but she was extremely alert. Thinking quickly, she became the aggressor. Moving to unburden herself of his weight, she allowed him to continue his grip on her arm and eased her body on top of his.

"You want me, don't you, baby? I knew it. Did the old cowboy come up a little short?"

She lay flat against him and kissed him hard, sucking his tongue into her mouth while lowering the hand that he was holding down to his zipper. He moaned as she slid her fingers up and down the front of his pants.

"You're wonderful, baby. No one can make me feel the way you do. I've suffered for months, knowing the woman I loved and wanted had left me. When I learned you were with another man, I damn near went crazy. I had other women, but I wanted you. I love you."

"Then let go of me. I don't want to make love this way."

Instead of letting go, he increased his grip. "If I let go, you'll run away, just like you did before."

"Okay, we'll do it your way." She now used both hands to navigate down his body. Each touch rendered him more relaxed and susceptible. She slid his pants down just enough to restrict any sudden moves from the sofa and tilted her body sideways, allowing her free arm to reach above the sofa back to a small bronze statue that sat next to the lamp. She strained forward and brushed it with her fingertips, but could not grasp the base.

"This is awkward. How am I supposed to enjoy being with you like this?" Moving slowly so as not to alarm him, she shifted further to the side and closed her right hand around the statue. Hesitating for just a second, she lifted it swiftly, and brought it down on the side of his temple. After jerking free of his grasp, she stood and backed away.

He tried to sit up, touched his hand to his head and felt the trickle of blood. His eyes rolled back in his head and he slumped backwards in mortified disbelief. "I'm bleeding! How could you do this?"

"Ask yourself that question! I came here to return your ring so you could comfortably continue your perverted games, but you're not playing them with me."

She buttoned her blouse and grabbed her jacket. "Let me tell you about those standards you spoke of. For all of your bogus class and sophistication, I'm now ashamed of having loved you, and even more ashamed of ever considering marriage. In my estimation, you're damn near the bottom of the barrel."

She ran from the building and took a cab back to the bakery. Her arm hurt and she felt in dire need of a shower, but instead of going inside, she went to the garage, sat in her Jeep. When the tremors of anger ceased, she drove to her mother's house and let herself in.

Amanda was alone, sitting quietly on the edge of the sofa. There was no television or music playing. The silence seemed almost eerie. She slowly lifted her head, but did not look at her daughter.

"Are you here to give me another of your frank assessments of my abilities as a wife and mother?" The shaky, tear-filled voice was bitter and sad.

"I'm sorry. That's what I came to say. Please forgive me. I had no right to say those things to you. I am truly sorry."

"Why be sorry if that's how you really feel?"

Small traces of mascara had lodged in the inner corners of her eyes. Her hair was flattened on one side, meaning she had been lying down. Lacey thought that at that moment, her mother looked nothing like the image she so vehemently sought to maintain. She looked human.

"You were a great mother and wife, but in your quest to ensure this lofty quality of life, you've taken a few too many liberties. I love you, Mom, and I value your opinion. I just want you to allow me to make my own choices."

"Fine. I'll do my best." She finally looked up and when she did, the sadness on her face changed to fright. "What happened to her jacket? Your face? Were you mugged?"

Lacey turned to the mirror on the wall. She had not realized that the arm of her jacket was torn. She had felt a burning sensation on her cheek and thought it was from the stubble on Mason's face. She moved closer to the mirror and saw that it was actually a small scratch that was swollen and red.

"Don't worry. I'm fine."

Amanda took Lacey's face in hands and inspected the scratch. "You're bleeding! Who did this to you? I'm calling the police."

"No, it's nothing, Mom." She tried to smile. "You should see the other guy."

"Tell me what happened."

"After what you said about Mason dating someone else and giving our relationship another try because you asked him to do so, I knew there was nothing left between us. I already knew it was over. I don't know, that whole episode in Oak Bluffs, losing Pearl and learning the man I had fallen for was someone else, I guess I wanted something to hold onto, and that was wrong. I went to see Mason, to return his ring."

"You didn't—"

"Please let me finish, Mom. I went to return his ring because I don't love him and I don't think he loves me. I guess he likes the way I look on his arm. Anyway, he tried to force himself on me, held me and wouldn't let go. I hit him with a statue and left."

"Oh, my God! Is he hurt badly? Is he going to be okay?"

Lacey nodded.

Amanda's eyes bulged and her face twisted in guilt. "I'm so sorry, Lacey. This is all my fault. Can you ever forgive me?"

"There's nothing to forgive, but I would like you to consider this the next time you decide that you know what, or in this case, who is best for me or for Nicholas. Let us make our own mistakes, and I'm sure we will, but then we'll have only ourselves to blame."

Amanda sobbed. "You should blame me. I can see why you and your brother hate me. I am a terrible mother, and I probably wasn't a very good wife."

Lacey sat beside her. "Mom, please don't cry. Nicholas and I do not hate you. We both love you very much. You were never a terrible mother. I shouldn't have said what I did earlier. You were a good wife. I know because Daddy was very happy."

Amanda turned to her. "I miss your father so much. I'm so lonely. You and Nicholas are all I have.

I need you both. If I appear too controlling, it's because I'm afraid of losing you and ending up alone."

Suddenly Lacey saw a different side of her mother. The side that Pearl had alluded to. Amanda wasn't good at showing her needs. Her dominance was the way she kept herself in their lives. "It's okay, Mom. I understand."

Amanda dried her eyes. "You do?"

"Yes." She smiled. "I think I do."

"I just wanted to be close to you." She dabbed her eyes. "I wanted you to talk to me the way you did with Pearl."

"I want that very much, Mom. I want to talk to you and I want your opinion, but you'll have to stop forcing me to see everything your way. If Nicholas and I can't make our own decisions, then we're not living our lives. We're living yours."

"You're right. It's just that you're all I have."

Lacey put her head on her mother's shoulder. "No, we're not. You have other family, lots of friends, and Mr. Rydell." She lifted her head and frowned. "Now, that's something I don't understand. You've been seeing that man for over a year, and I know you must have slept together by now, so why do you call him Mr. Rydell? I don't even remember his first name."

Amanda smiled. "You're right again. Maybe I should let you give me advice. You're so bright, and I'm an airhead."

"That's not true. You're the most beautiful, brilliant, and youthful mother anyone ever had, and I need you very much. I need your advice, so if you promise not to say those ugly things about Mother Pearl, I would like for you to help me with the apartment."

"Really?" She tried to smile. "I would like that, and I will never say anything bad about Pearl. I guess I was just jealous. You were always closer to her than you were to me. Even as a little girl, you wanted Pearl to tuck you in and tell you stories."

"Well, I'll have to admit, Mother Pearl did spin a good yarn."

They both laughed and hugged.

"I'm not perfect and I'm not the socialite you are. There can be only one Amanda Daigle, and I'm proud to call her Mom. Please be proud of who I am."

With the fences between her and Amanda mended, Lacey decided to concentrate on her own life and finding a job. She sat in the bakery with the ads from the *New York Times,* circling anything that was remotely in her line of expertise. She was aware of having left her last position in a hurry and hoped she would not appear irresponsible. She had given proper notice and stayed a week beyond her scheduled departure date to train her replacement. Thinking that should level the surface, she did not hesitate to list the name and phone number of her old boss on her résumé.

When the mail arrived, she hurriedly ripped into the envelope from Warren & Douglas, unfolded the contents, and removed the check that was stapled to the front of the letter.

"Tobias Ranch." She read aloud. "I miss you, John Jacob Tobias." She held the check to her chest. "More than you will ever know."

She held onto it for five days before taking it to the bank, painfully closing another chapter of her life. Pearl was gone, Camp Noepe was sold, and she would never see John again. The finality left her shaken, but firmly intent on keeping herself above pity.

Knowing the physical altering of the apartment would not take very long, she reviewed the plans and made a list of her major purchases. While searching for a calculator in the box of desk items from Camp Noepe, she found a green cloth-covered book. Thumbing through pages of slanted and curved handwriting brought a lump of sadness to her heart. It was Pearl's diary.

She stacked the book on top of her calculator and ledger sheet and went back downstairs to escape the construction noise. Taking a back booth, she ignored Elfie and Peter's stares and opened the diary. The first entry was dated July 21 of the previous year. Realizing that was before they left for Massachusetts, she succumbed to curiosity.

After reading the first three entries, she wiped her eyes and muttered under her breath, "My God! She knew she was going to die."

She took a long sip of coffee and turned the page. She could not believe her eyes. Pearl had more than a slight ability to see the future. By the time she read the last entry, her eyes were burning and her nose was glowing red. It was clear that Pearl knew she was going to die and clear that she had been convinced a marriage would take place. She shook her head. None of it made sense. John was out of her life. How would they ever get back together?

"Hey, sis." Nicholas was standing before her, and became alarmed when he saw she had been crying. "What's wrong?"

"I want to tell you, but I'm sure you'll laugh like everyone else." She clutched the book to her chest.

"Lacey, you can tell me anything. I've never laughed at you."

"Not at me, at Mother Pearl. She knew she was going to die, Nicholas. She knew before she left for the island that she would never come back to New York, that she would die there. That's why she made the will and detailed the kind of funeral she wanted."

When he looked skeptical, she tried to explain. "Contrary to what Mom thinks, Mother Pearl did have powers to see certain things. She saw pictures, dream sequences, but while she was awake. They showed events in the future. Here, read this."

She watched her brother's face as he read through the entries and saw his nose turn scarlet. "Do you believe it now?"

"I guess I have to." He sniffled and wiped his eyes with the back of his hand. "It all seems so…strange."

"It's not strange. I think we all have certain powers, even you and I. It's when you feel something is going to happen, or something doesn't feel right about a certain situation. Her power was just more refined. She saw specific events. She knew she was going to die, even after Doctor Max said she was very healthy."

"She also said you'll marry this man. What do you think about that?"

She clutched the diary to her chest and felt Pearl's closeness. Her lips parted in a broad grin. "I think if I'm going to marry Monroe Faulkner, better known as John Jacob Tobias, I'd better get to know the man a little better."

CHAPTER 15

After a lengthy search in the jumble of moving boxes, Lacey found the phone number of Abby DeLarusso, a college friend from New Orleans who was now a news anchor for a Dallas television station.

"Abby, it's Lacey. I'm sorry I didn't make the shopping trip back in December. My project was just getting started and I couldn't leave. I'm back in New York. Mother Pearl died and I'm renovating her apartment. When it's finished, we can have a shopping spree here in New York."

Lacey accepted Abby's condolences and spent a few minutes talking before asking for help. "Listen Abby, I need a favor, and, at the risk of sounding pushy, I need it right away. I need everything you can find on John Jacob Tobias."

When Abby questioned her request, Lacey said it was a business matter and asked Abby to fax the information as quickly as possible. The phone rang forty-five minutes later and Abby advised her to stand by for the fax. Her heart began to pound when she saw his likeness on the page. The faxed photo was of poor quality, but she didn't need a reminder; she knew each dimple and curve on his face.

There was even a wedding notice and photo of his bride. Lacey saw, with astonishment, the striking resemblance. "My God! He showed me a photograph of his wife, but in this one, she looks like my twin. No wonder the man freaked out when he first came to Camp Noepe. He was trying to recover from the memories of his dead wife and had to live with a constant reminder."

She read each article with interest. There were stories about his father, Nathaniel, and his grandfather. There were wedding announcements for his sisters and several articles about John. When she found the one about his wife's accident, she wanted to fly to him and hold him close.

"Lacey!" Amanda stumbled into the room. "When will the elevator be repaired? Those steps are murder, and how can you stand this noise?" She saw Lacey's expression. "I'm sorry. I promised not to complain and I start before I even say hello. It's just that I'm not good at climbing steps."

Lacey laughed. "It's okay, Mom. I didn't expect you to go cold turkey. I wouldn't want you to. You might blow a gasket."

"What are those?" She pointed to the clippings.

"I'm gathering information on your soon-to-be son-in-law."

"Excuse me?" Amanda's eyes popped. "What are you talking about?"

Lacey told her all about John and about Pearl's prediction that they would marry. "I know you don't believe that she could see into the future, but she could. She knew she would die on the island. She wrote it here in this diary."

"Honey, you can't just decide to marry someone based on what Pearl wrote or what she saw. Are you in love with John Tobias?"

Lacey straightened her shoulders and took a deep breath. "I am more in love with him than I ever could have been with Mason. I can't even describe how he makes me feel. I tense up when he enters the room, can't get my words out correctly when he's around, and when we were together, I was never happier." She felt his presence as she spoke. "After being with John, I don't know that any other man could ever satisfy me."

"I don't know about this, son." Nathaniel Tobias shook his head. "From what you've told me, the only reason this young woman turned on you was anger over being lied to. Why do you think this will be different?"

"It is different, Pop. Lacey doubted herself and me. I have to show her how much I care, and it can't be just a matter of spending money. If I went to New York right now, she'd think I was just there because I could afford the fare. It has to be more than that."

"So how does the Indian family fit into this?"

He thought of Pearl and laughed. "Native American, Pop. They're taking care of things on the island. They live in Aquinnah. One of Shale's sisters owns the catering business."

"I don't know Lacey as well as you do, but I do know women. This is something most of them dream of doing. Your sisters spent years planning theirs. I think Lacey will want to make some of these decisions herself."

"There will be plenty left for her to do, both there and here. I thought about offering to build her another house, and I will, but she might just like to redo the one I have and the one on her family's land in Oak Bluffs. We'll be the Tobias family of Denham Wells and Oak Bluffs."

He laughed and couldn't stop. "She's so sweet, Pop. Her mother is a big snob, and Lacey is about as down-to-earth as a woman can be. You should have seen with the horses, especially her favorite, Champion."

"Build her a house. I do know how much a house means to any woman with an ounce of domesticity. We'll let your brother have this one if he ever gets his life together. Is there anything I can do?"

"Pop, right now, I just need to know that you're in my corner."

Nathaniel shook his head. "I want more than anything in this world for you to be happy, to find another love. In addition to your happiness, I know that your progeny is the only chance I have to keep this business and the family name alive."

"You have grandchildren. Surely one of the five will be interested in the business."

"John, your sister Lorraine is married to a man she can't trust behind a light post. He disrespects his marriage, treats her like shit, and doesn't know the meaning of the word father. Ellen's husband is nice and kind, but he has the aspirations of a squirrel—a few nuts to eat, a branch to sit on, and a leaf over his head. If it weren't for me, Ellen and those children would starve to death."

"You're right. I wish both Lorraine and Ellen would come to their senses, but their lives are still respectable, even if the men they married aren't."

"They both appear to have respectable lives, but other than the perception, what do they have? So far, I've been praying that recessive genes would take over, but from what you've said, this Lacey is everything a woman should be. She'll make a good wife and mother. I know there's no guarantee when dealing with children, but being a logical, practical man, I'll put my money on you two."

"Lacey is great with children and she's really smart. I looked for reasons not to fall in love with her, and the best I could come up with is that she is headstrong and hates to show her weakness. Wish me luck, Pop."

"I wish you all the luck in the world, but it may just take more than that." He placed his hand on his son's shoulder. "If this young woman is that stubborn and headstrong, you'll need a miracle."

John watched his father walk away. Taking the frame from the large mahogany desk in front of him, he spoke to the smiling face. "This is it, Deb. I will never forget the joy of hearing that I was going to be a father. I want to hear it again. Lacey is special. I know you'd approve." He touched the glass with his fingertips. "I'll always love you."

He placed the photo back in the center of the desk, stood and walked over to stare out the window. There was so much land. Lacey loved horses and she loved the outdoors. Surely she could be happy there.

He returned to his desk and picked up the telephone. There was still much to be done and since he wasn't sure just how much time he had to complete it, he felt rushed and anxious. He hoped to win her back, hoped he was not making the biggest mistake of his life.

Lacey spent a restless night thinking of ways to bring John back into her life. By morning, she was tired, but she had a plan.

"What do you think of this, Mother? I'll send him an engraved thank-you for purchasing Camp Noepe and wish him well. He was very fond of Mother Pearl, so I'll tell him that I'm refurbishing her apartment and when the repairs are complete, I'd like to show him some New York hospitality."

"Fine, dear, but don't phrase it that way. New York doesn't have a reputation of being the most hospitable city in the U.S." Amanda lugged the thick pad of swatches to the bed. "Look at this against the finish. We want your guest bedroom to be perfect, especially if you're going to invite Mr. John Tobias for the weekend. Of course, if you're lucky, he won't need the guest room."

"I don't know. Maybe that's too long range. What can I do to get him here now?"

"Invite him to my house." Amanda gestured. "Since you refuse to move home, I have lots of unused space. Too much."

"So you do approve?" Lacey was still skeptical of her mother's new cooperative attitude.

"What's not to approve of? I saw this man. He's absolutely gorgeous. He's also wealthy. I'll have to trust your judgment on the rest," she said with a smile. "And I do. By the way, I told Mason how I felt about him this morning."

"Why did you even bother calling?"

"I didn't. He called me. Said you refused to speak with him and wanted to know if I would talk to you. I told him after what he tried to pull, the only one I would speak with is the police and have his ass arrested."

"Watch out, you're beginning to sound like Mother Pearl." Lacey laughed. "Nicholas came by. Mason apologized to him, but I hadn't told Nicholas, so he had no idea what Mason was speaking of. When I told him, he got raving mad."

"Did Nicholas punch him?"

"Mom! You have become a wild woman. Aren't you worried about Nicholas's job?"

"Not at all. As soon as you told me what happened, I began making other arrangements for Nicholas. I have connections, you know."

Lacey laughed and hugged her mother while answering the phone. "Yes, Douglas. How are you?"

Her smile disappeared. "What? Did you call the bank? Are they going to run it through again?"

Amanda waited until she hung up. "What's wrong?"

"The check John sent, payment for Camp Noepe. It bounced."

"What do you think happened? Did Douglas know?"

"The check was written on an account that the bank says was closed months ago. Douglas has left three messages for John and not a peep."

"I don't know what to make of this. According to Mason, this man is rich. His whole family is rich. Why would his check bounce?"

"Well, Mom, there's real wealth and there's purported wealth. Maybe this is one of those situations where the money is long gone, but the family continues on name alone. It happens."

"But if he didn't have the money, why would he attempt to buy your camp? It wasn't something he had to do." Amanda went into a thoughtful repose. "Something is fishy here, my darling. What did Douglas suggest you do?"

"He said to give it a couple of days and if John didn't respond to his requests, we would think of another option. He believes it was just an oversight."

Amanda gave her a sharp frown. "I don't believe in oversights. Not from someone like Tobias. That whole episode of impersonating a dead man and now this. I trust your judgment, but something is definitely wrong with this picture."

CHAPTER 16

"Yank, how's it going, man?" He cradled the phone to his shoulder. "It's John."

"Just fine, John. Everything's in place. I can't tell you how happy you've made my father. He gets up early every morning and goes down to visit Pearl's sister so they can share ideas on the center. He wants to make sure you bring in a lot of literature, some on natives and some on African-Americans. He also wants to be the a curator, or whatever you would call it."

John laughed. "That's fine with me. I'm just glad I was able to do something to help him get through his grief. I hope I can do the same for Lacey."

"How is that going?"

"It's all set. We just have to wait for her to take the bait. I'll call you the second I know something, so tell the family to keep a bag packed."

John had barely hung up when his private line rang again. "John Tobias. Yes, Doug. I see. Mad as hell, I take it," he said and chuckled. "I can't tell you how grateful I am for your help, and I promise not to involve you if things turn sour. Thank you."

He caught a glimpse of his father passing the door. "Hey, Pop. It's just a matter of time now. Keep you fingers crossed."

"I hope you know what you're doing. I don't want to think of what'll happen if this turns out poorly."

He answered the phone again. "Yes, this is he. Excuse me? Of course I remember you. It's no bother at all. In fact, I couldn't be happier to hear from you."

Nathaniel watched his son's face as J.J.'s bewildered frown slowly turned into a huge smile.

Lacey went to the spa to try and relax. When she returned, she found Mason pacing the bakery floor.

"What are you doing here?"

"I've got to talk to you, Lacey. First to apologize and try and explain, and then to make you understand how much I love you, really love you."

"Don't you think it's a little too late for that? Have you forgotten what happened the last time we talked? By the way, you look absolutely horrible. What happened? Did someone take away your class?"

She grinned at his discomfort and took a seat in a back booth. "Say what you came to say. I'm busy right now and I plan to be even busier in the days to come."

"There are some things you don't understand. I'm not…" He grabbed his face with both hands and shook his head. "My life started to fall apart the night you left me at the restaurant. I don't know what's happening to me, Lacey. Everything was so perfect until them. My career was going well, I was saving money, had our life together all planned. I was happy. Now everything I touch turns sour."

She had never seen him so distraught. "I don't understand. Tell me what you mean."

"I've lost the last three cases I tried, failed in damn near all negotiations, and lost a ton of money in an investment that went bad. I'm drinking because I feel my life spiraling out of control and I don't know how to make it stop. What I did the other night, you know that's not me. I don't have a violent bone in my body, especially not with women. In my right mind I would never try and force you to be with me. I'm losing it, Lacey." His eyes were wet. "You've got to help me."

"I'm sorry you're having problems, but I don't see how I can help."

"I love you, Lacey. I'm not just saying that. I love you with all my heart. You hurt me deeply when you left. I'm not accustomed to losing, especially not someone who means so much to me. Just give me another chance to prove it to you."

"Mason, why do you feel that me giving you another chance will solve your problems?"

"Because I just know that once I'm happy again, things will change for me professionally. This all started the day you left, just little things at first, but now everything I do is wrong."

Lacey was no longer listening. Fighting back a smile, she took Mason's hand. "I'm so sorry you're having problems, and I'll try and help you, but not by becoming your wife. That wouldn't work for either of us. Let's just try to be friends. You'll find someone else to love and get your life straight. I'm sure of it. I'll be here for you if you need me. I promise."

As soon as he left, she went up to her apartment and closed the bedroom door against the noise of hammers and saws. "Mother Pearl, I pray you can hear me, because I have something important to say. I never heard you mention placing a spell on anyone, but I do remember what you promised to do to anyone who hurt me. If you've done something to cause problems for Mason, please do me a favor and…" The old clock chimed and Lacey covered her mouth to stifle the laugh. "Oh, Mother Pearl, I miss you, so much."

"Okay Mother, I think I've waited long enough." Lacey swung the door open and began ranting. "I was going to instruct Douglas to turn this matter over to the authorities, but I received a call from Yank Whitefeather this morning. He and his family were offered work restoring the camp, and now they're sitting there waiting to hear from this impostor to call. They don't even know if they have employment."

"Maybe something happened to him. From what you and Mason said, he doesn't seem the type to just write hot checks and disappear."

"He didn't seem the type to do a lot of the things that he's admitted doing. Our relationship began on a lie. It might as well end the same way. You have no idea how hard I tried not to fall in love with him. I damn near suffocated from the emotions I kept inside, and I'll be damned if the same blasted day I allowed him all the way into my life, I find out he's a lying dog. There's one thing I know for sure, I'm swearing off men forever."

"No, dear, you can't do that. You're young. Your whole life is ahead of you. I know the right man is out there. Maybe John is the right man. You'll just have to give him a chance."

"A chance to do what? Break my heart, again? No way. The first time I saw this man, the first second, my heart almost jumped from my chest. Every time he walked into a room, my knees turned into products of Goodyear. He lashed out at me and I lashed back, when all I really wanted to do was fall into his arms. When that finally happened, I was like a kid, hungry, thirsty, and insatiable. I couldn't get enough of him. I wanted him so badly that when he tried to tell me the truth, I was busy trying to take off his pants."

Amanda was silent.

"I don't mean to shock you, but you wanted me to talk to you so I'm trying—"

"Oh, no," Amanda answered. "I'm glad you're talking to me and I'm not shocked. I saw this man, remember? If they grow them all this way down in Texas, I'm going to say goodbye to Larry Rydell and hop on a plane."

"Mom, it's embarrassing. We played cat and mouse for most of the summer and when he said he wanted to get to know me, I just fell into that trap. When I learned he had lied, I wasn't nearly as angry as I should have been, and I was about to forgive him. When Camp Noepe burned, I don't know, it seemed like some kind of sign. I just wanted to get the hell away from the island and not look back, but he followed me. His voice, his touch, he's here with me, day and night. Sometimes I think I'm losing my mind."

Amanda sat on the bed and toyed with the fabric swatches. "Sounds like you're in love."

"I've been telling myself that. When I read that Mother Pearl saw us married, it was all I needed to get my hopes up again. Now I'm sitting here with a rubber check, but that's okay. I figured out Mother Pearl's vision. In fact, I've had one of my own. John and I will be together, and I will be dressed in white, standing, victoriously, over his dead body."

"You have every right to be angry, but don't jump to conclusions. As I said, just wait until we've solved this riddle to determine if he's a heel."

"I know he's a heel, not just for what he's done to me, but for the agony he's caused the Whitefeathers. I feel responsible for them, Mom. I also feel like getting on a plane to Fort Worth and telling that bastard just how much I've grown—"

"That's it!" Amanda yelled. "Why didn't I think of this before? Go to Texas and confront John Tobias.

Know what? I'll come with you. I doubt that any man in the world could stand up to both of us. Let's do it, honey. What do you say?"

Lacey frowned. "Are you sure you want to do this?"

"Since your father's death, I've had a full schedule, but those evenings at the opera, dining with friends, none of those things made me happy. They were just ways of killing time so I wouldn't have to think of being alone. I'm so glad that you and I can talk now, and I want to be with you there in Texas when you confront this man. I want to be with you anytime you need me. Start packing. I'll make the airline and hotel reservations."

Lacey took the bag from the back shelf of Pearl's closet, the same one she had taken to Oak Bluffs. Since reading Pearl's diary, she had slept with visions of a wedding in her head, visions of standing next to John and placing her hand in his. Now, once again, a crushing boulder of disappointment had fallen on her dreams. She thought of Yank and Shale. Off-season employment was scarce on the island. Shale had taken a position as a teacher's assistant, while Yank and Tedera were doing light carpentry and hauling jobs. Micah had started college, but worked with them when he could.

Lacey packed hurriedly, then stopped and sat on the bed. "Why the hell am I rushing? I don't know when Mom will be able to get us out of here." She closed her bag and took the stack of articles and news clippings from the nightstand and studied each of them closely. Pearl had trusted and believed in this man. She wanted to do the same, but how could she?

Only knowing she wanted to look her best, she called for a spa appointment, learned there was a cancellation, and hurried down for a taxi. After a ninety-minute massage and a facial, she was still too anxious to relax. She headed back to the apartment with a container of takeout from Dang's. Noting the time, she called Pearl's accountant, hoping for a positive update.

"Prepare to be pleasantly shocked," he said. "The bakery's books not only balance, it's the best non-professional bookkeeping I've seen lately."

It was the one piece of good news she had received lately. Thinking Elfie and Peter were too afraid of Pearl to pocket profits from the bakery, she stopped in and informed them she would have the attorney draft a contract giving them twenty-percent ownership in the bakery. With one less uncertainty on her mind, the sale of Camp Noepe loomed large, as did thoughts of John.

She lay across the bed next to her bag, exhausted from anger and frustration. Hugging her arms around her body, she tried to recall each touch, each word that was said when they were together. "This is so unfair!" She pounded the pillow with her fists.

Overcome with fatigue, she drifted off to sleep. In her fitful slumber, she saw John's face. She was standing at an altar and he was there. He lifted her veil and pressed his lips against hers, and in the slow-motion trance, she saw Pearl's broad smile.

Amanda's voice, followed by sharp raps on the door, woke her.

"Mom?" Still groggy, she ran to the door and found her mother surrounded by her trademark designer luggage. "What is this? What's going on?"

"Aren't you packed? I told you I was going to make the arrangements. Don't worry. We have an afternoon flight. There's plenty of time. Get dressed and we can have a bite down in your bakery before going to the airport."

Lacey was still trying to clear her head. "Mom, you're here early in the morning, which is a rarity, packed and ready to go to Fort Worth. This is unbelievable."

Amanda grimaced. "You know something, Lacey, maybe this is what I need. I'm only fifty-three. I have a lot of life left, and I know your father would want me to live it. I want to do more things with you, travel, entertain, take in shows, dine in fancy restaurants. I'm not saying I want to be your pal. I'm proud and happy to be your mother, but I want to share as much of your life as I can. That goes for Nicholas as well."

"I want that, too, Mom, but what about Mr. Rydell? You do enjoy his company, don't you?"

"My world fell apart when your father was killed. I tried to carry on as before because I didn't want anyone feeling sorry for me, but I was still up in the air. Larry Rydell became my comfortable landing spot. I do care for him and I enjoy him, but he is just about the stodgiest man I know. He never wants to do anything fun. Your father and I used to dance together, we laughed, I don't know, did silly things. He called me his baby, and I wanted so much to remain his baby for the rest of my life."

She wiped her eyes and took Lacey's hand. "When I heard you talking about this John and how he made you feel, I realized that I haven't felt like that since your father left us. I want to feel that way again. I know I'm acting like a fool, but—"

"Stop, you're acting like a woman. A vibrant and very alive woman who wants to feel passion and the thrill a man's arms should bring. There's nothing wrong with that. You're a young woman. Even Mother Pearl found romance before she died. Those last months in Oak Bluffs were very happy for her."

Amanda's eyebrows lifted in a quizzical frown. "She did? I'm shocked. Who was it?"

"Tedera, Yank's father. She denied the attraction at first, but Tedera was persistent. In fact, he was with her on that last night. I saw him leaving her bedroom."

"I would never have believed it." She shook her head in wonder. "So Yank is the very tall man with the big shoulders, and his father is the man with the long braid down his back? If I recall, he was pretty good-looking for an old man."

"That's him," Lacey said as she finished packing. "Beautiful smooth tan skin, salt and pepper hair, and a sort of recklessness about him. I think that's what did it. He is a hard-living drinker, who probably never shed a tear in his life until Pearl's death. She obviously touched him, and I know he touched her. She was so happy with him, giddy almost."

"Well, I'm happy for Pearl. I'm glad she found excitement and love. I'm going to start looking for the same thing. I want to go a little wild while I'm still young enough to get away with it."

Lacey smiled. She had always suspected there was a hidden streak of untamed adventure in her mother, but was still surprised to see it emerge. There were times, back when her father was alive, when she would overhear private talks between her parents. She always hurried out of earshot, but the naughty things she overheard told her Amanda was more than a little risqué.

"I wanted everything to be just right for you and Nicholas. I wanted to protect you, to make sure your lives ran smoothly, but you've made me see that smooth can be very boring. We need the excitement of a roller coaster—up and down. Maybe it's the downs that make the ups so enjoyable."

"I believe you're right. I need someone like John in my life. I'm just sorry he turned out to be such a louse."

"Remember the motto of justice, innocent until proven guilty. There could be a simple explanation for what's happened." She winked. "Let's go find out."

Lacey fidgeted in her seat and wondered why Amanda appeared so calm. They arrived at DFW at four-fifteen and felt the steam of a Texas summer.

"Now I know where hell is," Lacey told Amanda as they waited for their luggage. "It's like a sauna. Did anyone tell them summer is over?"

"I'm sure it's something you could adjust to if you stayed here long enough." Amanda was still smiling. "Besides, it's good for the skin."

Lacey was still in shock at the change in her mother's attitude. "I don't understand you at all. You're usually the one complaining, and I've never known you to do anything on the spur of the moment. I thought words like spontaneous were totally absent from your vocabulary."

"Spontaneous is the way I intend to operate from now on. Predictability is boring." She pursed her lips in disgust. "Just watch me, dear. I'm going to prove to you, and to myself, that I can be spontaneous, a little wild, and very bad sometimes, all without losing my femininity."

Lacey laughed and pointed to the revolving carousel. "There's part of your luggage. They probably had to use two carousels. As usual, you packed enough for a month."

"Just tried to anticipate the weather here. From what I understand, it's very mercurial. Get one of those carts, would you dear? We can take a cab to the hotel. I have a rental car waiting there. We can drive on out to this man's place this evening."

"Do you think we should? Tomorrow is soon enough. We can rest and get an early start in the morning."

"No, I think it's best to go tonight. It's Friday. Who knows what plans these people might have for the weekend. If you don't go today, you might not be able to see him until Monday. Besides, I want to put this mess behind us so we can do a little shopping. Dallas is very urbane with lots of wonderful high-end malls, and I think we both deserve a little relaxation."

"Yeah! I can call Abby DeLarusso, the friend who sent the information on John." Saying his name reminded her of the purpose of their trip. "You're right, we need to get this over with so I can lose this ton of rocks in my stomach."

After the luggage was piled in the back of the taxi, Amanda giggled excitedly.

"I know this is an unpleasant mission for you, but I think once the mission is accomplished, we just might enjoy our trip to Texas. I've always wanted one of those western outfits, you know, with the hat and matching boots."

"Do you realize that anything we purchase will have to be shipped home? Either that or purchase more luggage. I forgot to ask, when are we returning home?"

"Monday, if everything goes well."

They checked into a two-bedroom suite at the Four Seasons and Amanda started unpacking.

"I'm going to shower and change for dinner, dear. Why don't you do the same?"

Lacey took the navy pantsuit from her bag and hung it over the bathroom door so the steam from the shower could loosen the wrinkles. She allowed the warm water to wash away some of her apprehension, but each time she thought of John, her insides contracted and her heartbeat tripled.

Amanda was waiting in Lacey's bedroom, wrapped in a hotel robe. Her face was plastered with cream.

"What are you planning to wear, dear?"

"Navy pantsuit. Very casual. There's no need for anything dressy. After all, this isn't a social call. I'm here to get my money or John Tobias's hide, and right now I think the latter would give me more satisfaction. I should wear combat boots, a pith helmet, and a mean-ass assault rifle draped over my shoulder."

"Well, honey, these people might be barbarians, but we're not. I say we dress in our finery and after we've made mincemeat from this John Tobias, we can go out on the town. I got a list of evening entertainment when I made the reservations. There's a lot to do here in Fort Worth."

"I didn't pack the way you did, Mother. What are you suggesting we wear?"

"Don't worry about it, dear. I assumed your mind was too clogged with anger to properly pack, so I brought enough for both of us. I thought a nice dinner suit for the evening. Come over to my room and choose one. Isn't it great that we're the same size?"

Lacey followed her mother across the living room and found her bed covered in designer finery.

"The cream would be stunning on you, and I have a Judith Leiber bag, and little rhinestone shoes to match. Take the black, if you like it better. It's your choice."

"You're something else, Mom. I didn't come here with a single thought of dressing for dinner. I could wear wading boots and a camouflage coat for the mission I'm on, as long as I had a long shotgun." She dropped her head.

"What's wrong?"

"Nothing. I just thought of Mother Pearl. She was never without that shotgun. I'm glad I gave it to Tedera before the fire."

"I'm glad she was there for you, and sorry she left us so soon. Right now, I dearly wish she were here. If two Daigle women are a formidable force, just think how intimidating three of us would have been."

"Thank you. I know Mother Pearl wasn't your favorite person, but I miss her so much."

"I was wrong about Pearl. I was wrong about a lot of things, and I wish I could take back every unkind word I said. There's no way to do that, so let's make the best of being together. I know Pearl would approve, so let's not fret. This man has never seen you as lovely as you're going to be tonight. He'll get the shock of his life."

"I'm beginning to think this plan was ill-conceived. How do we know Tobias is home, or if he is, how do we know he's not in the middle of something important? Isn't it rude to just barge in on people this way?"

"Lacey, this man gave you a bad check. What could be ruder than that? If we call and he doesn't want to see you, he'll just leave. This way we sneak out there and nab him when he least expects it. Anyone who writes bad checks doesn't deserve consideration."

"And he broke my heart, don't forget that."

"And we'll make him damn sorry he did those things. That's why I want you to look ravishing when we meet him. It would serve little purpose to go there in jeans." Amanda pulled a small box from her handbag. "Wear these diamond earrings. Let this man see what he's missing."

Lacey stared at the ensemble on her bed and thought, for once, she agreed with Amanda. John had only seen her in work and casual clothes. She applied more makeup than usual, stepped into the mist of cologne she spritzed in front of her, and dabbed another touch behind each ear. Allowing a few strands of hair to fall into her face, she pulled the rest back into a sheik little knot. Then the cream suit, burnished gold shoes with rhinestone straps and matching bag. After adding the diamond earrings, she practiced walking in the very high heels and then went across to Amanda's door.

"Are you ready, Mom?"

Amanda was wearing the black suit with pale pink piping. The look on her face was one of sheer excitement.

"You are stunning," Lacey said, opening her arms. "I love you so much. I'm glad you're my mother, and I'm glad you're here with me."

"Oh, thank you, dear, and you look ravishing. You're much too good for Mason. I'm glad you were more insightful than I was. You're beautiful and brainy. Full of grace and elegance. I look at you and know I've succeeded in passing the torch. That man won't know what hit him."

"And by the time he recovers, we'll be back in New York."

Amanda smiled and led the way to the elevator. "I'll get the car and you can get directions from the concierge."

Lacey watched heads turn as they walked through the lobby and swelled with pride as she hurried out to the car.

"According to the girl at the desk, the Tobias place is outside of town. She said to take the Turnbull exit off Highway 45, keep driving and you can't miss it. Okay, Mom. We're going out for a little Tobias hunting."

They drove and talked, with Amanda still trying to convince Lacey to calm down, which Lacey found impossible to do.

"I want to calm down, but can you imagine how this feels? I fought with this man the first day he arrived, and that was mild compared to the blowup we had on the beach. But when his arms were around me, I felt ten feet tall. Now we're back to square one."

Thinking they had driven too far, Lacey had Amanda consult the map.

"The hotel clerk said we couldn't miss it, but we've been driving almost an hour and I don't see anything that says Tobias."

"Everything is bigger in Texas. Remember? When you're told something is right down the road, it's usually the distance from New York to Massachusetts."

"I still think we've gone too far. See if you can read the name of this road at the next intersection."

Amanda unfolded the map and glanced up to read the green and white sign. "We haven't gone too far. From the looks of the map...oh my goodness, it's here. It's on the map."

"What's on the map?"

"The Tobias Ranch. It's on the map. Looks like about another mile. There's the exit. Turnbull Road. It dead ends into the Tobias Ranch. No wonder the young woman said we couldn't miss it."

❧

Lacey's hands were clammy and her chest heaved and caved. She was happy for her mother's company, but thought she would have felt much better to have Pearl and her shotgun in the passenger's seat. Overcome with misgivings, she took a deep breath and felt so lightheaded, she thought she might faint.

"Are you okay? Your face is flushed. I can see it under your makeup."

"I'm not okay, Mom, I'm nervous. John can be gruff at times. I'm not sure he'll appreciate us coming all the way to Texas to tell him off. What if the check is a mistake like Douglas said, and he isn't even aware of it? This is wrong. We should—"

"We should calm down. You fell in love with this man, so he can't be all bad. Other than show us the door, what can he do? If you feel this might be a mistake, then don't say anything about the check. Just play it by ear. If he's ugly, we'll get ugly right back."

"Do you even know how to be ugly?"

"If I have to, yes, I do. I'm as nice as I'm allowed be, but if I'm pushed, I can become very ugly. Don't you worry. Maybe I wasn't always there for you the way I needed to be in the past, but I'm here now. I'll be with you, no matter what. You're good for me. You've made me see a lot of things more clearly. I didn't tell you this, but I called your brother last night. I thought about what you said. He was happier with that girl than without her, just as you were happier with John than with Mason. I had no right to ruin their relationship, and I told him so. We're all going out to dinner when you and I get back to New York."

"You don't know how good that makes me feel."

"I'll tell you something else. I don't know how much of Pearl's visions I believe, but I do know that she loved you, and I believe she's here with you, too."

Lacey chocked back a sob. "That one of the nicest things you've ever said. Thank you. I know she's here. Tedera said I've gained a guardian angel, and I believe it."

"There. There's the sign. Slow down."

Lacey looked to the right at the endless blanket of green, the white fence, and the sign that hung on a large metal gate. Tobias Ranch. The name was arched over a circled TR. Panic set in.

"Now don't be nervous, honey. I'm not just saying this because I'm your mother, but there isn't a man alive who wouldn't melt at the sight of you. Don't give this John Tobias a second thought. We'll just knock on his door and ask for a moment of his time. Turn here."

"Mom! Look at the cars! They're having some kind of—"

"And aren't you glad we're dressed? Pull over there and park behind that Mercedes."

Lacey was awed. "This isn't a house, it's some kind of compound. Like the gangsters have. A wing for each family member. This looks like Southfork, that house on the TV show *Dallas*."

"As I said, this is Texas. Everything is supposed to be bigger here."

"Look back there! Horses." She heard sounds from the middle structure. Live music. "Oh, Mother, I'm not sure I want to do this. We can't interrupt these people's party. That really is a social no-no."

"We've come too far to turn back. Maybe it's good they're having a party. That means John is here, and we can just mingle with the guests until you feel like confronting him. We'll have our say and then find a place to have a little fun. I've never partied in Texas, but if these men all look like John Tobias, I think I'm going to like it."

Lacey followed Amanda down the paved path from the motor court to a bricked driveway and then slowed her pace, feeling scared and lost.

"Come on, dear." Amanda reached for her hand. "Let's go in and give them something to talk about."

"Tell me again why this is a good idea, because I've never felt so wrong in my life. There's no telling what kind of party they're having. Suppose someone is getting married. Oh, God! John could be getting married. That certainly would have kept him too busy to return Douglas's calls." She stepped to the grass and turned back. "Let's get the hell out of here."

Before Amanda could speak, the side door opened, and a short, round man in a butler's uniform smiled and bowed.

"Good evening, ladies. I will announce your arrival, and I do hope you enjoy your visit. Your names, please."

Lacey cowered behind her mother.

"Mrs. and Ms. Daigle," Amanda touted proudly.

Lacey peeped inside and knew they were not over-dressed. Designer outfits filled the large and lavish room. A band was set up just outside the glass doors. Beyond, a giant waterfall, surrounded by tropical foliage reminiscent of a Hawaiian landmark, cascaded into an Olympic-size swimming pool. She glanced over the crowd, searching for John.

The butler announced them in a deep, thick voice. "Mrs. Amanda Daigle, and Ms. Lacey Daigle."

"How did he know our first names?" Amanda whispered, as the crowd broke into frenzied applause. Amanda moved quickly to the side of the room, leaving Lacey alone in the spotlight. She looked around the room of strangers.

"Mom!" She moved to catch up with Amanda and stopped short when she saw her brother standing next to the Whitefeathers.

"There she is," John proudly announced. "What do you think?"

"Stunning," Natty answered, twisting his head for a better view.

"She is stunning, son." Nathaniel looked from Lacey to Amanda. "And if that's her mama, I wanna be her daddy," he drooled.

"Pop, please don't put the moves on Amanda until I've squared things with Lacey. Her mother helped me make this happen."

Lacey moved cautiously forward. "Yank? Shale? Tedera! What's going on here?"

They smiled, but no one answered. She turned in the direction of the band just as the volume and tempo of the music changed to a soft, dreamy melody. The crowd suddenly parted. Lacey looked to her right and saw John walking toward her. Tall, handsome, dressed in a black dinner jacket, and smiling cautiously. He towered over her and took her hand.

"Welcome to Texas." He studied her unsmiling face. "You take my breath away, and I want very much to kiss you."

"And I want you to tell me what's going here. Why are Yank and Shale here? My brother. Why is Nicholas here? What is this?"

"This?" He gestured around the crowd and shook his head. "It's just an engagement party."

"An engagement party? For whom?"

He took her hand. "You and me."

She quickly canvassed the room. Her aunts and cousins were there, as were several friends. Everyone was smiling. Lacey was too stunned to speak.

John took her hand and turned to his guests. "For those of you who might not have heard, I went out East some months ago to take a job as a riding instructor for a girl's camp."

He held his head down until the murmurs died. "You heard right. As most of you know, I've been quite distraught lately."

"Impossible is what you were!" Nathaniel yelled.

"Okay, Pop. I was impossible. I didn't know how to go on, so I left. I used an assumed identity and taught horseback riding to a group of delightful young girls. In the process I fell in love."

His soapy admission was punctuated by a collective "Ahhhhh," and he continued.

"I learned a lot this summer. I met some wonderful people whom I will always hold dear. I met a very wise woman who looked inside my heart and advised me to be honest with the woman I loved, but I didn't do it soon enough."

Looking at John, so dapper and charming, Lacey felt her heart would burst.

"With the help of an attorney who felt sorry for me, a family that adopted me, and a woman who will hopefully welcome me into her family, I was able to trick again the woman I loved."

He shook his head in protest of the resounding boos. "I had to do it. It was the only way I could get her here, and I had to get her here. Douglas? Where are you?"

"I'm right here." Douglas stepped forward and Lacey's mouth hinged open.

"I never met this man until today. He's a distin-guished attorney, but he took a chance and helped me get his beautiful lady here today. See, he knew I loved her too much to ever let her go."

He looked into Lacey's eyes and slipped his arm around her waist.

"Everyone, this is Ms. Lacey Daigle, the woman I love."

The band played and Nathaniel stepped forward.

"This is my father, Nathaniel Tobias."

"Hello, Lacey. Welcome to our home. My son said you were perfect. You're that and more."

She mumbled, "Thank you," and watched him give John a blue box. Her body went limp when he kneeled before her.

"Lacey, in front of my Texas and my Massachusetts families, as well as the family I hope to call mine, I humbly ask you to be my wife. To allow me to love and care for you." A sheepish grin crossed his face. "And allow me to make up for the hot check."

She looked at him and then at her mother, Nicholas, Abby DeLarasso, Yank, Shale, Tedera, and Micah.

John moved aside. "Let me introduce my family while you take a minute to think this over. This is my grandfather, Nathaniel Tobias, Sr. We call him Natty. My brother, Chris. My sisters, Lorraine and Ellen."

Lorraine rushed forward and took Lacey's arm. "I know this must be a shock. Would you like to sit down?"

"No," she managed to say. "I'm fine." She looked at John. "How did you do this? I mean the

Whitefeathers, Abby, how did you get them all together like this?"

"I had a lot of help, and this is just the beginning. We've also reserved the lighthouse at Oak Bluffs for our wedding, but don't worry, you can change anything you don't like. The wedding is for you. I want what comes after that, and I want it forever."

Amanda batted the tears from her eyes and took Lacey's hand. "Honey, everyone who loves you and John knew the two of you should be together, so we conspired behind your back. I hope you're not angry." She squeezed Lacey's right hand while John waited with the ring poised over her left hand.

Micah stood behind John. "I've got good news, too, Lacey. John got me a scholarship, so you don't have to worry about my tuition. I feel like I have another set of parents. Please say you'll marry him."

Lacey looked at the ring in his hand, and in the brilliance of the diamond, she saw a smiling face. Faded eyes filled with love. Pearl had been her telescope to the future. Now she was her guardian angel. She also saw white and lace and a lifetime of love and happiness.

Joan Early was raised in a family of cultural diversity and takes great pride in the sprawling roots, varied traditions, and many tongues of her ancestors. She finds true inspiration in the rich history and breathtaking scenery of Martha's Vineyard and Nantucket. Joan currently resides in Houston, Texas, with her husband and children.

2010 Mass Market Titles

January

Show Me the Sun
Miriam Shumba
ISBN: 978-158571-405-6
$6.99

Promises of Forever
Celya Bowers
ISBN: 978-1-58571-380-6
$6.99

February

Love Out Of Order
Nicole Green
ISBN: 978-1-58571-381-3
$6.99

Unclear and Present Danger
Michele Cameron
ISBN: 978-158571-408-7
$6.99

March

Stolen Jewels
Michele Sudler
ISBN: 978-158571-409-4
$6.99

Not Quite Right
Tammy Williams
ISBN: 978-158571-410-0
$6.99

April

Oak Bluffs
Joan Early
ISBN: 978-1-58571-379-0
$6.99

Crossing the Line
Bernice Layton
ISBN: 978-158571-412-4
$6.99

How To Kill Your Husband
Keith Walker
ISBN: 978-158571-421-6
$6.99

May

The Business of Love
Cheris F. Hodges
ISBN: 978-158571-373-8
$6.99

Wayward Dreams
Gail McFarland
ISBN: 978-158571-422-3
$6.99

June

The Doctor's Wife
Mildred Riley
ISBN: 978-158571-424-7
$6.99

Mixed Reality
Chamein Canton
ISBN: 978-158571-423-0
$6.99

2010 Mass Market Titles (continued)

July

Blue Interlude
Keisha Mennefee
ISBN: 978-158571-378-3
$6.99

Always You
Crystal Hubbard
ISBN: 978-158571-371-4
$6.99

Unbeweavable
Katrina Spencer
ISBN: 978-158571-426-1
$6.99

August

Small Sensations
Crystal V. Rhodes
ISBN: 978-158571-376-9
$6.99

Let's Get It On
Dyanne Davis
ISBN: 978-158571-416-2
$6.99

September

Unconditional
A.C. Arthur
ISBN: 978-158571-413-1
$6.99

Swan
Africa Fine
ISBN: 978-158571-377-6
$6.99

October

Friends in Need
Joan Early
ISBN:978-1-58571-428-5
$6.99

Against the Wind
Gwynne Forster
ISBN:978-158571-429-2
$6.99

That Which Has Horns
Miriam Shumba
ISBN:978-1-58571-430-8
$6.99

November

A Good Dude
Keith Walker
ISBN:978-1-58571-431-5
$6.99

Reye's Gold
Ruthie Robinson
ISBN:978-1-58571-432-2
$6.99

December

Still Waters...
Crystal V. Rhodes
ISBN:978-1-58571-433-9
$6.99

Burn
Crystal Hubbard
ISBN: 978-1-58571-406-3
$6.99

Other Genesis Press, Inc. Titles

Title	Author	Price
2 Good	Celya Bowers	$6.99
A Dangerous Deception	J.M. Jeffries	$8.95
A Dangerous Love	J.M. Jeffries	$8.95
A Dangerous Obsession	J.M. Jeffries	$8.95
A Drummer's Beat to Mend	Kei Swanson	$9.95
A Happy Life	Charlotte Harris	$9.95
A Heart's Awakening	Veronica Parker	$9.95
A Lark on the Wing	Phyliss Hamilton	$9.95
A Love of Her Own	Cheris F. Hodges	$9.95
A Love to Cherish	Beverly Clark	$8.95
A Place Like Home	Alicia Wiggins	$6.99
A Risk of Rain	Dar Tomlinson	$8.95
A Taste of Temptation	Reneé Alexis	$9.95
A Twist of Fate	Beverly Clark	$8.95
A Voice Behind Thunder	Carrie Elizabeth Greene	$6.99
A Will to Love	Angie Daniels	$9.95
Acquisitions	Kimberley White	$8.95
Across	Carol Payne	$12.95
After the Vows (Summer Anthology)	Leslie Esdaile T.T. Henderson Jacqueline Thomas	$10.95
Again, My Love	Kayla Perrin	$10.95
Against the Wind	Gwynne Forster	$8.95
All I Ask	Barbara Keaton	$8.95
All I'll Ever Need	Mildred Riley	$6.99
Always You	Crystal Hubbard	$6.99
Ambrosia	T.T. Henderson	$8.95
An Unfinished Love Affair	Barbara Keaton	$8.95
And Then Came You	Dorothy Elizabeth Love	$8.95
Angel's Paradise	Janice Angelique	$9.95
Another Memory	Pamela Ridley	$6.99
Anything But Love	Celya Bowers	$6.99
At Last	Lisa G. Riley	$8.95
Best Foot Forward	Michele Sudler	$6.99
Best of Friends	Natalie Dunbar	$8.95
Best of Luck Elsewhere	Trisha Haddad	$6.99
Beyond the Rapture	Beverly Clark	$9.95
Blame It on Paradise	Crystal Hubbard	$6.99
Blaze	Barbara Keaton	$9.95
Blindsided	Tammy Williams	$6.99
Bliss, Inc.	Chamein Canton	$6.99
Blood Lust	J.M. Jeffries	$9.95

Other Genesis Press, Inc. Titles (continued)

Other Genesis Press, Inc. Titles (continued)

Eve's Prescription	Edwina Martin Arnold	$8.95
Everlastin' Love	Gay G. Gunn	$8.95
Everlasting Moments	Dorothy Elizabeth Love	$8.95
Everything and More	Sinclair Lebeau	$8.95
Everything but Love	Natalie Dunbar	$8.95
Falling	Natalie Dunbar	$9.95
Fate	Pamela Leigh Starr	$8.95
Finding Isabella	A.J. Garrotto	$8.95
Fireflies	Joan Early	$6.99
Fixin' Tyrone	Keith Walker	$6.99
Forbidden Quest	Dar Tomlinson	$10.95
Forever Love	Wanda Y. Thomas	$8.95
From the Ashes	Kathleen Suzanne	$8.95
	Jeanne Sumerix	
Frost on My Window	Angela Weaver	$6.99
Gentle Yearning	Rochelle Alers	$10.95
Glory of Love	Sinclair LeBeau	$10.95
Go Gentle Into That	Malcom Boyd	$12.95
Good Night		
Goldengroove	Mary Beth Craft	$16.95
Groove, Bang, and Jive	Steve Cannon	$8.99
Hand in Glove	Andrea Jackson	$9.95
Hard to Love	Kimberley White	$9.95
Hart & Soul	Angie Daniels	$8.95
Heart of the Phoenix	A.C. Arthur	$9.95
Heartbeat	Stephanie Bedwell-Grime	$8.95
Hearts Remember	M. Loui Quezada	$8.95
Hidden Memories	Robin Allen	$10.95
Higher Ground	Leah Latimer	$19.95
Hitler, the War, and the Pope	Ronald Rychiak	$26.95
How to Write a Romance	Kathryn Falk	$18.95
I Married a Reclining Chair	Lisa M. Fuhs	$8.95
I'll Be Your Shelter	Giselle Carmichael	$8.95
I'll Paint a Sun	A.J. Garrotto	$9.95
Icie	Pamela Leigh Starr	$8.95
If I Were Your Woman	LaConnie Taylor-Jones	$6.99
Illusions	Pamela Leigh Starr	$8.95
Indigo After Dark Vol. I	Nia Dixon/Angelique	$10.95
Indigo After Dark Vol. II	Dolores Bundy/	$10.95
	Cole Riley	
Indigo After Dark Vol. III	Montana Blue/	$10.95
	Coco Morena	

Other Genesis Press, Inc. Titles (continued)

Indigo After Dark Vol. IV	Cassandra Colt/	$14.95
Indigo After Dark Vol. V	Delilah Dawson	$14.95
Indiscretions	Donna Hill	$8.95
Intentional Mistakes	Michele Sudler	$9.95
Interlude	Donna Hill	$8.95
Intimate Intentions	Angie Daniels	$8.95
It's in the Rhythm	Sammie Ward	$6.99
It's Not Over Yet	J.J. Michael	$9.95
Jolie's Surrender	Edwina Martin-Arnold	$8.95
Kiss or Keep	Debra Phillips	$8.95
Lace	Giselle Carmichael	$9.95
Lady Preacher	K.T. Richey	$6.99
Last Train to Memphis	Elsa Cook	$12.95
Lasting Valor	Ken Olsen	$24.95
Let Us Prey	Hunter Lundy	$25.95
Lies Too Long	Pamela Ridley	$13.95
Life Is Never As It Seems	J.J. Michael	$12.95
Lighter Shade of Brown	Vicki Andrews	$8.95
Look Both Ways	Joan Early	$6.99
Looking for Lily	Africa Fine	$6.99
Love Always	Mildred E. Riley	$10.95
Love Doesn't Come Easy	Charlyne Dickerson	$8.95
Love Unveiled	Gloria Greene	$10.95
Love's Deception	Charlene Berry	$10.95
Love's Destiny	M. Loui Quezada	$8.95
Love's Secrets	Yolanda McVey	$6.99
Mae's Promise	Melody Walcott	$8.95
Magnolia Sunset	Giselle Carmichael	$8.95
Many Shades of Gray	Dyanne Davis	$6.99
Matters of Life and Death	Lesego Malepe, Ph.D.	$15.95
Meant to Be	Jeanne Sumerix	$8.95
Midnight Clear	Leslie Esdaile	$10.95
(Anthology)	Gwynne Forster	
	Carmen Green	
	Monica Jackson	
Midnight Magic	Gwynne Forster	$8.95
Midnight Peril	Vicki Andrews	$10.95
Misconceptions	Pamela Leigh Starr	$9.95
Moments of Clarity	Michele Cameron	$6.99
Montgomery's Children	Richard Perry	$14.95
Mr. Fix-It	Crystal Hubbard	$6.99
My Buffalo Soldier	Barbara B.K. Reeves	$8.95

Other Genesis Press, Inc. Titles (continued)

Naked Soul	Gwynne Forster	$8.95
Never Say Never	Michele Cameron	$6.99
Next to Last Chance	Louisa Dixon	$24.95
No Apologies	Seressia Glass	$8.95
No Commitment Required	Seressia Glass	$8.95
No Regrets	Mildred E. Riley	$8.95
Not His Type	Chamein Canton	$6.99
Nowhere to Run	Gay G. Gunn	$10.95
O Bed! O Breakfast!	Rob Kuehnle	$14.95
Object of His Desire	A.C. Arthur	$8.95
Office Policy	A.C. Arthur	$9.95
Once in a Blue Moon	Dorianne Cole	$9.95
One Day at a Time	Bella McFarland	$8.95
One of These Days	Michele Sudler	$9.95
Outside Chance	Louisa Dixon	$24.95
Passion	T.T. Henderson	$10.95
Passion's Blood	Cherif Fortin	$22.95
Passion's Furies	AlTonya Washington	$6.99
Passion's Journey	Wanda Y. Thomas	$8.95
Past Promises	Jahmel West	$8.95
Path of Fire	T.T. Henderson	$8.95
Path of Thorns	Annetta P. Lee	$9.95
Peace Be Still	Colette Haywood	$12.95
Picture Perfect	Reon Carter	$8.95
Playing for Keeps	Stephanie Salinas	$8.95
Pride & Joi	Gay G. Gunn	$8.95
Promises Made	Bernice Layton	$6.99
Promises to Keep	Alicia Wiggins	$8.95
Quiet Storm	Donna Hill	$10.95
Reckless Surrender	Rochelle Alers	$6.95
Red Polka Dot in a World Full of Plaid	Varian Johnson	$12.95
Red Sky	Renee Alexis	$6.99
Reluctant Captive	Joyce Jackson	$8.95
Rendezvous With Fate	Jeanne Sumerix	$8.95
Revelations	Cheris F. Hodges	$8.95
Rivers of the Soul	Leslie Esdaile	$8.95
Rocky Mountain Romance	Kathleen Suzanne	$8.95
Rooms of the Heart	Donna Hill	$8.95
Rough on Rats and Tough on Cats	Chris Parker	$12.95
Save Me	Africa Fine	$6.99

Other Genesis Press, Inc. Titles (continued)

Secret Library Vol. 1	Nina Sheridan	$18.95
Secret Library Vol. 2	Cassandra Colt	$8.95
Secret Thunder	Annetta P. Lee	$9.95
Shades of Brown	Denise Becker	$8.95
Shades of Desire	Monica White	$8.95
Shadows in the Moonlight	Jeanne Sumerix	$8.95
Sin	Crystal Rhodes	$8.95
Singing a Song…	Crystal Rhodes	$6.99
Six O'Clock	Katrina Spencer	$6.99
Small Whispers	Annetta P. Lee	$6.99
So Amazing	Sinclair LeBeau	$8.95
Somebody's Someone	Sinclair LeBeau	$8.95
Someone to Love	Alicia Wiggins	$8.95
Song in the Park	Martin Brant	$15.95
Soul Eyes	Wayne L. Wilson	$12.95
Soul to Soul	Donna Hill	$8.95
Southern Comfort	J.M. Jeffries	$8.95
Southern Fried Standards	S.R. Maddox	$6.99
Still the Storm	Sharon Robinson	$8.95
Still Waters Run Deep	Leslie Esdaile	$8.95
Stolen Memories	Michele Sudler	$6.99
Stories to Excite You	Anna Forrest/Divine	$14.95
Storm	Pamela Leigh Starr	$6.99
Subtle Secrets	Wanda Y. Thomas	$8.95
Suddenly You	Crystal Hubbard	$9.95
Sweet Repercussions	Kimberley White	$9.95
Sweet Sensations	Gwyneth Bolton	$9.95
Sweet Tomorrows	Kimberly White	$8.95
Taken by You	Dorothy Elizabeth Love	$9.95
Tattooed Tears	T. T. Henderson	$8.95
Tempting Faith	Crystal Hubbard	$6.99
The Color Line	Lizzette Grayson Carter	$9.95
The Color of Trouble	Dyanne Davis	$8.95
The Disappearance of Allison Jones	Kayla Perrin	$5.95
The Fires Within	Beverly Clark	$9.95
The Foursome	Celya Bowers	$6.99
The Honey Dipper's Legacy	Myra Pannell-Allen	$14.95
The Joker's Love Tune	Sidney Rickman	$15.95
The Little Pretender	Barbara Cartland	$10.95
The Love We Had	Natalie Dunbar	$8.95
The Man Who Could Fly	Bob & Milana Beamon	$18.95

Other Genesis Press, Inc. Titles (continued)

The Missing Link	Charlyne Dickerson	$8.95
The Mission	Pamela Leigh Starr	$6.99
The More Things Change	Chamein Canton	$6.99
The Perfect Frame	Beverly Clark	$9.95
The Price of Love	Sinclair LeBeau	$8.95
The Smoking Life	Ilene Barth	$29.95
The Words of the Pitcher	Kei Swanson	$8.95
Things Forbidden	Maryam Diaab	$6.99
This Life Isn't Perfect Holla	Sandra Foy	$6.99
Three Doors Down	Michele Sudler	$6.99
Three Wishes	Seressia Glass	$8.95
Ties That Bind	Kathleen Suzanne	$8.95
Tiger Woods	Libby Hughes	$5.95
Time Is of the Essence	Angie Daniels	$9.95
Timeless Devotion	Bella McFarland	$9.95
Tomorrow's Promise	Leslie Esdaile	$8.95
Truly Inseparable	Wanda Y. Thomas	$8.95
Two Sides to Every Story	Dyanne Davis	$9.95
Unbreak My Heart	Dar Tomlinson	$8.95
Uncommon Prayer	Kenneth Swanson	$9.95
Unconditional Love	Alicia Wiggins	$8.95
Unconditional	A.C. Arthur	$9.95
Undying Love	Renee Alexis	$6.99
Until Death Do Us Part	Susan Paul	$8.95
Vows of Passion	Bella McFarland	$9.95
Waiting for Mr. Darcy	Chamein Canton	$6.99
Waiting in the Shadows	Michele Sudler	$6.99
Wedding Gown	Dyanne Davis	$8.95
What's Under Benjamin's Bed	Sandra Schaffer	$8.95
When a Man Loves a Woman	LaConnie Taylor-Jones	$6.99
When Dreams Float	Dorothy Elizabeth Love	$8.95
When I'm With You	LaConnie Taylor-Jones	$6.99
When Lightning Strikes	Michele Cameron	$6.99
Where I Want to Be	Maryam Diaab	$6.99
Whispers in the Night	Dorothy Elizabeth Love	$8.95
Whispers in the Sand	LaFlorya Gauthier	$10.95
Who's That Lady?	Andrea Jackson	$9.95
Wild Ravens	AlTonya Washington	$9.95
Yesterday Is Gone	Beverly Clark	$10.95
Yesterday's Dreams, Tomorrow's Promises	Reon Laudat	$8.95
Your Precious Love	Sinclair LeBeau	$8.95